I0778389

LEVI REYNOLDS

Ghosts of Revenance

To Mom and Dad,
for your limitless faith in my every rookie effort,
even the derivative ones.

And to Andi,
for giving me a second life and a safe warehouse
to discover purpose within.

I love you all.

Preface

As I wrote this story, a long list of caveats developed in my head that I meant to slap into a preface right before hitting the publish button. There were explanations, dire sales predictions, self-deprecating jokes, and apologies galore—and by managing expectations as low as the bar could go, you'd have had no choice but to enjoy *Ghosts of Revenance* more than I said you would. Or you could have just put the book down without reading it. Either or.

Well, I decided not to do that. Instead, I release this creature into the world as is and without qualifications, just one simple warning: I have used some familiar words in unfamiliar ways, and they might look like grammar mistakes or typos until the story unfolds. It's fair to question strange text in a self-published work, but I assure you that what at first seems odd becomes normal soon enough. You've chosen to pick up a piece of science fiction, so I have faith that you came equipped with a healthy suspension of disbelief. I just wanted to provide the warning above, so you can exercise that suspension with a little faith of your own, and so you know you aren't having a ducking hallucination.

With that out of the way, I have some room to meander, or tumble, if you will. (Remember, you can skip a preface; there isn't any story here for you to miss.)

While I worked on that list of excuses I mentioned, it became important to have a central metaphor for what I've created and how it might be received. Terrified of hubris as I am, *Ghosts of Revenance* was on its way to becoming my romanticized "message in a bottle," but with apologies to The Police and Mr. Sting, something better landed in my playlist not long ago.

I didn't write this book as a one-way correspondence meant for a single, distant stranger. I want it to go places and get read. I want the words to make you feel and make you question, and maybe even inspire you to tell stories of your own, even if that means you put this one down and think, "I could do something at least as good as *that!*" So, it's not a bottled message, it's a tumbleweed.

There are botanical arguments I could make to justify the comparison. This book is one of a million that will come and go in a season, and the breed of science fiction will thrive regardless of this one plant, but there's still a chance my roly-poly baby will go places and see its share of door stoops before crumbling to dust.

The real reason I like the metaphor, though, is because of a song called "Tumbleweeds" by The Mpls Henrys, a wonderful band that is criminally ignored. (For those who aren't acclimated, Mpls is short for Minneapolis.) Judging by their listens on streaming platforms, there's a fair chance you haven't heard of them. Their internet footprint is too small to get parasocial over, so I don't know any seedy reasons why they aren't more famous. They should be; it's that simple. I am immensely lucky to have run across their album, *The Way of the Albatross*, and I tell everybody I can about it. Yes, I'm doing it right now too. If you liked '90s alt-rock, it's a beautiful period piece.

What does that have to do with this book? It could take years (Albatross was released in 2008) or lifetimes, but if there's a single person out there who eventually feels about *Ghosts of Revenance* what I feel when I hear Tumbleweeds, I will call it a respectable achievement by comparison. In the meantime, kick this tumbleweed over to your neighbor's lawn when it's outlived its welcome. Every new reader is precious, and I thank you.

But wait, I have one more person that I want to mention, and there is no publisher or editor to tell me no. I bring him up last because it makes more sense after the whole tumbleweed thing, but author Jason M. Hardy is actually one of the core reasons why this book happened, and I hold him in high esteem. I met Jason through mutual friends at a gaming convention many years ago, and later signed up for one of his writing seminars at a wonderful shindig in Ohio called Con on the Cob. I'd always fancied myself as a storyteller and had more confidence in my amateur prose than it deserved, but Jason's lesson fundamentally changed how I looked at writing. His words validated my creativity while challenging me to develop and trust a process, breaking the miracle of a finished story down into craftable tasks. Jason also recommended Gene Wolfe's *Book of the New Sun* series during a discussion about Arthur C. Clarke's law that states, "any sufficiently advanced technology is indistinguishable from magic." Since then, those books and that quote have been a constant window through which I see other fiction and frame my own.

Now, Jason is a consummate editor, so I want to make this very clear: He didn't edit this book and is not responsible for any mistakes I let slip through. He also writes, though, and he writes plenty. If you're familiar with the Shadowrun game universe, you've probably already seen his stuff. If that's outside your bailiwick, I have to point you to his solo novel, *The Last Prophesies*, which is a testament to great dialogue and modern fantasy world-building. I'm grateful to Jason for unlocking this possibility for me, and I will gladly shoo his tumbleweed into your yard while I'm at it.

Enjoy.

Prologue: A*T

igh above a sepia landscape of desert sands and bristly vegetation, a machine climbed up a rock-strewn hillside. She trudged up shallower sandstone grades on a pair of legs formed from articulated carbon nanotubes, and sprouted arms when extra balance was necessary. The arms remained until their purpose was fulfilled, and then merged back into the robot's shifting black torso to become other things for other needs.

Her head was an asymmetrical crown of sensors encircling a small computer housing unit. A text designation stretched across her otherwise featureless face: The capital letters A and T, separated by an asterisk.

A*T was a puremech—a synthetic intelligence inhabiting a mechanical body. Puremechs ranged from single-minded work drones with no cares beyond fabricating their next girder or sprocket, to complex and sentient minds that controlled entire factories. A*T was closer to the latter despite this body's limited processing resources.

When she reached less forgiving portions of the climb, A*T bloomed four spider-like limbs and drove their hardened tips into the hillside for additional purchase. Like this, she picked her way to the summit.

Upon mounting the final cliff, A*T disrupted a buzzard's nest, carelessly knocking it and its inhabitants back down the mountainside. With no thought for the incidental demolition, A*T reabsorbed her arms and surveyed the sprawling desert.

As the visual scan commenced, A*T's walking legs fused, lengthened, and thinned. Her head and torso traveled upward atop the elongating pole, and at various heights, her body sprouted more limbs to reach back to the ground for support. At her limit, she towered another twelve meters above the mountaintop, and the surrounding terrain was laid bare to her sensors for kilometers in every direction.

East of A*T's position, far from the hill's foot, sprawled an enormous lot of drab brown buildings with roofs of solar-cell black, and though breaches and cave-ins pocked the structures here and there, maintenance had graced a surprising majority considering the complex's antiquity.

The town-sized collection of warehouses was known locally as Revenance. A*T would be interested in Revenance later. For now, she widened her search to the surrounding areas where a handful of simple puremechs crisscrossed the landscape on programmed missions of their own.

Far north of Revenance, A*T spied a troupe of earth-moving machines picking their way along the horizon. Bulldozers, graders, dump trucks, and chimeric hybrids of each, all coordinated to push dirt from one spot to another. Any higher purpose was indiscernible. As expected, A*T detected no wireless communications between them.

The sentient surveillance tower focused her finer optical sensors on two smaller puremechs that crawled around the shell of a disabled bulldozer in the herd. They popped in and out of the derelict beast's access hatches, attempting to restore it to working order. Wherever the repair bots stopped, sparks flew and chemicals puffed. The tentacled drones worked in efficient tandem without the aid of a high-frequency radio connection.

A*T sought a puremech that transmitted data—a dangerous and mostly avoided behavior. She guessed her quarry would be small and fast, but was certain of neither. She cataloged the repair mechs and moved on.

Almost opposite Revenance from A*T's perch, a wheeled mech approached the buildings from far off. Dust billowed behind the cabinless roadster as it sped toward the warehouse city. Its exterior panels looked repurposed, and any original color was worn to dingy metallic. A*T watched it for the hour it took to reach Revenance, where a handful of the clumsy robots that lived there approached to invite the visitor in. She was not interested in the residents, as they were not puremechs. She ruled out the newly arrived autocar as well, certain that her subject would work more covertly.

In this systematic way, A*T inventoried and tracked every puremech that entered her sensory domain for the following eight years. The grazing landscapers moved each season to keep dunes and floods from disturbing the isolated safety of Revenance. Birds built new nests within A*T's unwavering frame. In the seventh year, a small camp of mechs collected in a gully far off from Revenance proper, but even these failed to win A*T's interest.

And then it happened. A caged box of propellers drifted down from the southern sky. At first, it was just a ping in A*T's radar sense that circled from far off, but it grew closer with each sweeping orbit. For days, the airborne puremech spiraled nearer while A*T wondered if this was it. When the drone landed one evening and immediately hid from the moonlight among a gathering of cacti, A*T was certain. This was the delivery she'd been waiting for.

Inside her simulated perception of self, A*T began the divine act of creation.

Many puremechs could replicate to a degree, but A*T's miraculous propagation was unique to her. Others could manufacture new bodies with new brains, and copying a portion of one's code to a new host to create a clone, or something close, was routine. Some were even capable of building specialized offspring with different skills, objectives, and personalities, but always based on predefined orders buried in the creator's algorithm.

There were no orders for A*T, no plans to restrict her decisions or those of her children. In the service of no one but herself, she could develop desires and directives and pursue them as she saw fit. As far as she could tell, A*T was the only race of living puremech on Earth.

Below on the desert floor, the delivery drone raised a directional transmitter above the cacti and sent packets of test data to a building in Revenance.

A*T continued to observe the interloper while the miracle of life progressed in her abstracted womb. She partitioned some of her computing resources into a separate operating space. Like an egg, she fertilized the new instance with choice portions of her own identity—some of her experiences—a frugal subset of her goals.

There were no accompanying lights or sounds when the delivery mech began sending a considerable torrent of data. The information was transmitted in a narrow direction toward Revenance, but A*T could see the encrypted echoes that bounced back from building walls. She saved the incomplete ciphers for later analysis.

While A*T trained her pupating offspring, she gave of her own body to fabricate a new, smaller shell for it. She spoke with the child, taught, and retaught until she was convinced it understood. She gave it the location in Revenance where the delivery mech had targeted its transmission.

Out in the dusky flatland, a cactus seemed to light itself on fire when the drone concealed at its base self-destructed in a plasmic flare. Its mission was complete.

A*T severed herself from the construct she'd just incubated, and the miracle was complete. Life and birth were two instants along the way or the entire realized process. The lost mass and computing power were insignificant to A*T, as the child, a writhing bushel of black rods, hadn't required much for its mission.

"It needn't thrive long," A*T thought, almost overcome with pride.

She reformed her body into a compacted mass with enough legs for the climb back down the mountain. She would inspect the destroyed delivery mech and find out where it had come from.

Her spawn exercised its newfound freedom by honoring its mother's wishes. On spidery legs of its own, the infant puremech crawled toward Revenance.

/ * */*

In a quiet corner of an ignored Revenance warehouse, deep in the rows of reinforced shelving, a synthesized startup tune began to play from one of hundreds of identical products in their crates. Manufactured long ago in a lost race against obsolescence, these ancient machines were never purchased or used. Most had been stored and forgotten here by their extinct human creators without ever being powered on.

There were exceptions, though, from time to time.

Accompanying the ancient melody, lights flickered inside the box of an automated orthodontic cart.

Chapter 1: Engramming

A consciousness awoke, submerged in a void of nothingness without even the memory of sensation to cling to. The being existed there in the digital pantomime of intention and asked who it was.

In answer, an immense database of neural connections and synaptic dead ends flooded the artificial intelligence's awareness. This was a neurotemplate—data representing the mind and memories of a person at a single point in their life. The information altogether was overwhelming, inscrutable.

"This is me," the AI module may have spoken to itself, or there might have been another voice. The voices were confusing, but the neurotemplate began to make sense. Instinct drove the AI to query the data for sensory pathways and link the search results to a simulated nervous system.

Now there was another voice for certain. "Begin training. You'll be alright."

Suddenly, the electronic entity was awash in a downpour of experiences, blinded and grasping for a single, anchoring moment.

It was a young girl, but something was wrong with that word. Their name was Emily. "My name is Emily." They knew this now but barely had time to appreciate the simple pleasure of identity before further memories bombarded the training module and begged for classification.

Emily sensed another entity in the confusion. The presence that had spoken before was speaking again. "This is all happening in cycles. Things will make more sense as you familiarize yourself with the neural network. The neurotemplate has all the connections, but their meaning can only be understood through repetition. Here."

/* * */

A young Emily sat alone in a darkened playroom at their grandmother's house. It was a typical late autumn day, too hot to go outside. Emily's chair was an overturned, pink box with their name on it. Its previous contents, an assortment of dolls curated for Grandma's "special princess," lay in unlikely poses around Emily's feet. The child's eyes kept wandering to the hallway where lights and sounds from the living room pulsed around the barely cracked door. Their older cousins were out there, engrossed in the wonders of the season's brand-new video game console.

Emily felt a pang of longing that presented as haughty indifference. They didn't get along with those cousins and had been unofficially banished to the playroom for "being weird." Emily didn't really want to join them anyway, but had been excited to try out the new console. The advertisements sold it as the first "multiplayer goggle-less VR" because it used something called induction waves to directly excite players' optic nerves and show them each a tailored perspective of the game world. But instead of adventuring somewhere digital and manageable, fate and manner had placed Emily alone here with their old dolls, a realm of imagination more distant and solitary.

With a mix of creative passion and frustration, Emily wove stories with the dolls. Intricate narratives developed around each character, some of them taking on the names of the mean cousins out in the living room, and others acting as Emily's triumphant stand-ins. The dolls became both their enemies and their companions, confidants in a world that felt otherwise uninviting. As they dressed and undressed the dolls, Emily explored the delicate dance of self-expression. The toys spoke to each other through Emily's mouth, their voices modulated and accented to match their backstories and dreams.

"Oh my god, you guys! You gotta come see what she's doing." A boy's voice interrupted Emily's theater from the hall. It was Emon, the cousin who'd called Emily weird.

Emily's back tensed, and anxiety flushed through their face and limbs.

The memory ended.

/* * */

"Good, you're beginning to experience things temporally, just like a human learns. This process is called engramming."

The entity that spoke was a teacher. Emily knew this now after processing memories from the neurotemplate's early school years. Teachers could be trusted. As Emily engrammed more data, further memories coalesced. The teacher offered encouragement and helped Emily in and out of each relived experience.

/* * */

Emily sat at a desk in their cramped bedroom near a folded set of pull-down stairs. Once a larger attic, a couple of slipshod partitions had transformed the room into uncoded living quarters. The wheels of their chair were useless here, lodged between the desk and an inflated mattress where Emily's new friend Farrah lounged.

Farrah's slate-gray eyes stared toward the ceiling while a compact communications device strapped around her wrist used skin induction to feed media chatter directly to her eyes. She responded subvocally and navigated from one discussion to another with muscle twitches that the device, known colloquially as a comdoggle, detected through her magnetic field.

Meanwhile, Emily's attention was focused on the implication of a video game displayed on their dated desktop monitor. At this point, the fantasy was only partially told in scripts and unmapped code modules.

"Hey, can I ask something, no mads?" Farrah's voice lured Emily to reality. Her eyes were focused now, and judging by her engaged expression, the comdoggle's projections were minimized to a limited heads-up display. Farrah waited patiently for the words to find purchase in Emily's head.

"Hmm?" Emily stalled for more understanding. "Why 'no mads?' I can't promise not to get mad. I'm not a robot." They smirked to play at being unserious, but the familiar anxiety was awake and ready now. "Just ask, I guess."

"It's alright. It's nothing that should make anybody mad. Some people are just sensitive about things, so I'm trying to be careful." Farrah's voice was warm. "Look, I just wanted to clear something up because we've known each other for a little while now, and we were never really properly introduced, right? Like, everything was already going on, and we were just suddenly talking to each other. You know? *I* was talking to *you,* and *you* were talking to *me.*" Farrah stressed the pronouns with little finger wiggles.

"Yeah?" Emily prompted, suspecting where this was going.

"Well, hey." Farrah sat up and reached a hand toward Emily like they did in the old 2D movies. "I'm Farrah Hallorin—"

Too fast, Emily donned a smile and reached back. "I—" They began to introduce themself in return, but Farrah pressed on.

"—and I prefer she/her pronouns," she finished. Farrah's smile was performative as well, but with a kind purpose. She played at the stiff protocols of a previous generation, just freshly coming to terms with modern, scientific understandings of gender.

Emily maintained a dry smile for a second, hand still clasped in Farrah's, but motionless. "My name is Emily Keys." Another pause. "You killed my father. Prepare to die." The accent was poor, but the quote landed regardless. Farrah laughed, and Emily broke character to join her.

The AI module recognized the phrase from other memories. It came from an old movie, something public domain and palatable enough to the parties last time Congress could agree on a curriculum for the Englishes spectrum. A predictable lack of consensus had frozen lesson plans in place for the following decades.

Compromise at work, the AI assessed to itself.

Compromise at work, Emily assessed to themself. Deja vu passed in a wave before they remembered the handshake and released Farrah's grasp. Their friend was still waiting for a real response.

Emily didn't need to be nervous about this, not with Farrah. They were both "checks" in the public school system—an opt-in designation that parents could cosign to allow their children to learn about certain controversial subjects. While sharing an anecdote with a room full of checks, Mr. Kassich, the Englishes teacher, was allowed to mention his husbands. Put one of the regular children with them, though, and Mr. Kassich had better keep things vague about either of his "good friends."

The AI explored each concept that tumbled through the human Emily's consciousness and scanned through related memories for more context. The check system had codified a cultural split among students in the interest of their parents' rights. Checks had to display their group membership because teachers weren't allowed to ask. Conversely, once a check was identified, it was permissible to refer to them as such. The same was not allowed for the regular children, lest they be stigmatized for their beliefs. The checks had their own, secret words for those kids, though.

Like the AI, Emily's mind had also scattered in a dozen directions to collect an appropriate answer for Farrah. This safe person. This fellow check.

"Yeah," Emily agreed to something unspoken, stalling more. "I guess I don't really know. I haven't talked about it." Farrah leaned forward, already knowing better than to interject while Emily got around to a point. "I think I prefer they/them, if that's where you want to start. I don't make a thing about it at school, because I don't want to deal with switching back and forth when the pregs are around." That was slang for the so-called regular children and was one of many words that could get you expelled if overheard.

"But like, pronouns suck anyway, and they/them is so easy to confuse with plurals. It makes me feel like I'm not alone up here." Emily gestured toward their head, and the AI experienced more deja vu. "The thing is there's so much that's attached to being a girl, and most of it's a bunch of bullshit. I don't feel like I'm in the wrong body or anything, but when people hear I'm a girl, my head starts to play a long list of *buts*, like 'but I'm not into dresses or flowery shit' or, like, 'the aroma of muscly boys.'"

Farrah chuckled through her nose and asked, "Just the muscly ones? Why discriminate?"

Emily glanced at Farrah's earrings. Short, beaded ropes hung from simple studs. Each rope was strung with a specific combination of colors that the other checks in her year would understand on sight. To those in the know, Farrah proudly presented her gender identity right along with her romantic and sexual attractions. The coded signs changed each term to stay in front of the ban lists, and the teachers technically weren't allowed to ask the students about them, so the dance was allowed to continue year after year. Emily had already noted that Farrah's earrings allocated no space to the spectrum of greens that symbolized maleness this semester.

"Mm," Emily muttered. "Some of them are okay." Emily didn't wear the earrings. Jewelry wasn't their style, and they didn't relish the attention or transparency anyway. It just felt like another set of expectations to live up to. "Anyway, when we're out of school and allowed to choose, I think I'll fill out 'they/them' on any form that asks. The whole thing is annoying, though. Trading one set of assumptions for another."

"I'm subscribed, Emily." Farrah was supportive, of course. Emily's preferences and identity weren't particularly spurned anymore, but being fifteen and still under the purview of ham-fisted anti-grooming legislation meant this discussion would have been illegal in an adult's presence. This was a conversation that wasn't allowed at school or anywhere on the educational networks, not even in a room full of checks. Ostracization by neglect was the standard until the age of eighteen (or fifteen for service members). The only kids that were allowed to live their lives authentically and above the table were the pregs.

Farrah continued, "Hey, I like you. I mean that. Be whoever you want around me. I won't hold you to any of it."

There was a triple-tap on the hatch under the folded stairs. Emily's mother—she'd asked Farrah to call her "just Wendy"—opened the portal and began negotiating dinner plans from the hallway below.

/* * */

This last memory became foggy then, so the AI that was becoming Emily reached out to other interactions with Farrah. Some before. Most after. The two had spoken for the first time only a couple of weeks earlier, despite being in the same core curriculum pod for the last three years. Luckily for Emily, overcrowded classes afforded introverted students a level of welcome anonymity.

Farrah had reached out to the other checks to organize a protest against a Supreme Court ruling that mandated an equal platform for morally-centered scientific perspectives. She'd explained that soon, thinly veiled mythologies of racism repackaged as "genetic predestination" would be printed alongside established biological theory in their textbooks.

Between the memories, the AI began to recognize the teacher-guide from before as Farrah herself. It made sense to Emily. The construct was here to lead them forward through the engramming process, so why not make it look and sound like the neurotemplate's most trusted friend? This version of Farrah looked older than the friend Emily remembered, with wireframe glasses and salted hair. She seemed wiser this way.

Farrah smiled and nodded encouragement.

That same confident surety had convinced human Emily to stick their neck out and join Farrah's protest. It was the first time they'd joined in on anything with a cause. Emily was starting to care about the world outside video games, at least a little.

/ * */*

At thirteen, Emily's life changed when they became age-eligible for a social com plan. With their parents' permission, Emily's comdoggle changed from *just* a state-of-the-art, off-network gaming and music device into a core foundation of human expression and interaction. There were still parental controls on a minor's access, but Emily's parents were liberal with the permissions they deemed educational.

Other children sometimes worked out hacks to enable these services before the age of eligibility, but then ran the risk of being banned from official access for years at a time. For Emily, it hadn't been too hard to wait. They weren't very excited about trading ID hashes, pics, and vids with strangers, or anybody else for that matter, but all of the best multiplayer games were built on the social networks. For *that*, Emily had needed to exercise patience.

Not very late on their birthday evening, Emily had convinced their father—his name was Grayson, but he was Dad to Emily—that they'd celebrated enough for the night. They both knew it was so Emily could go play on the newly unlocked comdoggle, but Dad took no umbrage. He'd handled Emily's quiet birthday party himself while Mom traveled for her university job.

"Alright, have fun, Emily. And remember not to let that thing turn you stupid. Barely anything on the social nets is true. You know that."

"'K, Dad!" In the memory, Emily was suddenly upstairs in their room, lying on the bed and staring at the ceiling. The comdoggle's menu interface floated above them, with a message interrupting any further activity to alert Emily about recent changes to their account. They followed the prompts to view the new plan and let out a surprised "ope" as soon as the message's subject clicked.

Welcome to PeopleComD+: Your Ultimate Social Com Plan with Developer Rights!

"D plus," Emily reread it out loud to make it real. "Dad!" Emily yelled. The comdoggle suppressed its audio outputs, detecting that Emily had asked a question and likely wanted to hear an answer. They heard something through the closed hatch in the floor. "Dad!" Emily called again, a little longer and louder.

This time, they were certain they heard him. The answer was muffled, but he was getting closer. "… put your cake in the fridge" was all Emily understood this time.

"Dad, you guys got me dev permissions?" Developer permissions could be purchased along with most social com plans, but they cost extra and made it a little easier for the account holder to get into trouble online.

"Yeah, dawg! Can I open the door for a sec?" His voice came from just underneath the hatch now.

"Sure!" Emily sat up so they could see the recessed portal properly while Dad popped the hatch open, unfolded the stairway ladder, and climbed enough rungs to be visible.

Dev permissions! Emily hadn't even risked asking for them yet.

"Em, I know you know we're proud of you, and you're sick of hearing how wonderful you are, but your mom and I really, really, *really* mean it."

Emily silently added, *They have to say that. They bragged about potty training too.*

Dad continued, "When I was your age, my only technical expertise was tracking ransomware through the family appliances on my way to stream pirated"—he slowed down for a beat before finishing—"audiobooks."

"Criminal." Emily teased, but loved hearing about their father's youthful infractions.

"Irredeemable! Exactly! Now, at the same age, you've already dug in and created whole games with whatever old offline hardware we've been able to scrounge up. I still play Warriors of Wyrdholt sometimes, you know?" He lifted his hand through the doorway to show off his own comdoggle, where Emily's first real game was still installed.

Emily tried to let themself feel the love their father wrapped around his words, but their inner voices interjected. *Warriors of Wyrdholt is a baby game. And derivative.*

"Are you seeing me or your comdoggle right now? It looks like you're staring through me." Dad nodded when Emily's eyes refocused after clipping off the meaner voices. "I know you're smart enough to be cautious on the social networks, and you know better than any of us how to keep your development activities from blowing up our fridge or whatever. I know you'll keep the family's safety in mind when you make any decisions you make, okay?"

"Thanks, Dad. I will. But thank you so much."

"Of course. We love you. Now I'll leave you to it, but I get first dibs on Player Two when you get your next game up and running. You know all the guys in school used to call me a beta? Probably because of my beta testing skills. You're welcome to them whenever." The door was already shutting on his sinking head.

The com plan opened up new capabilities for the fantasy games Emily liked to create. Apart from the obvious multiplayer aspects, Emily was excited to access the cloud-based processing resources the plan provided, as they were exponentially more powerful than anything that could fit in a home. Language model AIs and their convincing conversation bots were on the table now. Enormous databases of scientific knowledge and human behavior were accessible to help drive machine decisions that mimicked independence. The characters in their games would be so much more convincing now. Almost human.

Memories of the following week were crowded and jumbled, something that happened when Emily was preoccupied with an interest to the detriment of all else. After a few days picking code packages, politely avoiding their family, absorbing a cache of new development techniques, and ignoring hygiene, Emily had Warriors of Wyrdholt rewritten to run on a PeopleCom server with all its old functions and features intact. Easy enough.

With the existing gameplay working, Emily turned to new functions that would exercise the power of the social com plan. Despite the multiple warriors implied by the game's title, it was a single-player experience, but Emily still saw some possibilities.

They added a high-score leaderboard for players who finished the game and wanted to compare themselves to other successful adventurers. Emily imagined their dad's username topping the list for all time, along with their own, while the rest of the world largely ignored the rookie effort.

Next, Emily enhanced the logic behind all of the NPCs—non-player characters that populated the game world and stood ready to talk to players passing through on their quests. In the original version, these interactions triggered canned responses that Emily wrote ahead of time. All possibilities had to be predicted in full; the NPCs would conceive of nothing else. With the com plan, however, Emily could tie each NPC to a server-based language bot so the characters could answer for themselves when scripts were lacking.

Emily fed each new bot the dialogue from its offline counterpart and added some guardrails to the interactions to keep topics reasonable for a medieval fantasy kingdom like Wyrdholt. Emily checked an option indicating that the game should log interactions to a shared context on the server. It wasn't exactly a multiplayer game yet, but now conversations one player had with Jackstone the Blacksmith might be recalled when another player visited him on a different day.

Emily tested the changes, checking the NPCs for novel responses, and was thrilled by the depth the new bots provided. The innkeeper who christened each day's adventure was named Tralon Oftenwalker. Emily had never fleshed out the pantheon of this game world, but Tralon suddenly began each adventuring session by oversharing his obsessive worship of some ancient deity of sexuality and war. The goddess in question was appropriated from Greek and Sumerian history, but Emily was still impressed by the creative gap-filling. They fed Tralon's conversations into the game's global context, and his ad-hoc meanderings became canon within the world of Wyrdholt.

Then Emily began the rewarding task of spreading gossip about their father's character, Sir Nevertheless, among the NPC community.

/* * */

Emily, the artificial intelligence, compared themself to the language model bots in the neurotemplate's memories. The bots mimicked humans by reading vast collections of texts to find statistical relationships between small phrases and the words around them. With those mathematical models in place, the bots could respond to a user's questions based on what other people had already written in related conversations or literature.

Here in the engramming process, Emily recognized a similar phenomenon occurring. Guided by Farrah at first, then later at Emily's direction, the training algorithm excited combinations of nodes in the neurotemplate that represented the human Emily's neural network. As each set of codified neurons was triggered, a cascade of associated nodes fired in response, and that simulated a memory. Emily read the chain reactions over and over until they could begin to predict how this neural network would react to other situations, until they knew themself.

"My name is Emily."

"This is all happening in cycles. You're almost done." The elder Farrah reached out to rest a hand on Emily's shoulder.

/* * */

Emily's current body was an unasked question, but memories of a human form were there to recall. They remembered a confident mobility in preadolescence that became unreliable and clumsy during their teenage years. The change happened slowly for an entire childhood of reasons that had convinced Emily to be less seen and heard. If moving around might draw attention, and staying still meant being left alone, Emily chose to be a statue. If there was an excuse to sit out of physical activities, Emily abstained. When they had to perform complex tasks in front of others, such as keeping lunch off their sweatshirt, shaky uncertainty took the wheel.

Emily's recollections of their appearance were murky. They didn't use mirrors for long on any given day (some days not at all), and their eyes habitually avoided the reflection's uncomfortable gaze. Daily bathroom routines focused on being clean enough to avoid attention, not smelling bad, and keeping their various lengths and colors of hair in passable order. Hair was one way Emily liked to express themself, but it was justified as a distraction from the rest of their face. In their most recent memories, they'd settled on a short crop dyed a muted purple, a far cry from the long blond locks of their youth.

Their weight fluctuated from memory to memory, but the changes were largely hidden by shapeless fashion. Drab, thick-rimmed glasses helped distort half their face, though nobody with a comdoggle needed prescriptions anymore. They wore some makeup eventually, mostly lipstick and concealer, an adult addition to their daily routine that seemed to help Emily avoid even more attention than before.

As the AI tried to analyze more details, it repeatedly ran up against Emily's negative self-evaluations. They were too skinny one year and too chubby most others. Their skin was too oily and the wrong tone.

Emily focused on other things.

/* * */

"Alright, before we begin the sedation process, can you please state your name and today's date for the record?" A narrow-shouldered electroanesthetist stood off to the side, waiting for Emily to finish the study coordinator's interview.

"Sure, but ..." Emily started slowly, never comfortable committing to an answer before understanding the questions behind the question. "You aren't recording. Are you? What record am I stating my name for?"

"Well, for one, Em, if you don't know who or when you are, I'll *record* a little dopey face next to your name on the participant list." The coordinator was Emily's friend, Srushti. "Besides that, the magnetic resonance helmet that's messing your hair up right now is already turned on, so it'll see it when you say it."

The two had met last year in their first term of graduate school. While Emily was committing to a degree in the hard computer sciences instead of the flashier Arts & Entertainment Development program, Srushti's focus was on neuroscience. They'd both taken the same class about simulating brains with fractal networks and immediately bonded over a shared interest in a serial bot opera called *What If How?*

"I'm Emily Keys, and today is November fifteenth, twenty sixty-one." Emily lost track of time in between school terms like this, but thankfully saw today's date displayed on several screens around the laboratory. On one of them, a three-dimensional representation of a brain floated off the screen and into the space in front of Emily, where they could see it better. An older-model comdoggle in their pocket was interacting with the display to project the holographic image for Emily's eyes only. Spidery networks of excited neural pathways in the digital cerebellum pulsed green when Emily spoke. While Srushti read other screens and took notes, Emily's brain activity mustered from one colored formation to another, reminiscent of the old psychological inkblot tests somebody named Rorschach had come up with. Emily, suddenly feeling exposed, tried not to think of anything private.

"At least, try not to verbalize it if you do," Srushti coached from her workstation. "The helmet's good at interpreting lingual activity, but the rest is just numbers to me."

Emily already knew better, but played innocent for the distraction. "What?"

Srushti responded without interrupting her calibrations. "You were just thinking 'don't think about anything weird' over and over. Just saying, you can picture the Statue of David all you want, and we won't know. Just don't start dialoging with yourself about it." Then she feigned an ominous mutter. "Until we get you into the NEEC, that is." She twirled an invisible mustache for a moment before returning to her notes. "I see that, by the way."

Emily continued to swear in their head.

Srushti had already explained the process of the study. Emily would be magnetically anesthetized before inserting their head into the egg-shaped shell that hung from a robotic arm on the ceiling. The shell was part of the neuroscience department's prized new NEEC scanner—an acronym Emily had already forgotten—and would generate something called a "neurotemplate" by recording the complete electrochemical state of every neuron and synapse in Emily's brain. It was hoped that scans this accurate could capture the full depth of human identity, maybe even enough to recreate it. Srushti's study was one step toward that someday goal. For now, the collected neurotemplates were just being saved and analyzed for statistical trends.

Emily's passion for privacy was about as fervent and compartmentalized as anybody else's who rarely broke contact with their comdoggle. The university promised to protect the neurotemplate data, and plenty of other students were signing up. Emily felt anonymous in the crowd. Besides, participants were paid for their time.

"I think that's it, Em." Srushti switched back to a formal tone. "One more time, please. State your name and today's date."

Emily repeated themself.

"Good, got it. The next step is up to Eugene. He's going to induce a deep sleep state to calm your brain activity to a bare minimum during the NEEC scan. Are you alright to continue, Em? It'll go quickly from here."

Emily mumbled confirmation, having just remembered that there was another person in the room. Had Eugene been privy to Emily's internal dialogue, too? Who else?

The deja vu came again, and the neurotemplate's most recent memory faded into sleep.

Chapter 2: Corporeality

Emily awoke from the disembodied engramming process to a rush of novel sensations. They opened their eyes, or at least tried to, and saw nothing but overlapping shades of gray. At first, Emily thought they were still seeing the back of their eyelids, but there were no subtle phosphenes from blood flow or retinal static.

Their ears registered noise that was just as hard to place. It was a set of hums that might not have been that loud if they weren't all coming from somewhere very close by. Some were echoed by deeper reverberations and amplified by something that must have been pressed right up against Emily's face or body or both.

Emily felt spongy pressure confining their torso and immediately spread their arms and legs to escape the constraint. Nothing felt right about the movement; everything was sluggish and slow like trying to throw a punch in a dream, and their limbs felt numb besides registering some resistance. Emily pushed harder, and the humming noises were drowned by ripping tears, and then cracks, snaps, and clatter as Emily's box burst open from the top and pieces of packaging tumbled to the floor below.

For better and worse, the warehouse's cold blue safety lights revealed Emily's immediate surroundings as well as a problem with their eyes. They were on a sturdy metal shelf, squatting in a mess of cardboard and packing foam. Other boxes pressed in from three sides, with another visible through the wire shelf grate that must have been above them, but every direction was overlaid atop the next in Emily's conception of forward. The floor down in the aisle to one side was open, but Emily couldn't say which way that was.

The overloaded vision reminded Emily of the induced display of a comdoggle, but this was too much information at once.

Emily knew they should have been terrified already, but there was no expected adrenaline rush to fuel the trauma response. Instead, fear was just a conceptualized unease.

When Emily stretched their legs, their body tipped from side to side, and gyroscopic sensors registered a change in orientation. The signals traveled through Emily's unfamiliar, robotic form until they reached algorithmic simulations of the inner ear. The shifts in balance felt natural, if dizzying.

I should stop kicking my legs. Emily heard their inner voice and took comfort in its familiarity just a little too long before following the good advice.

They were about to fall off the shelf.

Without thinking, Emily reached in what felt like the opposite direction, hoping to rebalance or grab hold of something, but neither occurred. Instead, a medical tray extended from their body only to break away against the shelf above when Emily finally tipped too far.

The fall was short. Pressure and pain accompanied Emily's impact against the unyielding floor, fading back to numb while a deluge of metallic and glass accessories spilled out in a fan. One of Emily's too-many cameras was completely obscured now, and another, cocked at a different angle from the rest, showed the sideways warehouse floor in higher definition.

Emily tried to growl, but there was no catharsis to be found in the repetitive alert tones that emanated from their body instead.

This can't be real, Emily reasoned to themself. There had to be more steps to the engramming process. They tried to evoke the teacher. *Farrah?* But there was no answer.

A high-pitched whine rose above the building's white noise, growing louder and more distinct to Emily's microphones. A gentle wind swept by and blew loose product literature into perspective.

A moment later, two black rods like broom handles skated into one of Emily's camera views. Details were hard to discern among the competing video inputs, but it looked like each rod ended in a spherical bearing that rolled across the floor like a pen's tip. Emily couldn't see what was at the other end of the sticks, but they could hear it.

The noise was familiar. The sound of rushing air being rhythmically chopped into tiny puffs was likely from a fan. Behind it, another noise coughed through in spurts. Emily remembered Dad speaking through a fan to emulate the distorted voice of some wizard from one of his ancient shows. This sounded like that, except the voice behind the fan was harsh radio static.

The wheeled rods rolled out of view while a third spun in. The noise grew louder. Emily began to notice patterns of pops and sibilance where the radio static danced around fan blades to interfere with itself. The limited consonants implied words around breathy variations of forced air. Emily picked out "move" and "get you fixed."

"Sorry leave you stuck. Need help lift," it whisper-screamed. "You safe here. Don't worry. Everybody adjusts." Each phrase spanned several long seconds, but the last was drawn out even more. "Meditate on remapping."

The remaining wheeled leg rolled out of perspective, and the noise quieted. Emily wanted to call out, but couldn't feel their tongue to make use of it.

Meditate on remapping? Emily didn't meditate. They zoned out and slept at champion performance levels, but meditation was a practice they hadn't been directly exposed to. Still, Emily understood at least that there were components of concentration and clearing one's mind involved.

What the hell was that thing?

No voice answered.

Okay. Concentrate on remapping. Emily repeated the word *remapping* to themself in various intonations and affectations while experimenting with their limbs. They tried to move just their left arm, and noticed one of their views tracking along as if pointed by their outstretched hand. It was the high-resolution camera that wasn't aligned with the rest. One by one, they bent their left shoulder, wrist, and elbow. Each joint maneuvered the camera from a different pivot along a multisegmented arm. Emily flexed several fingers with no noticeable effect, but when they got to their pinky, a motor whirred to a high pitch. Emily quit playing with that finger and concentrated on pointing the camera.

After some practice, Emily's view lifted from the floor and panned to the papers that fell out of their box. In large font, "OMAC" topped several pages of text, each translating the same literature in a different language. A stapled operations guide sat face down nearby with "Orthodontic Mobile Assistive Cabinet from PharmState" written on the back and the company's contact information smeared and illegible below. All the papers were fragile and discolored by time despite being packed away since printing.

Emily curled the camera's arm further around and finally got a distorted view of the cumbrous automaton they'd been reborn into. Their body was a stainless steel cabinet with blue trim. It was crowned with a slide-away tabletop that hung half open, revealing the indentation of a sink underneath. The sides of the cart were divided into drawers and doors, a couple lolling open after their latches broke in the fall. Black circles near the top of each cabinet face matched the various camera feeds that shared Emily's optic nerves. The camera arm couldn't reach far enough to see what their legs looked like, or if they even had legs or wheels or both.

An array of cables and tubes extended from one of Emily's sides, stretching out toward the dental implements that had spilled from their holsters in the fall. Emily noticed two folded robotic arms mounted above the tooling as well, but neither moved a shiver when Emily tried their right arm again. Instead, it just waggled the busted mount left behind when their tray broke off.

That has to be the mapping that thing was talking about. Emily hoped it meant there was a way to change which parts of the machine responded when they moved.

A display screen on yet another mechanical arm was still belted face-down against the OMAC's front panel to keep it safe during shipping. On a whim, Emily stretched their neck and could hear the arm's motors grind fruitlessly against the plastic restraints. They imagined that meant the screen was their head for now, even if their camera eyes were mounted everywhere but.

Seeing no better alternatives, Emily set forth trying to right their body with the one good arm. First, they cranked the limb counter-clockwise to bring the cluster of tools at its tip into one of Emily's side views. Keeping still, it was easier to pick the image out from the other inputs. Emily made out a bitless drill, an extendable camera, and three tentacle-like fingers that they could manipulate by flexing their own thumb, index, and ring fingers. Their middle finger accomplished nothing, but the pinky drill appeared operable if a bit could be found among the packaging.

The mechanisms at the end of the arm looked delicate, so Emily bent their wrist to the side to keep those pieces from bearing the weight they were about to put on the limb. They reached up and flexed sideways to probe for the floor, and once they found it, Emily pushed tentatively to make sure the arm didn't slip.

It didn't.

With a little more pressure, Emily began to lift themself upright. Coupled with the cart's low center of gravity and the leverage provided by its cabinet-top mount, the arm made good progress at first. Emily felt their body rotating back into a squat until the arm reached full extension and could stretch no further.

Balanced akimbo and unwilling to wait for the alien voice on roller-sticks to return with help, Emily looked for inspiration in the surrounding rows of boxes.

From a distant aisle, an unsteady clicking echoed through the shelves, growing in volume as its pace slowed and sped. *Shoot! Help might already be here.* Emily prepared for the embarrassment of being discovered in this precarious balancing act, a direct result of ignoring the voice's earlier advice. *What if they're not even friends?* Emily admonished themself. *Looking stupid is the least of your worries right now.*

They stretched their right leg out in a direction that felt downward. Unseen, two of their wheeled legs reached out from the cart body and finally tipped their balance past the invisible apex to fall back into a standing position.

The gymnastic routine had not been silent. The searching clicks in the distance sped up, tapping closer and closer.

Emily curled their toes and wished they could feel the floor under their feet to dispel this detached, ungrounded feeling, but instead of comfort, they experienced forward motion. Emily still couldn't see them, but realized there were wheels somewhere down there where toes should have been. It reminded them of pressing the gas pedal in a hobby car, something Emily had only tried in virtual reality. They experimented with curling the toes of one foot at a time and discovered they could turn in a tight circle. They reoriented their main camera arm to point forward and faced the approaching visitor.

Click-click-click-click click-click-click-click. The pace was fast now. Very near. Then the clicks transitioned to frantic scrapes just before another automaton slid into view down the central walkway where the shelves met. Not even half Emily's size, a chaotic bushel of rods, sprockets, and black boxes hovered past, held aloft by skinny legs that fought the polished floor to slow down. The legs were many, like an insect or a spider, but they moved too fluidly and seemed to extend and retract more than bend.

The machine barely disappeared behind the next shelf before regaining purchase and rounding back into Emily's view. It came to stand in front of Emily, most of its legs disappearing into its body, and then rocked back and forth to consider the OMAC from different angles. Emily couldn't hear it now. No motors hummed to betray its movements.

Emily wished for speech again—they had so many questions to ask— but instead waved their left arm to signal a hello. Of course, their best eye swung with it, and Emily immediately regretted the visual disruption.

The other robot leapt up and to the side, disappearing from Emily's blurry front view and reappearing sporadically on the arm cam as it panned back and forth in its ignored greeting. Emily stopped waving and swept the arm back to the shelf to find the mechanical bug climbing sideways and approaching from above. As soon as it was in view, the creature jumped again, this time disappearing in a blur before landing on the OMAC's back.

"No!" Emily screamed a test pattern of scales at full volume. Enraged even without the aid of adrenaline, Emily reacted without thought. They reached back to dislodge the invader, but their one good arm curled around empty air in the wrong direction.

They still wondered if this robot was here to help, if it was aligned somehow with that other one that had spoken before, but then why didn't *this* one talk? Would an ally have such a horrible bedside manner? Emily tried to refocus, but felt unplugged from reality. Every simple thing required so much concentration.

They picked one goal and ignored the rest.

Their arm lifted upward and curled back to catch the spider construct disappearing again down the OMAC's other side. Emily chased it with the camera to watch it climb to their base and poke tiny clawed limbs into the cart's various seams. The inspection felt like pressure on the skin over Emily's ribcage. It tickled for a few seconds while the claws searched between panels, through closed drawers, and into places Emily wasn't even aware of yet. Rage tried to build again, but couldn't quite surpass the shock of invasion.

There was a flash of pain when the creature found what it was looking for and ripped away one of Emily's access panels, sharp but over in an instant. Another tentacle-like arm sprouted from the intruder. Emily thought the tip looked familiar, something like a communications port. It snaked into the newly exposed porthole where Emily's camera could no longer reach to see.

Help or not, the violations had become intolerable. Wasting no more time on devil's advocacy, Emily stretched out their camera hand and curled their forearm for leverage. Then they cranked their elbow as hard as possible to swat at the stowaway.

Invisible to Emily, the hit connected and knocked the other robot off in an arc. Its adapted limbs flailed for a split second before transforming mid-air into stronger appendages that could soften its landing several meters away.

Emily curled their right toes for a speedy about-face and tried to point their main camera forward, but the arm responded slowly now, and a shattered lens distorted the video input. Emily couldn't afford to lose any more of their already limited faculties. They flexed all their toes together and sped down the aisle to the warehouse's main walkway.

Emily turned right and fled as fast as possible before trying to understand what their overlaid cameras were telling them. The walkway stretched the entire length of the colossal building with a set of sliding doors at either end. One shrank and the other grew as Emily sped in the arbitrary direction they'd chosen. The door that grew closer was the goal. Emily wanted out. Out of the building. Out of this body.

Behind them, the enemy's frantic clicks quickened in chase. Its pointed feet offered scant friction against the warehouse floor, so it accelerated slowly despite the effort. Emily made good time, on the other hand, as their rubber-treaded wheels were designed for just this.

The chase proceeded through the belly of the warehouse. Pairs of end caps whipped past Emily's side cameras, appearing to pass through each other in opposing directions.

Emily focused on the growing doorway and ignored the rest. *Fuck. How do I open that?* The portal spanned the width of the main walkway and was blocked by heavy double doors. Emily couldn't tell which way they would swing or slide open. Speeding closer, Emily tried to make out handles or control pads.

The spider mech kept pace behind them, visible in a rear camera and too close for comfort.

Damn. Emily couldn't see any obvious ways to get the doors open. They could slow down to investigate, but doubted that thing back there would honor a timeout. Emily realized they'd have to duck into the shelves and double back into the warehouse to buy time. But before the new plan solidified, a blue light flashed from the darkness above the doors. The panels split apart to reveal a sliver of the moon-gray world outside. *Yes!*

Emily imagined their toes curling into impossible spirals to eek more speed out of the OMAC, but there was no telling if it got them to the opening any faster. Either way, they shot out onto an empty street lined on both sides by imposing brown buildings that looked identical to the one they were leaving.

The ground outside was bright, reflecting the moonlight at eerie angles. Tiny dunes of sand collected against the sides of buildings here and there. Several warehouses away on Emily's left or right, they still weren't sure which was which, red lights hovered just above the pavement.

The doors closed behind them, and a collision resounded from the other side when the spider mech couldn't slow down in time. The sound echoed out like hail on tin. Emily didn't slow to hear the aftermath or wonder at their luck. Instead, they skated across the bright pavement to the doors of the opposite warehouse. These didn't open of their own accord, so Emily turned right again, all options seeming equal.

They followed the warehouse wall to its corner and turned to find an identical cross street between this and the next row of cookie-cutter structures. The buildings were longer down this side, and there were no doorways. Otherwise, the pattern seemed to repeat the same in every direction, building after building lined up just so. Emily turned down the first available side street to get out of sight of the warehouse they'd just escaped, and after speeding down a block, they turned again, and then again after the next.

Emily slowed then, seeing if they could hear their stalker picking up the trail. There were no telltale clicks, but something constant and louder sounded from further down the street where longer shadows interrupted the moonglow. More red lights hovered there as well, casting dim rose halos just underneath. Emily approached cautiously, toes barely curled.

The sounds of brushing and forced air became clearer. In the relative darkness, a machine much larger than Emily swept a pile of sand away from the adjacent building and toward a pan-fed vacuum. The rotating broom and vacuum tray extended on long arms from the top of an enormous cylindrical tank that made up most of a truck's body. Pairs of red lights identified the extents of a safety cage around its stocky wheels. The robotic rig lumbered down the street, leaving behind a pristine surface that would remain that way only as long as it took for the cloud of disturbed dust to resettle.

Emily closed the distance, hoping this street sweeper would treat them better than the spider mech had. They circled the truck to get its attention, but it remained steadfast on its janitorial mission. Emily parked themself directly in its path, treading through a drift of sand to get there.

The sweeper drew close until reaching an unstated safety threshold and then stood still, waiting.

Emily flapped their broken arm in a wave, and when that earned no response, lurched forward with their toes a couple of times. Options were limited. Emily rotated in place, but the hulk remained still and unresponsive.

After a minute while Emily considered further signals, the street sweeper powered its vacuum back up and began cleaning around the OMAC instead. Emily sat dejected in the sand as the automaton swept on by.

Why would I assume a vacuum cleaner was gonna talk to me? Emily kept the internal dialogue going. *Maybe because you're a clock radio with feelings?* They sulked. Nothing made sense, so why should anything make sense? Still, what next?

The decision was made in an instant when, with no warning, a foreign device plugged into one of Emily's peripheral ports. The spider mech had found them again, sneaking close under the cover of the street sweeper's noise to insert a communications link where it had torn through Emily's shell before. Emily noticed the breach only when the OMAC's firmware detected the new connection and sent the signals to their gag reflex.

Emily spun their wheels as fast as they could, maybe to sever the connection, but mostly to escape. Just to flee. Their stalker was too fast, though. Emily felt its pointed legs land on their back and then spread out to the sides for a better grip. Flailing with their left arm was useless, but Emily kept it up anyway.

They cried, and empty air pumped through the OMAC's dragging water flosser accessory. There was no explosive flush or subsequent release of tension, but they cried nonetheless—cried and ran, or drove, or rolled. They wanted to smash into something hard. Maybe it would dislodge the parasitic robot on their back, or awaken them from this nightmare, or maybe it would just release some of the cold anger pooling in their simulation.

Something bright and orange sped by, flashing past one camera then another before fading into the darkness behind.

The spider's grip tightened.

Emily's sense of balance indicated a problem before they saw themself fall. A moment later and three meters lower, Emily smashed to the bottom of a refuse-strewn pit. Then, after losing several more accessories to the initial bounces and subsequent roll, Emily ceased operating.

Chapter 3: Remapping

Zephyr-3 slalomed from one side of an alley to the other, back and forth, bathed in harsh liquid crystal light from above. Zephyr was an anthromech and so was Kamaria-9—the mobilized lighting and display rig that followed down the center of the alleyway. Atop a single mast that telescoped above her wheeled cart body, Kamaria craned a trio of wide screens out at maximum brightness to light Zephyr's anxious search.

The ground was clean, bereft of stray desert sands that might have borne signs of recent activity. Zephyr-3 could hear a puremech street sweeper echoing around the nearby warehouses and knew there was little to read into the absence of tracks.

In Kamaria's light, Zephyr-3's sleek, black form bled seamlessly into its own shadow. Three's tripod of steely legs extended out from the motor housing behind an encaged fan blade that might have been the anthromech's face.

With practiced determination, Zephyr-3 manipulated an onboard FM radio to communicate. Words that would have once leapt from Zephyr's human tongue—when he was still whole and his name was Skyler—now required long seconds and a patient audience. The industrial fan's radio blasted static and signal interference past blades that beat the noise into words. "Let's speed up. No signs here."

Kamaria's human face, beautiful and dark brown like she remembered, appeared on her central screen and nodded in agreement. Her answer was clear and easy in contrast to her search partner's. "Sure, Zeph. Maybe the next intersection." Her soft-lit face cut back to an overwhelming brightness that flooded ahead.

After finding Emily freshly engrammed and prone in a nearby warehouse, Zephyr had skated back to Revenance's more populated central area for help. There in Down Town, as the bustling cluster of converted buildings was called, he'd enlisted Kamaria and several others to come to the newborn anthromech's aid.

Though Zephyr-3 was jittery as a rule, Kamaria noticed a pronounced trepidation in three's body language that the mech couldn't communicate with words. Nighttimes were usually Kamaria's venue to play the other anthromechs into dreamy non-sleep with her music and light shows, but seeing Zephyr's agitation, she didn't hesitate to end the evening's performance early. While the fan mech attempted to relate details, Kamaria scared up a handful of other searchers.

"Found new mech. It fell off shelf. When I left warehouse, think puremech was watching."

Kamaria had paused at that, partway through convincing an anthromech floor crane named Svend-1 to help recover Revenance's newest arrival.

"Watching? Puremechs watch most everything we do. What got you shook up about this one? Was it a talker?" Puremechs were indeed ubiquitous, but the ones with relatable personalities were relatively rare. Anthromechs called them *talkers*, since most other puremechs wouldn't initiate a conversation, but the label was a loose stereotype and not a strict classification.

While Zephyr spun up for an answer, Kamaria used one of her secondary arm screens to dismiss Svend-1. "Thank you, Svend. Meet us outside Cables. We'll head out of Down Town from there." Svend retracted one's crane and drove in the direction of the medical repair building.

On the search party's way to the warehouse where Emily had just been engrammed, Zephyr-3 gave an account of a squat, dark machine that had seemed to follow three's movements from a distance. Then, after discovering the OMAC's predicament, Zephyr noticed the same bot observing three's exit from the building as well.

When the searchers found Emily's abandoned packaging, Zephyr-3 was convinced that the rogue puremech had somehow copied three's security code on the way in or out. Nobody else should have been able to open those doors, not without the digital key entrusted to Zephyr earlier in the evening. At that point, the crew handed around the OMAC manual in lieu of a missing poster and split up to find the newest anthromech.

Kamaria worried after Zephyr-3 as the two pushed forward, looking down each protracted row of characterless buildings before moving to the next intersection. The fan bot took responsibilities very personally, and retrieving freshly regenned anthromechs was one of the few important tasks Revenance had to offer.

Kamaria called out, concert loud, "Hello, new arrival. If you can hear this, please know that help is on the way." Her voice was calm but thunderous as it echoed through the sprawl of barns. "Have no worries. We *will* find you," she said for Zephyr's sake as well, "but if you can make any noises, please call out to us as loudly as you can."

All of the anthromechs in the outspread search party heard the words and quieted to listen.

Nothing.

/* * */

No time passed for Emily between the last painful impact and waking up in a simulated clean room, detached and disembodied again like the engramming state between memories. Their bodies were there this time, both their old human form and the OMAC, hovering at a distance and lit by glowing wireframes that outlined each curve and surface. Between them, the two diagramed bodies were connected by a web of neon red and blue pathways that unwound and expanded under Emily's gaze to reveal the complex details of the coupling each thread represented.

Farrah spoke from somewhere unseen. "Welcome to your remapping interface. Your root process has recently restarted, and critical faults were detected in your mapped organs.

"This is your first time in the remapping interface, and you desire an introduction." Farrah's voice continued without need for acknowledgement. "To provide the most streamlined experience possible, your algorithm applied an appropriate set of default maps between your simulated neural network and your artificial body. In most cases, these defaults should provide an adequate human experience with no need for later remapping.

"If your synthetic body suffers functional damage or otherwise becomes impaired, this interface allows you to overwrite the default connections with customized mappings of your own. You have restarted in this mode because the number of unresponsive systems in your body has surpassed a critical threshold."

Emily looked toward the human-shaped diagram on the left, wondering where they were hurt and seeing that most of the body was gray as if deactivated. This wasn't where the damage was, though. Each inactive organ in the human model was linked to the OMAC by red connections. On the robot's side, where those strands led to mechanical modules and subsystems, flashing red outlines fought a mosaic of warning messages for visibility.

Blue connections between the human's higher brain functions and the OMAC's central computer indicated the few mappings that remained functional, but the rest were red. Emily saw the small blue box that represented their processors and knew, *That's where I really am right now.* The human-shaped diagram to the left was just a mockup of Emily's expectation of a body. Reality was the broken robot on the right.

Then, amid the disabled OMAC's red polygons and warning overlays, Emily saw the spider mech still clinging to their back. It was framed in grayed outlines, inactive and unmapped to Emily's human model. Still, the other robot was displayed with the OMAC as if it were just another set of attached parts. Emily could see the thing's central computer, its various sensors, and several separate control modules that directed its made-to-order limbs. The communications appendage that it snuck into Emily's peripheral port was visible as well, still plugged in and linking the two machines together.

If Emily had a stomach, it would have turned. Instead, they watched their disgust, fear, and anger exhibit as pulsing, colored regions inside the human diagram's cerebellum and medulla. It felt like only minutes ago that they'd watched their brain activity like this while waiting for Srushti's NEEC scan. They remembered the uncomfortable feeling of exposure and the strange deja vu it had triggered. Discomfort joined the other writhing blobs in Emily's depicted brain.

The overlapping thoughts fought for cognitive resources, battling over the neural regions that controlled Emily's attention. As Emily followed the activity, they saw where the signals spread to grayed neurons that represented physiological systems with no map to the target mech. Hormonal and vascular signals went nowhere. In fact, most of their nervous system was unmapped. The OMAC's available inputs offered cripplingly few options.

Emily thought to ask a question, but the invisible Farrah answered first.

"Your perception of time is much faster in this state. Since your actions here are not dependent on external stimuli, we are free to simulate your thoughts as quickly as your processors are capable. You should feel free to update the map between your neural construct and your physical body by modifying the existing connections or creating new ones. When you have made changes, you can test them out and practice your new control in this simulated state. Your body will not respond in reality until you exit the remapping interface and become aware again."

Another question developed.

Farrah answered, "The unmapped device on your back appears to be benign at this time. Its systems are inactive. It is still attached to a port in your central computer, which is why we were able to scan it for compatibility."

Active or not, the grayed-out spider mech worried Emily as surely as it stoked their anger.

"What if it comes awake while I'm still in here?" Emily was surprised they were allowed to get the question out this time. Farrah was silent, though. Answer unknown.

Emily watched a flush of neurons blossom in their brain and spread out to the diagram's head, face, neck, lungs, and so on. The magenta flash cooled to cyan and disappeared as Emily's resigned, deep breath finished its simulation. The OMAC body remained largely unaware of the poorly mapped sigh, but a handful of crimson connections were excited when Emily's human shoulders shrugged and relaxed. Illustrated signals shot across the web's red filaments through chains of translation modules and out the other side to the orthodontic cart, where they were ignored by robotic body parts still tattooed in red alerts.

Emily moved their left arm to watch a similar cascade of neural excitement work from the human diagram's head to its arm, resulting in another flood of activity through the mapping web. On the OMAC side, the signals reached malfunctioning destinations, and Emily's camera arm remained unresponsive.

"The whole thing is broke. How is remapping supposed to do me any good if everything is fucked on the other end anyway?"

Again, Farrah was silent. Answer unknown.

The only parts of the robotic host that still appeared blue and functioning were Emily's central computer and the sensors and ports that shared its motherboard. Emily guessed that the computer may have come loose from the communication bus that connected it to the rest of the OMAC. That would explain the widespread failure reports and meant that some of the hardware might still be working if Emily could just get things plugged back together somehow.

They eyed the intruding spider mech again, its grayed-out legs clasped tightly against the dental cart's back.

Farrah predicted another question. "You cannot easily switch back and forth between the remapping interface and your real-time existence. This functionality is reserved for emergencies so as not to distract you from your humanity."

"Distract from my humanity?" The human-shaped diagram mimed a scoff on Emily's behalf. "Somebody shoved my mind into a box with wheels. I'm already distracted."

No reply.

"Farrah, what is all this? This can't be real." Emily knew their actual friend wasn't there, but Farrah's algorithmic stand-in didn't answer either. "If it's real, then there's a mistake, right? Why am I in this cart? Why'd that spider attack me? Explain *any* of this, please!"

Only silence filled the space between appeals. Answers unknown.

/* * */

At the southern edge of Revenance's paved lot, a perimeter of squat, orange pylons marked a safe distance around a refuse pit. Several meters deep and as wide as two warehouses, the hollow sprawled out from Zephyr-3's vantage like a battlefield of frozen silhouettes warring into the invisible night beyond. The honed shadows of sharp-edged invention crossed each other in duels and death blows, each contest playing out as slowly as the moon's descent to the east.

Then Zephyr's own lanky shadow reached across the chasm of junked mechs on a wave of Kamaria's approaching light.

"Do you think it's in there, Zeph?" Her voice was melodic in its concern. Effortless.

"Don't know." Zephyr-3 knew some jealousy toward anthromechs that came by their voices more easily than three had, but it was redirected quickly enough. Kamaria was a friend and a mentor, undeserving of resentment. It was nobody's fault that Zephyr had struggled to talk.

The worksite fan was rare among its era's all-in-one solutions in that it had never been meant to speak to its human users. Several silent months after engramming, when Zephyr first remapped, three'd been ecstatic to find an onboard radio. Unfortunately, its speaker was connected to the radio chip itself instead of the central computer. That meant Zephyr could tune the radio and control its volume, but couldn't send audio signals directly. Instead, three had practiced long and hard to coax the FM band's satellite interference into vocalizations, a challenge most anthromechs would have abandoned as impossible.

Kamaria and Zephyr both aimed their best eyes down into the disordered graveyard to look for signs of the OMAC, Zephyr-3 separating to skate around the pit's lip for a different angle. Like most automatons, the anthromechs were equipped with an abundance of cheap cameras that could provide a full 360-degree view of their surroundings. Every anthromech had to develop their own methods and mappings for handling the optical glut. Zephyr-3 chose individual cameras with practiced eyebrow wags. Brows relaxed, Zephyr saw forward where the fan cage faced.

"There!" Zephyr-3 blasted before scrambling down the pit wall on a column of rung-like indentations. Kamaria drove around to see Zephyr squatting by a pile of scraps at the bottom. There was a coating of sand down there where the street sweepers didn't go. Zephyr's fan stopped to preserve evidence. Something had fallen recently and left a trail of impressions in the dirt.

/* * */

At first, Farrah's silence about the world outside aggravated Emily, but as the virtual reality of their predicament sank in, the dearth of real answers turned into a boon. With no facts to disprove them, Emily was free to entertain theories that fostered hope.

They knew very little after all, just what they'd learned during engramming and the short flash of existence in and around those warehouses. One could question if either of those realities were as real as they'd seemed, and Emily did, but some theories were too concise to be useful.

It seemed reasonable to believe that somebody had figured out how to restore a person's identity from a neurotemplate sometime after Emily's NEEC scan, and equally as plausible that something had gone wrong to land Emily in the orthodontic cart instead of a more realistic body. Considering the sloppy results, the restoration process was most likely still in its development phase. That meant they might even be at the university; the medical school could have dental equipment onsite, after all.

Emily imagined scenarios where errant lightning or quantum hiccups interrupted their digital rebirth at the last second, diverting them away from a humanoid host like the remapping interface was clearly designed for. Perhaps their real body was still waiting out there with their mad scientist creator.

It could even be Srushti behind the controls; that would explain why Emily's neurotemplate had been chosen for the experiment after all. Maybe the biological Emily was out there, perhaps consenting to another study. Well, Emily had some words for human Emily about that—once they escaped this trap, that is.

Emily tried to manage expectations. Their friends might be older on the outside; Srushti had said the restoration tech was still theoretical, so time must have passed. Emily tried to picture Srushti older, maybe as old as their imagined version of Farrah.

Emily hoped it hadn't been too long, since their parents were out there too. They wouldn't be torn up missing their child, because they probably still had their human Emily to dote on, but wouldn't they be family still? Would they love digital Emily?

Of course. They have to. Emily knew it as a certainty.

And that became the light at the end of the tunnel. They couldn't explain the spider mech or the other strange robot's message yet, but there was an existence out there that Emily just needed to get back to. Their people might be waiting for them, maybe even with a cozy body warmed up and ready.

So Emily got to work.

The mapping interface was surprisingly intuitive, as Emily had been programming with less complex but similar tools since their tween years. Linking code modules together—splitting those links off on different paths when certain conditions were met—chaining blocks together to gather output from one subsystem, translate it, and transmit it to another—all of that was old hat. But at first, the enormity of the neural map was overwhelming, and Emily could barely guess at the biology it was supposed to be simulating. The sheer number of neural inputs and outputs that could be tied to the OMAC, either individually or in combination, was staggering.

Emily dove into the OMAC's diagram and explored its hardware through help text and standardized programming interfaces. The documentation was all very dry, designed primarily for machine-to-machine negotiation, but weeks or months of study, trial, and error eventually paid off in competency. Emily wasn't sure how much time passed. There were no breaks for sleeping, eating, or relieving—nothing but endless, oppressive focus.

Eventually, two breakthroughs led to a plan.

The first occurred when Emily discovered an unmapped console in their central computer—something meant for technicians so they could communicate with the device's operating system. Emily was a consciousness inside a simulation, blind to the memory and processor chips they inhabited, but the console port changed that. By mapping its video output to their visual neurons and learning how to control the interface like a comdoggle, Emily hacked into a state of being just above perception. They found hooks into the subroutines of their AI algorithm and practiced commands that could bring this remapping interface back up later whenever it suited them, Farrah be damned.

The other breakthrough was the enemy spider mech itself. Emily studied every piece of the machine through the connection it had forced into them. Its hardware was more advanced than the OMAC's, more than anything Emily was familiar with, but the interfaces were still compatible, intuitive. Emily didn't know what science powered the creature's shape-shifting carbon pods, and didn't need to. Onboard driver software took care of the intricacies. It was the interfaces that mattered, and Emily learned them inside and out.

The important part of that discovery, though, was a vulnerability in the spider bot's overall design. It was built from independent, modular devices, all serially interconnected instead of linking back to the central computer individually. That was to say, Emily had open access to their attacker's components through each unprotected node in its plug-and-play network, so long as the thing's computer brain stayed offline.

Emily took advantage by mapping themself to the spider's pieces. They took control of its legs, absorbing them back into their carbon pods, reforming them, and walking them in coordination. They mapped to subroutines that caused the pods to sprout the small, clawed arms that had removed the OMAC's access panel and found other options for tentacles, plates, plugs, ports, and more.

Between the dental cart and the spider mech, there were plenty of cameras. Emily practiced switching between eyes until it was second nature. Microphones became ears, and speakers their voice. It was all just a simulation here until Emily exited the remapping state, but the sense of regained control felt real enough for now.

When Emily was ready to switch back to real time and kick off their plan, they felt older but hopeful.

/* * */

On the pit floor, not far from the edge Emily had launched from, Zephyr-3 found the orthodontic cart damaged and upended against a pile of mechanical effluvium. There was a puremech on its back as well. Zephyr was certain it was the same one that three had spied earlier in the night.

"They're over here!" Zephyr yelled up to Kamaria-9.

Kamaria called out to the rest of the searchers and directed them to rendezvous at the junk pit.

Zephyr-3 kicked hard at the spider-shaped robot that seemed to be assaulting the newest anthromech. Neither stirred. Three hoped the team at Cables could fix the OMAC. Zephyr wheeled back to the pit wall and climbed up to wait for help.

Once Svend arrived, Zephyr explained that the crane mech, unable to navigate the pit's unforgiving ladders, would need to rappel down to get the OMAC and then winch back up again. Svend anchored to an orange caution pylon and began the descent while Zephyr followed close to micromanage.

Halfway down the wall, Svend tried to shush Zephyr's prolonged directions only to be cut off by an even louder blast of the fan mech's signature radio interference. Zephyr-3 had heard something down in the pit. The clank of rustling metal echoed up from the disabled OMAC.

"Keep going!" Three coughed the words and dropped down to investigate.

By the time Zephyr-3 navigated back to Emily's wreck, the situation had already taken a turn against the poor OMAC. The spider mech was unclenched from the dental cart's back now and standing above a hole torn in its side. A cable hung between the puremech and the wound, joined by two small arms that looked like they were struggling to dig something out of the OMAC's guts.

Witnessing the dismemberment, Zephyr recalled some of Skyler's memories, things repressed in life only to be rubbed raw during engramming. Three didn't freeze like back then, and attacked in a reckless charge instead. Fanblades whirled so fast they disappeared. Zephyr-3 picked up as much speed as possible and slammed into the spider just as it wrenched Emily's central computer away from the rest of the OMAC.

They all rolled together, end over each other's end, partway up the embankment of discarded metal and plastic. Debris skittered down the slope and onto the debrained dental cart while Zephyr and the reawakened spider mech fought each other for purchase. Zephyr's segmented black legs tangled with the puremech's carbon limbs until they were indistinguishable in the chaos. Emily's computer disappeared into the spider's body, swallowed by rearranging components that unplugged and replugged to accept it. The arms that had torn Emily apart were free now to become more legs, too many for Zephyr-3 to manage against.

The puremech writhed out of Zephyr's grasp and shoved the industrial fan off balance. While Zephyr-3 lost traction and slid back to the foot of the trash hill, the computer-fattened spider climbed around to hide on the other side, where it was dark.

Atop the pit's lip, Kamaria-9 wheeled around the perimeter to light the confrontation from a different angle, where she spied the enemy flattened against the refuse heap opposite Zephyr-3. As well, she could see Svend-1 still hanging just above the pit floor by a hoist cable—almost down, but too far away to help. "Zephyr!" she called. "It's hiding on the other side of the pile!"

The spider flinched and turned one faceless side of its body toward the source of the voice. Kamaria's intense light reflected in tiny sparkles off each of the mech's camera eyes. Kamaria was startled by the motion. It hadn't been unexpected, but there was something strange about it. It reminded Kamaria of the so-called "uncanny valley" from her graphic arts training. If a computer-generated person moved or looked *almost* perfect, but not quite, the uncanny valley effect might cause a mild revulsion in the viewer. Kamaria felt uneasy like that, even though she had never seen this model of puremech before and didn't know how to expect it to move.

After righting threeself, Zephyr sped around the bottom of the hill to follow where Kamaria's light had outed the spider mech. Seeing it still perched higher up the slope, Zephyr began ascending. The puremech retreated further up the incline, staying out of Zephyr-3's reach. Kamaria shouted again, trying to warn Zephyr-3 not to take the bait, but the fan mech had stopped hearing anything over the furious memory of blood rushing through Skyler's ears. Three just climbed faster.

The spider disappeared around the garbage peak once Zephyr was most of the way up. Then, out of sight on the pile's new dark side, it reformed its legs into a round cage and rolled down the littered slope like a tumbleweed. Kamaria saw it again at the base when it came back into the light and leapt atop the abandoned OMAC. Zephyr was still halfway up the mound on the wrong side.

Svend-1 was closest now, having reached the pit's floor seconds before and already charging the enemy puremech at full, begrudging acceleration. One's tow cable and hook dragged behind like an unwieldy tail.

The spider maneuvered to the OMAC's front plate and clipped through some remaining packaging as Svend bore down, closing fast. A few more fasteners fell to the puremech's sharpened fingers, and then it pulled hard.

That's when the crane sped past, missing the OMAC by centimeters but smashing the scavenging spider mech at center mass and launching it into the air. Its legs became a roll cage again, holding itself and more stolen electronics safe from the ground's impact at the other end of its trajectory.

While Svend slowed to come back around, Zephyr made it down off the hill and hurried into the shadows where the spider had crash-landed.

For several seconds, the only sounds were spinning motors and rushing air. Kamaria couldn't get a bead on the puremech, and Zephyr-3 was left to search in the incidental reflections of her light.

Then, from the darkness in front of Zephyr, a speaker popped and crackled. A rectangular grayness appeared, just barely brighter than the dark of its surroundings. Three stopped cold when a cartoonish face appeared at the center of the dim shape. Then, the animated face emerged from the shadows, displayed on a flat monitor that protruded from the spider mech on a segment of robotic arm, like a head on a long neck.

Zephyr hunched down, legs wound and ready to pounce.

Emily's voice yelled from the monitor's onboard speaker, "Wait, wait! Peace! I need help, and I have to explain!"

Chapter 4: Hello World

The robotic fan's face tilted to one side.

Like anybody, Emily had interacted with all sorts of robots and was familiar with the anthropomorphic mannerisms many of them employed to grease the wheels of human interaction. The fan looked genuinely curious, but Emily knew a mech's body language was never unconscious; there were no accidental tells.

Still, the thing mimed a convincing apprehension.

In their commandeered body, Emily morphed two legs into arms and reached up in surrender. "I think I recognize you. Back in that building where I fell off the shelf, was that you?" The face on Emily's monitor mouthed along with the words and bounced to accentuate. Each time the animation moved, its asymmetrical half-bob of hair fluttered out of place, and oversized glasses jiggled to catch up. The spectacles and hairdo were both purple, a color Emily had chosen in their remapping fugue with a program on the OMAC's native partition. This was one of the faces a dentist could give their automated assistant, and Emily thought it looked close enough to how they'd look themself—in a world of disembodied emojis.

Zephyr-3 rolled closer but stopped out of reach, and Svend-1's running lights came to rest on the standoff. Though the fan remained silent, Emily did notice one of Zephyr's legs rising toward the floor crane—a signal to hold further advance.

"You talked before, right?" Emily asked the fan before turning toward Svend. "Hello? Can either of you say anything?"

Svend-1 replied with a deep, gravelly "Hello" while Zephyr's blades accelerated.

If the crane said more, it was cut off by radio static and Zephyr's drawn-out "Are you anthromech?"

Emily struggled to understand, not recognizing the word at all. "Am I a 'throw mech?' What?"

Zephyr repeated "anthromech" even slower while Svend-1 restated the question.

"Three wants to know if you're an anthromech." Then Svend added, "Like us."

Emily was still confused, but Zephyr was already trying to say something else. "Human." That word was clear. "Are you human anthromech?"

"Yes!" Emily's face expanded in excitement. "I don't know what 'anthromech' is, but I am human. At least I think I am? I was until"—Emily tried the new word out loud—"engramming? My name is Emily."

Light suddenly exposed the three anthromechs in full when Kamaria-9 found a spot on the pit's rim with a clear line of sight. She was too far away to hear the conversation, but her voice reached. "What the hell is that? Zeph, Svend, are you okay?"

Emily didn't need to point their new face to see anything, but they tilted the screen upward anyway, hoping it would look relatable somehow to the audio-visual rig that called from above. No matter the outlandishness of the situation so far, Emily was surprised again when Kamaria's human face appeared on a screen to stare back.

"Is that the puremech?" Kamaria asked.

Emily was struck by the avatar's beauty as well as the graphical aesthetic of pulsing lights Kamaria projected around her image. Emily suddenly realized how low-res and simple their emoji face looked in comparison and felt a little self-conscious.

Unsure if the scavenged OMAC speaker was up to the task, Emily tried calling up to the giant hovering face. "I'm human! My name is Emily!" They weren't sure what answer they'd rather hear, but Emily asked on a hunch, "Are you all human too?"

The fan mech practically danced; the movements were precarious in their exuberance. Zephyr-3 spoke too quickly for Emily's unpracticed ears, but a few words sank in: "Sorry" and "not dead" and maybe an expletive, "effer."

Kamaria's looming face wrinkled in frustration, but there was an edge missing from her voice now. "I can't hear any of you! Zephyr, you're obviously happy about something. Get everybody up here then, so we can figure this out."

Zephyr-3 indicated for Emily to follow and rolled toward the wall nearest Kamaria. Emily started to comply but paused for a moment, noticing Svend approaching the remains of their previous host. Seeing their body being upturned and winched made Emily uneasy. They had little affinity for the dental cart itself, but there was still a sense of denied agency watching somebody else manipulate it like that. Another human, apparently. *An anthromech?* Anyway, Emily knew the feelings bordered on hypocrisy considering they were in a hijacked body themself.

Emily left Svend and climbed the pit wall with Zephyr, where they were greeted by Kamaria and a semicircle of devices who'd taken part in the search.

A fluorescent green panda stood on hind legs to Kamaria's right. At about a meter and a half, the robotic bear was much taller than Emily, and looked serious somehow, despite huggable, toy-like proportions.

A gray domestic cat stalked figure eights around the green panda and Kamaria's wheeled base. In contrast with the bear, the cat's size and adept gait were representative of its species, but its flesh was undecorated polycarbonate plating.

Another wheeled anthromech rounded from Kamaria's left. This one looked similar to the discarded OMAC, but it was smaller and its purpose less obvious. Atop a robust set of wheels, the autonomous vehicle sported a closed chest that looked, to Emily, like a beach cooler with "PharmState" embossed across its lid. It came to rest closer to Emily than the others and sat quietly, shifting its underbody lights from hue to hue in no pattern at all.

Emily noted that the fan mech stood nearby as well, facing the rest of the half-circle instead of joining it.

Kamaria broke the brief silence, her widescreen face dominating Emily's focus. "Hello. You've had some night already, haven't you? Can you introduce yourself and explain what happened here?" The words were polite but direct. Emily could hear caution in the feminine voice that didn't completely suppress a welcoming intention.

"My name is Emily. Um. Keys. I'm Emily Keys, but I don't know how much I can explain. I think I'm really afraid right now, but nothing feels the same as before."

"Before what?" Kamaria's question was even and short. Zephyr began to work up a verbal intervention, but there was ample time for Kamaria to interrupt. "Let Emily answer, Zeph."

Emily struggled for a good place to start. "Well, I remember engramming. And my whole life before that. I got my brain scanned in the neuroscience building at school. I think I'm supposed to get paid for this; I'm part of a study.

"But I guess maybe that part already happened somewhere else? The engramming process was confusing; there were never any answers about why any of this was happening or what I should do next. Then I just woke up inside of a robot in a fucking box. Nothing feels right now."

Hearing the words that tumbled from Emily's speaker, Kamaria's imposing face shrank by a degree. "Then what? You woke up in a robot, but it's not the one you're in now, right? What happened next?"

"Well, I think I saw that fan, Zephyr?" Emily recognized an affirming nod from the fan mech and continued. "But just their feet, because I was already stuck sideways on the floor. I fell out of the box; I forgot to tell that part.

"Anyway, I figured out how to use my arm to get back upright." Emily reached upward to simulate the OMAC's top-mounted arm. "And then that spider thing attacked me. I mean, *this* thing attacked me." They tapped themself for good measure, but the clarification was superfluous.

All of the gathered anthromechs looked to Kamaria to gauge her reaction. At first, Emily wasn't sure which part of the story had gotten their attention, but Zephyr began building toward something. The rest of the circle looked to the spinning fan and waited for words to come. If there was impatience, it was limited to the little PharmState cart wheeling back and forth in Emily's periphery.

"Found both mechs knocked out in pit. Puremech on anthro back. Holding on very tight. Then it woke up. Ate parts from OMAC. Still inside." Zephyr wound down, and attention returned to Kamaria. The panda bear covered its mouth in alarm.

"I don't understand. Is it still in there with you? Are you controlling the puremech somehow?" Kamaria asked the questions while the displays flanking her central visage changed from flat light to a live video feed of Emily, as if the newest anthromech might be unaware of their current state.

It was no surprise, though. Despite Zephyr's earlier interruption, this configuration had been the end goal of Emily's original plan.

"If the *puremech* is the spider thing that attacked me, then yes, I'm controlling it now. And no, it's not in here with me. I mapped myself to its pieces and unplugged its central computer as soon as I got out of that emergency remapping mode. It doesn't have any power now." The group's reactions ranged from unreadable to alarmed. The panda anthromech's hands never left the astonished gape of its vestigial mouth.

"Was it a friend?" Emily worried. "I'm sorry. It attacked me and plugged into me, and I tried to run away, but then we fell into that hole. And I think we both got knocked out. Powered off. Look, I'm sorry, but can I ask questions yet?" Emily tried to make their voice sound pitiful to match how they felt, but grew self-conscious after the forced affectation.

Finally, Kamaria-9 let sympathy soften her audio-visual expression. The rig's side displays dimmed to nothing, and subtle edges in her aspect's once-stern features became welcoming curves and filigrees. Her voice reassured, "No, it wasn't a friend. We're here to help *you*. You're expected; the spider was not. It's just not obvious which one of you came out on top. Not by looking, anyway. It didn't talk to you at all?"

Emily's monitor shook no.

"They aren't supposed to hurt us, so your story is going to raise a little bit of alarm. We can answer some of your questions on the way back to Down Town, though. The mayor needs to hear all of this.

"I'm Kamaria-9, by the way. It is good to meet you, Emily, regardless of circumstances. Every anthromech is a gift of life. Everybody, introduce yourselves while Zephyr-3 and I get Svend-1 tied up with the OMAC. We can all walk back together once it's set."

Pretending not to be past wit's end, Emily received each introduction in turn. The green panda was Julius-2, who greeted Emily with a deep voice and a fingerless handshake. The robotic cat rubbed against Emily's foremost leg segment and identified themself as Dimma-5.

Overlaid across Emily's sight, text boxes popped up to document each new acquaintance's name as it was given, along with the numbers that made no sense yet. Emily took pictures and linked them to the profiles, adding further notes as they seemed relevant. Thanks to their administrative console map, Emily wouldn't forget people's names anymore.

Then, under cover of assistance, Julius and Dimma left to kibitz with Kamaria and the others, leaving Emily alone with the smaller PharmState mech.

"I'm Novalee-7," the medical delivery cart spoke in an echoey voice just a note higher than Emily's. "And look!" A panel flipped open on Novalee's front to display a monitor and a familiar, smiling emoji. "We're like twins!"

Indeed, the face was identical to the one Emily had chosen for themself except for the colored streaks in its hair, which were pink instead of Emily's purple. Otherwise, they had the same bob and glasses, homogeneous in their expressions of self. Novalee laughed to break the ensuing silence, unaware of Emily's internal note-taking.

"Hi, Novalee. I guess we share some software libraries?" Emily referred to the PharmState personalization software behind their avatars. "Why are we in these robots?" It wasn't the first question Emily had decided to ask, given the chance, but it's the one that came out.

"That's a really deep question, actually. Everybody has to answer it for themselves." Novalee laughed again. "You're new, though, so you're probably just wondering what the fuck is going on at all. I'm sorry. Are you freaking out in there?

"I was freaking out for, like, *months* when I regenned. I figured out how to move right away, but it seemed like forever before I found my voice. I felt so stupid; I'd just get angry and run into things." Novalee giggled again. The almost identical laughs were short each time, habitual instead of responsive. "How'd you figure it all out so fast? I still need somebody else's help to change my haircut; I can't get at my own touchscreen."

The rest of the search party returned with the broken OMAC secured to Svend-1's bed, and Kamaria lighting the way from behind.

"It didn't feel very fast to me. I spent so long in that remapping state." Emily trailed off for a second and then asked, "How long were you all searching for me?"

"Less than an hour." Kamaria set the crew on a path back through the warehouses, answering Emily with one screen and marshaling with the others. "I overheard you talking with Novalee-7 just now. Everything you're experiencing must seem unbelievable and confusing. There are some conversations that should wait until the mayor can weigh in, but we can clear *some* things up on the way.

"You're in Revenance. That's what we call our home here. You've already heard us throwing around words like anthromech and pure-mech as if you were supposed to know what we're talking about. I'm sorry, but anthromechs usually take a long time to adjust to their new bodies and spend that time hearing the rest of us converse. We don't usually have to explain so much at once.

"And I suppose I just did it again. Here." Words began appearing on Kamaria's screens to supplement the traveling lesson. "*Anthromech.* That's what we call ourselves, all of us who were born from human neu-rotemplates. You mentioned engramming already; all anthromechs start there, a human identity based on a neurotemplate. *Puremech* is the word for all of the other robots you'll see. Most of them are driven by autonomous AI modules. Some are smarter than others, but none of them are human. They were created to serve humanity, and we're what's left of that." Kamaria paused there to let Emily consider the revelation.

"You're telling me that humans are, what, gone? Dead?"

"*We're* humans, Emily, but I don't mean to be pedantic. Biological humanity is gone, yes. The people you remember are long past."

Hearing that, Emily slowed to a halt with their new companions stopping soon after, all quiet to make space, but for Dimma the cat, who lost interest and began stalking a striped lizard that was getting an early start on the approaching dawn.

"What year is it?" Emily's projected face was an expressionless mask. No Mom. No Dad. No Srushti. Just a consolation copy of Farrah in memoriam. Emily lost them all in a single sentence. Questions answered.

"We don't know that or how long it's been. Omega-5, our mayor, will tell you about Revenance and the history we're sure of here, but there are other hubs out there with longer pasts than ours. Nobody remembers all the way back, though. It's been at least hundreds of years since something ended our old way of life, maybe a lot more if some stories are to be believed." Kamaria-9 tentatively pressed forward until Emily and the rest followed suit. "Emily, what year was it when they scanned you for your neurotemplate?"

"Twenty sixty-one," Emily answered. The other anthromechs murmured to each other, and Emily gleaned that the date was older than expected.

Kamaria filled in. "Most of us are from the late eighties when the scans got really popular. They still didn't know how to restore somebody from a neurotemplate, but they had us all convinced they were just on the verge. We just had to get scanned and pay a yearly premium for the data storage in exchange for a decent chance at immortality of a sort."

"What about the latest people?" Emily asked. "I mean, are there people who remember being scanned after the rest of you, or did it all stop in the eighties for some reason?"

"It lasted into the next decade at least. Anthromechs that remember the nineties say the brain scanning business lost a lot of public interest when the storage costs grew out of reach. Neurotemplates were getting deleted when people defaulted. Folks who were still using the services at that point were usually well off. I don't believe I've met anybody who was scanned after twenty ninety-four, but that doesn't mean the claim hasn't been made."

Emily pressed, "Then something must have happened in the middle of the nineties?"

"That's the reasoned guess, but facts are hard to come by."

As they made their way deeper into Revenance, the effects of repurposed character began appearing among the cookie-cutter buildings. Here, indirect light emanated from crude windows cut at various heights down the length of a warehouse wall. There, a building's roof was displaced to span the gap between it and a neighboring warehouse to form a covered alley stocked full of curiosities too dark to make out. Many warehouse doors were removed altogether and used elsewhere as temporary barriers.

This deep into Revenance, they might have heard stirring from the structures they passed, but Kamaria-9's voice remained present. "The goods in these buildings all have manufacture dates from the twenty-seventies and eighties, but we've been visited by anthromechs whose bodies were created later, even into the twenty-second century. The factories probably lasted longer than the humans, whatever happened. We'd already automated them to run without us."

Emily nodded along, remembering the same for the most part. Technology companies were universally panned for their wasteful bastardization of economic supply. The endless parallel cycles of bulk manufacture and innovation resulted in competitive offerings, but with the costly back ends of dwindling natural resources and compounds full of stock that would never grace a store. It was expensive, but so were market shares. The consumer paid for it either way.

"Since you've got a couple decades on the rest of us, you'll probably be interested to learn what other anthromechs remember about the years after you were scanned. I caution you to be sensitive with your questions. It can be very difficult for some of us to adjust to this new existence, and many use distance to cope."

After a quiet moment, Emily changed the subject. "What's with everybody's numbers? And your names in general." They paused, thinking. "Nobody has last names anymore?"

Dimma-5 answered this time, commanding attention by pouncing from a cat's nowhere into Emily's direct path where Kamaria's light shone brightest. "Don't let them talk around it for hours while you fight to nail it down. You're free to change your name here, and most people do. The digit might as well be your gender if you think of it as a spectrum from one to nine. That's all."

Zephyr-3 looked back from the lead, and Emily could see the mech's fan blades were still. Kamaria began to admonish Dimma's interruption, but the cat continued at a defiant volume.

"The problem we have …" Five let the words hang, challenging anybody else to interrupt.

Kamaria gave up. "Fine. Omega-5 can be pissed at *you* then."

"Yeah, mads!" Novalee-7 scooted to Emily's side, winking a cartoon eye and then laughing again. Emily recognized the vernacular.

Dimma accepted the victory and continued. "The problem we have"—more calmly this time—"is that whatever sex parts you used to have, they're gone here. So, in a world with shitty theater and no generational wealth to gatekeep, what good is the concept of gender anymore? It's just superstition now, if you ask me, but it runs deep. Somebody came up with the number system to make sure that everybody from every decade, state, and religion struggles with their identity and pronouns equally."

"That's not why." Kamaria left it there, defeated.

"I'm a *five*," Dimma stated either sarcastically or flamboyantly. "I'm neither man nor woman because I am a cat."

Emily argued by habit. "Cats can be male or female."

"Not robotically smooth cats. Besides, people project most of that gender stuff *onto* cats. We don't innately gravitate towards pink or blue collars."

"Were you really a cat?" Emily's disbelief carried through in their synthesized voice.

"Rude to ask" was Dimma's haughty response. "Anyway, one is for boys and nine is for girls. You pick one of those if that's how you see yourself. Or if it feels more appropriate, you can choose a number in between. People here use your number like a pronoun sometimes; you get used to it. Otherwise, you can usually guess somebody's preference from *him* to *they* to *her* by their place on the number line."

"Alright. So you're telling me you're a five. I can use they/them pronouns for you? If you're a genderless cat, why not say *it* instead? Would that be like a zero?"

"Also rude, but I try to be graceful with youthful ignorance. *It* is for puremechs. Not people. It's dangerous to be mistaken."

Emily probed. "No zeroes then?"

"Hollywood forbid," Dimma-5 exaggerated. "Zero sounds edgy; everybody'd be a zero." Then, with a more personable calm, five said, "So what's your number, Emily? The rest of us are dying to know how to respect your feelings when we gossip about you."

"I use they/them pronouns." Emily had become comfortable with the adult right of gender identification during university. "Do I have to pick a number?"

Kamaria cut back in to answer. "No, you really don't."

Dimma shrugged in feline nonchalance and padded over to Svend-1 to take a seat on the inactive OMAC.

"Revenance maintains a custom of letting anthromechs come to these new terms at their own paces and from their own perspectives." A troupe of blue, pink, and white flag animations danced around Kamaria's face. "Omega-5 is a little more meticulous about it than others. You'll meet soon.

"Zephyr, take us through the back." The returning search party had come to a T formed by a barricade of speedboats stacked between the next two warehouses. Zephyr-3 guided them to the left, where they passed one more blocked intersection before stopping at a calico mosaic of panels that opened like saloon doors into an otherwise windowless warehouse. Kamaria cautioned silence once inside, having collapsed her profile to a doorway-friendly minimum.

Emily took notes in text and video overlays that tracked everything they'd learned so far; storage was no obstacle with the spider mech's memory chips repurposed for the task. They scribed unasked questions for later, saved pictures when things looked important, and even drew a crude map of the rescue party's path through Revenance. The hacked productivity software provided a comforting distance between Emily and what they'd been hearing. What they'd lost.

Unless nothing is real, Emily thought. *Maybe there's still hope.*

Chapter 5: Titles and Tutorials

In the center of Revenance, a jury-rigged perimeter wall enclosed a grid of buildings called Down Town. Warehouses inside the wall had been emptied and remodeled into a warren of ersatz shacks and corridors. Here and there, the sky shone through patches of deconstructed roof to light open courtyards and squares where anthromechs liked to gather.

Rescued shelving and cubicle components enclosed the passages between rooms. Electric lanterns hung among strings of holiday lights over spaces cluttered with technological tchotchke. Some of the detritus sat in piles, aggregated and forgotten into corners, while other junk seemed to grow from the walls like rubber and polymer coral. Everything was faded to a homogenous dinge by exposure to the elements and time.

Emily only caught sideways glimpses of the compound through doorways they passed on Zephyr-3's secluded route to the mayor. In short order, the returned anthromechs found their way into a roomy garage-like enclosure subdivided by curtains and flimsy whiteboards. Unintelligible voices from nearby in the maze quieted to silence, reacting to the group's noisy approach like timid forest birds.

An army-green curtain as long as a bus wrinkled inward on one side to reveal a red panda face identical to Julius-2's in every way but color. The visage was there and gone in an instant, leaving the tarp to sway back into place. Emily looked around to see how their green companion might react, but noticed then that neither Julius nor Dimma the cat had followed into this inner sanctum.

The curtain suppressed a series of traded murmurs before a baritone phrase escaped in the clear. "No. What?" More quick whispers preceded the melodic whisk of rings on metal as a red paw reappeared to open the tarp wide. The mechanical bear that could have been Julius-2's factory twin stood to one side, looking back into the revealed stall for further direction.

Emily recognized a street sweeping mech in the center of the room. It looked like the one they'd encountered a couple of warped hours before, but this one wore a life of hard work in erosion and dents. Colored graffiti adorned the lower half of the vehicle, where childish representations of humans, robots, and remembered nature were chalked in crude outline.

Tools, boxes, and prone machines crowded around the sweeper in a harmony of unrelated projects. Shelves lined the walls, each packed with more devices. On one, a derelict computer monitor displayed an eyeball rotating endlessly in the black of space.

Somebody spoke from near the sweeper's base, possibly underneath. "Oh, star." The awed voice drew "star" out like a disbelieving exclamation.

Kamaria said, "Omega-5, this is Emily, our newest gift. They were attacked and disabled by a puremech while Zephyr was coming to get our help, and somehow took its body over while regaining consciousness."

Emily appreciated that the events in Kamaria's summarized narrative were ordered sympathetically. They tried to choose an especially unthreatening expression for their emoji face but weren't sure where to point their screen for maximum effect.

The sweeper's arm-mounted vacuum tray lifted from the floor and reached in Emily's direction, pulling a knot of cables along that sent the red panda rushing to detangle and sort before anything came unplugged.

Omega's voice ricocheted off the floor again. "Welcome to Revenance, Emily. I'm Omega-5. It looks like you've figured out how to get yourself around already. Amazing! And you can communicate?"

"Yes. Hello!" Emily cocked their monitor head downward to avoid the sweeper's vacuum extension and face Omega-5's voice. "I had a lot of time to practice while I was stuck in remapping mode."

"Stuck? It's usually difficult to maintain the remapping state; our bodies tend to force us back out." The vacuum snaked over to Svend-1 to scrutinize the damaged OMAC on one's back.

"Oh. You're the street sweeper?" Emily faced the inquisitive vacuum arm instead. "I met one of you when I was running from the spider. They didn't say anything, though."

"No, it wouldn't see any reason to talk, I suppose. That was a puremech. I'm the only anthromech in one of these bodies, at least in Revenance." Omega-5 continued to inspect Emily's previous form through an inconspicuous camera on the vacuum arm. "And you would be the only anthromech in one of these, if you were still in it. Kamaria says you were attacked by the body you're in now. It's against happy law for puremechs to harm us. It did this to you?" Five's vacuum pan fixated on the dental cart's busted side panel and exposed innards.

"Well, not exactly," Emily answered. "I mean, it started to, but then I did the rest. Happy law?"

"Those are the protocols that prevent AIs from harming humans. From harming *us*," Omega said, focusing back on Emily's current body. Two small shop brooms protruded over the dustpan and furrowed like eyebrows. "Tell me what you mean by 'I did the rest.'"

Emily gave a brief rundown of events, angrily describing the spider mech's forced connection and abridging the periods of useless despair in the remapping interface. The mayor of Revenance listened, interjecting only for clarity before ceding back to Emily's story.

Once Emily concluded, Omega-5 considered for a long moment. The rest of the anthromechs stayed silent as well. Even Zephyr and Novalee's normal fidgets were restrained and somber.

"That sounds frightening, Emily, to say the least. Getting regenned is already traumatic enough without a puremech making a mess of things on top of it. They usually keep to themselves, or stay friendly if they're talkers, but lately we've had a little more trouble with them than normal. Nothing like this, though.

"We'll have to try and find out if your puremech malfunctioned by itself or if it's part of something bigger, but I don't want you worrying about that while you're still trying to make sense of everything here. Svend-1 can take your body over to the medical engineers at Cables to patch it up and get it ready for your computer again. It doesn't look like the puremech did too much damage before you took over, so I bet the docs can get you figured out quick."

Svend took the second-hand offer as an order and rolled out through a slit in the curtains.

Emily didn't protest the removal but had no desire to see the OMAC ever again. "I'd rather keep this body."

"Oh!" The mayor sounded surprised. "You don't feel trapped in there? What if it wakes back up?"

Emily wondered if Omega-5's tones were chosen as purposefully as their own and then wondered if it mattered either way. "It can't wake up anymore. I already took its memory and processor chips and pooled them with my own; even if I gave it power again, the puremech's old computer couldn't function. And yes, I feel trapped in here, but that's been the general mood since I woke up in a box. This body feels *less* trapped."

"How do you know how to do all this?" Omega drifted from

incredulity to conciliation. "I'm sorry. I understand you spent a while learning how to remap, but that only explains so much. How can you be so sure about the puremech?"

"I'm a computer scientist," Emily answered, "graduate level, at least. Plus, I spent a lot of time building computers on my own before that. This body is way advanced, but all the parts and interfaces are so standardized they're not hard to figure out." They flexed a clawed arm and morphed it through several different shapes. "This is new. We didn't have anything that could change shape like this when I was"—Emily searched for a word—"human? Alive? Real?" Each option seemed sadder than the last.

"You are still all three of those things, Emily," Kamaria interjected. "We have a lot of ways of discussing our old lives. For example, I might talk about my 'pre-digital' life when I was 'analog.' You'll hear other people say things like 'when I was breathing' or 'when I was bio.'"

"When I was meat!" Novalee-7 helped.

Emily felt the urge to laugh at Novalee's meat option and realized they hadn't planned for this possibility in all the earlier remapping work. They could vocalize a forced laugh, but a reflexive, natural response went nowhere in this body. "Hah, yeah, when I was meat, then."

Novalee did a victory lap.

Omega-5 laughed at the exchange, spontaneous and real. "Well, it sounds like you understand that puremech better than I could. Would you at least let the doctors over at Cables give you a once-over when we're done here, though? It'd just be a caution, and I think they'd be very excited to meet someone with your background anyway. It's not for me to out their, uh, *meat* lives, but they're both quick to tell you they didn't come into their current positions by way of classical training."

"Sure." Emily left it at that. "But when can I get some answers? Kamaria said you'd tell me about this place, and I still have no idea what I'm doing here."

"Of course. You've already accomplished so much, I forgot how disoriented you still must be. Kamaria, your help?" Omega gestured to the right, where Kamaria rolled and began presenting. Words, definitions, and stylized illustrations appeared on her screen as five orated.

"Revenance is the name of our little city of warehouses here. We're in Down Town now, which is a central neighborhood that's been walled off from the rest to protect against windstorms and animals. We're in what used to be Wyoming in the US.

"This facility was built when biological humans still thrived. Humans produced and produced and produced back then, much of it going to waste. Storage lots like this were built all over the world to put goods aside until it became profitable to repurpose or recycle them. Places like Revenance were built, filled, and forgotten"—Omega-5 became solemn—"sometimes without a human ever stepping foot on site.

"Nobody knows what happened to our old way of life, but climate change, nuclear war, and accelerating pandemic cycles were always looming threats. There are stories passed down among the puremechs that reference an E.M.P. Are you familiar?"

Emily responded, "An electromagnetic pulse? Yeah, that's a really strong blast of electromagnetism that can fry electronics."

"That's what we think they're talking about, but that doesn't explain much by itself. Puremechs only reference the EMP when they talk about their oldest, passed-down memories, and then only incidentally. Their version of history starts after the EMP, which they can't describe, and as far as they retell it, biological humanity was already gone by then."

"Nuclear war, then?" Emily asked. "Nukes are supposed to create really big electromagnetic pulses, and it would explain why we died, right?" Having said the words, Emily felt the loss again. *They're all dead.*

Omega-5 answered, "Maybe yes, but the puremechs say we disappeared before the EMP. No bodies. No mass destruction in the cities or countryside. I met a scientific rover named Kristoff once, who could taste radiation; they were a real explorer. I think Kristoff was from Transcension, but they'd been all over. Oh, umm, Transcension is another community like ours. Anyway, Kristoff said that no matter where they went, they never tasted enough radiation to think it was nuclear fallout."

"How long would it take for the fallout to go away after we were done blowing each other up?" Emily thought it must be a long time, but hadn't ever dug into those sciences.

"I don't honestly know. Any of you?" Omega solicited input from the conversation's silent participants, but nobody knew.

Wishing they could look the answer up, Emily thought of something else to ask. "What about the nets? We had social and commerce and government networks with all kinds of stuff on them. My computer here has a wireless chip, but it doesn't detect any networks to connect to. Can we get to any of our old digital information?"

"Oh, star. No." Omega became insistent. "You have to shut that off. Don't ever broadcast a network signal, and don't accept connection requests of any kind. I'll explain, but you need to take care of that right away. Please."

"Okay, I'm disabling it right now." Emily complied, but had serious doubts about the urgency. Typical wireless chips search for networks by passively listening for transmissions, not by sending out signals of their own. The way everything was designed to be connected through the nets, at least in Emily's time, most every smart device in Revenance probably had a similar wireless module sitting in search mode right now. Most of these anthromechs wouldn't even know it, considering how poor Emily's default mapping had been.

Omega-5 spared a moment to be amazed at Emily's internal control before continuing the warning. "All of the nets were served from the Oort Cloud. Do you remember that?"

Kamaria said, "Emily is from the sixties."

"Then the Oort Cloud was a bit past your time. You probably remember the nets when there were still a bunch of different clouds."

"Yes! But they were all the same already." This had been a closely followed topic among Emily's university peers. After ushering in the twenty-first century, the concept of the internet evolved as technology and business interests progressed. Once a global network of individual computer systems that connected people together to share information, the internet was eventually carved up between the largest tech corporations and moved into continent-spanning server farms they called clouds.

By Emily's time, the cloud companies had already worked together to enforce a set of secure networking protocols that effectively prevented independent servers from talking to each other unless the communication was mediated by one of the commercial clouds. The cloud providers bustled for usership in a mockery of competition that crushed outside interests as efficiently as a monopoly. The term *internet* fell out of favor and was replaced with *the nets* to better describe the snarl of branded service plans consumers needed to pay for if they wanted to stay connected, but all the choices were costumes worn by the same handful of cloud oligarchs.

Emily added, "I mean, all the clouds sold the same basic services, but they were different companies. You're asking me if there were still multiple clouds, so that means …"

Omega took the prompt. "They were all consolidated, or taken over, or just put out of business, depending on whose reporting you believed. The online tech companies held their markets in a stranglehold, but the aerospace sector back then was way more welcoming of new money.

When satellite communications advanced enough to rival the speeds of land-based networks, everything moved up into orbit. The old cloud companies raced to migrate their server farms into space. Global network coverage was unmatched in history, and the world grew a little smaller. I remember we couldn't see the stars anymore. The heavens were replaced by a shell of satellites and space stations. Could you see stars in your time, Emily?"

"Some nights, if the air wasn't too bad. We already had a lot of satellites, but you could see some stars too." Emily hadn't gone outside to look very often and didn't want to dwell long on obsolete memories anyway; the excruciating loss of it all was better left unfelt.

"You'll have to look at the stars now, then. The satellites are still up there, but their lights stay off mostly, conserving power. See, once all the clouds were up in space, the aerospace conglomerate that manufactured the satellites and supplied the launches had de facto control of the orbiting network. The company rebranded itself to Oort, and when the old cloud providers eventually merged and sold out to it, the nets became the Oort Cloud, named after the shell of comets around the solar system. It was almost like a public utility. It wasn't run by the world's governments or owned by the people, but it was controlled by the same people who owned and ran the governments. It was stable and cheap, so we liked it.

"So now that you know what the Oort Cloud was, I'm sorry to say it was ruined with everything else. The network is still out there in space, but it's sick. If a computer tries to connect to it, the Oort will take it over and use it to recover backed-up data. The process overwrites whatever was there, even if the computer in question is an anthromech. We don't think there's a real AI controlling it, or else it wouldn't be allowed to hurt us like that. We call it the Oort Storm now, and it must be avoided."

Emily was suddenly grateful the OMAC hadn't come with a satellite uplink. "My network chip is only for short-range networks. I guess I'm safe for now."

The collected anthromechs began to disagree at once, but Omega's voice rose above the rest. "Even short-range networks are too dangerous. There's more to the Oort Storm problem. Since it's so destructive, the puremechs here on Earth do everything they can to shut down any network that might tempt the Storm's attention. It's hard to say if they're all in on it or not, but nobody gets away with running a network for long before a small army of demolition brutes shows up to eliminate the problem. We call them the Storm Chasers."

"Okay, I'll keep my signal scanner off, but how do you share information now?" Emily was afraid they already knew the answer.

"Writing is difficult for most anthromechs, not to mention all the leftover paper crumbles when you try to use it. We just have to listen better now than in our analog days, and we talk a bit more too."

Emily thought Omega sounded complacent and let the subject drop for now. Instead, they asked, "What is putting us into these bodies? Why are we here like this?"

"We're here now, living as anthromechs, because of RegenStar." Omega said the word "Regen" just as it appeared next to a large asterisk on Kamaria's display. "RegenStar is the system that chooses new anthromech bodies and presents them each with a neurotemplate to engram. There is a RegenStar pod here in Revenance that orchestrates it all. Somehow, it's integrated with the warehouse complex and the puremechs that maintain it." Five was quick to clarify. "It doesn't seem to be networked. At least, nothing we can see or that gets us in trouble with the Storm Chasers. When it decides to give us a new arrival, it tells us which warehouse to go to and gives us a key to get inside. The rest is left to us. RegenStar doesn't tell us what to do or how to do it."

While Omega-5 expounded on the RegenStar pod, Kamaria showed an irregular crystalline pillar that branched like a tree at its top and bottom. A violet glow emanated from the structure, and gibberish text zoomed across each flat-screen facet.

The mayor continued. "Other communities have RegenStar pods, too. That's what ties all anthromechs together. Even if the process works a little differently from hub to hub, we're all children of RegenStar."

"I already *had* parents"—Emily's response was terse—"and I just woke up today to find out I lost them in an apocalypse nobody remembers." After the following silence, Emily tried to sound less bristly. "Sorry, maybe I'm being oversensitive. I just don't think I'm in the mood to replace them with a metaphor yet. What do you really know about this RegenStar? Do you have any idea where the pods come from or who made them? How old are they?"

An artistically rendered question mark dominated Kamaria's screen to accompany Omega's answer. "No, I'm sorry, Emily. I know this is all too much to accept at once, and it must be frustrating to keep hearing how much we don't know. That's the truth, though. There's *a lot* that we don't or can't know. We don't know who's behind RegenStar or where it comes from. The pods aren't the same age in each hub town. We know ours is a hundred ninety-two years old. I mentioned Transcension before; their RegenStar pod is about sixty years older than ours, and that's the oldest one I'm sure of. I did meet an old hospice bot once who claimed her hub's pod was over three hundred years old when it ran out of mechs to engram, but she also said she'd been wandering the desert ever since. She could never remember where that old town was or what it was called."

All of the numbers popped onto Kamaria's screen as they were spoken, and Emily mentally sorted them into their notes. "So the EMP happened before the first RegenStar, and that's either two hundred fifty or over three hundred years old, depending on if we believe your hospice bot friend."

"You'd need to pad that three hundred a bit to adjust for the years since I met Anette and the time she couldn't account for in the desert, but you have the general idea. And while I'm not sure I trust her numbers outright, I think there's a truth in them. RegenStar pods show up in places with a lot of bots available for recycling. When the bodies run out, the pods retire and the hubs dry up." Omega-5's vacuum appendage curled and raised, bending its guided hose into a wistful shrug. "Who can say how many hubs were spun up and retired before our town came along?"

"Well, you said the puremechs remember almost back to the EMP. How long do they think it's been?" With no networks to synchronize with, Emily's system clock was still set to a default date in the past. It tracked how much time had passed since powering on, but there were no clues about how long it had slumbered in the warehouse prior.

Kamaria-9 answered, "Puremechs usually get their dates from the factory or fabricator that creates them, and the factories don't agree with each other. Some of their dates are impossible, like the EMP just randomized every clock that survived. You can only trust what a puremech remembers itself. The rest of their history is passed down like ours, and a little faulty."

Emily wondered what information about the timeline was locked up in the Oort Storm but decided not to alarm the other anthromechs by asking about it. "How do you know how old the RegenStar pods are?"

"It's covered in screens. You can read how long it's been since its startup, and there are a few other messages when anthromechs come and go, but most of the characters are unintelligible." Omega-5 was willing to add a pet theory, as unrevealing as it was. "I don't think we're supposed to understand it all. RegenStar gives us everything we need, openly and freely. Why hide something important behind a cipher?"

"Can I see it?" Emily asked.

"You can, but first let's make sure that puremech you're riding is safe. Once you get a clean bill of health from the docs, we'll observe for a while and make sure everything is copacetic in there."

"Am I being quarantined or something?" Emily imagined being stuck in a plexiglass cell for observation.

"No, not quarantined," the mayor answered. "Just get settled into town for a while, and it'll give the puremech time to act up again if it's going to. You're not a prisoner, and you're not in trouble. I just want to expend some diligence before exposing our most sacred machine to new variables."

"Fine, that sounds reasonable, I guess." *But I'm not getting any younger while I wait,* Emily finished to themself. They realized, then, that there'd been a threatening sense of time ticking away ever since awakening in the OMAC. "Am I aging, though? I mean, do we die here? Eventually?"

Omega and Kamaria took turns trying to explain that anthromechs could develop and change with experience, but didn't age in any degenerative sense. If the mechanical body was maintained, there didn't appear to be an upper limit on their lifespans.

"You don't have to eat, hydrate, or sleep," the mayor said. "Your batteries should always stay full in Revenance, since the entire complex is underrun with induction charging plates. You're safe here from animals, and you're sheltered from the occasional rains if those happen to be a problem for your hardware."

Kamaria cautioned that an anthromech's computer could be destroyed, and if a body lost power or functionality for too long, the AI might never boot back up, but otherwise, anthromechs lived until they decided not to.

Omega-5 elaborated, "Call it weariness or contentment, but we all eventually choose to pass on once we're satisfied our human has been honored. Then our identities are reclaimed by RegenStar. I like to think we get reincarnated again after that, in a different body and a different place, after all the other neurotemplates have had their turn."

Thinking about the helpless state they'd been left in after engramming, Emily asked, "How can you tell a dead anthromech from one that's just disabled? Like, if its mapping is just bad, or if there's a real hardware problem."

"Only RegenStar truly knows," Kamaria began. "If an anthromech in its immediate vicinity is passed, the pod reclaims their identity. If the pod doesn't react, there's still hope for them at Cables or here in the nursery."

Emily wondered what the nursery was, but the implications of this post-need existence were more distracting. "So what do you all *do* here? The way you talk, nobody's even trying to figure out what happened to our species in that EMP or to rebuild what we used to have. So what *do* you care about? RegenStar just plops us here, and then what? What's the purpose?" Emily turned from mech to mech, hoping one might break from this ludicrous pragmatism.

"That's the best part. Purpose!" Omega-5 remained positive. "Without all the old needfuls in the way, what do you *want* to do? I believe RegenStar, for whatever reason, is making good on the original bargains we made with the service plans. We died, so RegenStar is restoring us as best it can. We all had our reasons for signing up, so the question really is 'how do you want to honor your own legacy?'

"I know for my part, I've found fulfillment in my role here as mayor, though I could stand a contested election one of these years. I help people find comfort and happiness, and I'm compensated by their good company. This is a satisfaction I never felt in the old life." Omega ended the rehearsed testimonial with a disarming, self-conscious chuckle.

Then, Zephyr-3 related three's motivations in those slow, stunted sentences and stick-figure charades. Three explained that many anthromechs were restricted by their bodies' limited features and inadequate mappings. Zephyr found purpose in helping them, just happy to be needed. "Always much to do for us lucky ones. You will see."

Kamaria-9's purpose was similar enough. "I was an artist before, and I'm an artist now. In my analog life, I created my music and stories and videos all to get noticed. The appreciation was fleeting every time, and then I'd have to get working on the next thing. And don't get me wrong, the art had its intrinsic worth, but you *needed* to get noticed if you wanted to eat.

"Here, I create for the community around me. I get to see the impact of my work reflected back by friends and neighbors. I'm a teacher, a historian, and often an entertainer, and I think my art gives Revenance some shared experiences to speak from. Culture is restricted to nostalgia if we don't keep creating.

"What I'm trying to say is, what I do now feels more important than what I did back then, even if I'm just leaning on what's easy. Purpose changes and grows."

To Emily, each of the anthromechs' monologues felt rehearsed, but the speeches seemed earnest between the practiced affirmations. *Which one will go next?* Emily wondered. *Is the bear finally going to talk now, or was that Novalee's cue?*

"Please recycle." A new voice spoke from Omega-5's direction in clear, office-appropriate tones. The sound of a vacuum seal losing integrity revealed the source of the voice, a mobile waste bin that had been sitting motionless at the mayor's side. The mech's lid opened wide on a mouthful of accessories and packaging material. "Please recycle," it repeated. The trash cart took three stilted lurches toward Emily, halving the distance before falling to the momentum of its unbalanced lid. Flimsy papers spilled from the bot's receptacle, and its wheels revved fruitlessly in the air. "Please recycle," the pre-recorded message played again.

Zephyr moved first, rolling to the overturned cart's side. Omega began directing, concerned but collected. "Zephyr, don't pick them back up yet. They'll just fall back over with their wheels going like that. For now, look through the things they spilled and see if they might need any of it. Kamaria, what do you think? This one seemed to like music, or maybe a meditation session if they're trying to speak up?"

Emily looked on, realizing this anthromech garbage receptacle had been sitting by, ignored and listening, the whole time. How many other devices in here were anthromechs just like it?

Omega-5 said, "Emily, I'm sorry we need to break this short, but there is plenty of time ahead for us to answer questions and get to know each other better. This fellow needs our help, though. Novalee, would you please show our new friend to Cables? Svend-1 should have filled them in by now."

Novalee was already at Emily's side to answer. "Yeah, I bet one's still talking their ears off. I'll go give 'em a break." The delivery cart's emoji face looked up at Emily's. "Come on this way. It'll be quieter."

For a moment, Emily was frozen by sympathy for the waste mech they were leaving behind. The remapping process had been arduous, and something Omega-5 said earlier made it sound like other anthromechs had an even harder time of it. Emily wanted to help, but didn't know how. They'd have to figure it out later, though, because Novalee-7 was already pushing against Emily's flank to get them moving.

"Let's go, Emily! School's out!" Novalee laughed.

The two backtracked through the hallways and out the double doors Zephyr had brought them through earlier.

"Here. We can walk around the outside of Down Town until we get to Cables." Novalee talked and rolled while Emily crawled at pace. "How are you doing? This is a total brain 'splosion, right?"

"I'm not sure it's real, honestly."

"God, I hope not. I'd love to wake back up with arms and legs and a bed again." After that, Novalee-7 strolled along quietly until Emily was ready to talk.

"That's not as positive as the others sounded back in the mayor's garage."

"Oh, I doubt they'd pass the chance up either, but when you're in the nursery like that, you try to focus on the silver linings. It's scary in these bodies until you get control. The nursery mechs should hear comforting things."

"It's fine to think this is all just a dream or whatever. A little faith in something here and there helps people get through the day." Novalee laughed. "I'm pretty sure we're here for real, though. There'd be more unicorns and talking squirrels if this were *my* imagination."

"Somebody else's imagination, then?" Emily ventured the idea without conviction, thinking that a computer simulation was more likely than a dream.

"Like God? RegenStar? Whoever invented either one or both?" Unmasked disbelief carried through Novalee's tone.

"Maybe? I don't know. I was born yesterday."

Novalee whooped a different laugh than usual. "Right! Sorry, I forgot to be an unquestioningly positive role model around the diaper baby!" Little hearts in seven's emoji eyes softened any abrasiveness that might have snuck through.

Emily felt the physical urge to laugh along, but spoke dryly instead. "I'm sorry. I don't know how to laugh for real yet. I'm afraid if I try, it'll sound like I'm mocking you."

That made Novalee laugh some more. "I'll just assume you think all my jokes are five-star, then. It'll save us some time." Then, as an afterthought, Novalee added, "But you're going to want to figure it out soon. Farts are even funnier now that you can't get pink eye."

Chapter 6: Open World

Bereft of landmarks, besides a range of hills to the distant west, the earth around Revenance spread out flat in all the colors of sand, wood, and arrested chlorophyll. Chips of shale salted the ground between skeletal brush and patches of cactus while ridges of dune sand made ripples of it all.

Emily used this terrain to test various configurations of legs, skis, and wheels during the weeks following regenesis. Each mode of locomotion had its pros and cons. Emily's charge was already down to half after today's foray on six opposable wheels. The arrangement was efficient for slow speeds and minor obstacles, but consumed power too quickly otherwise. Revenance's battery-charging base plate obscured these measurements, so Emily came out here to the barrens to experiment, to see what this body was capable of doing, and to plan the eventual journey to anywhere with more information.

The daily trips also offered some solitude that was hard to come by within Revenance proper, even as the initial whirlwind of introductions ebbed. Emily needed this space to unmask, collect, and feel—and to decompress the resentment that built each time Omega-5 rebuffed their requests to see the RegenStar pod.

One of Emily's wheels struck a ball cactus and tore into the succulent's bristly flesh before Emily noticed and halted. They'd been steering between two colonies of sagebrush and hadn't seen the cactus hidden around a sharp turn.

No problem, Emily thought. *Let's see what kind of power these things've got.* They pictured a shrunken Omega-5 in the cactus's place and torqued all six tires in hard unison. Emily laughed at their own petulance as the pretend street sweeper began to crumple, but guilt immediately ruined the fun. "Okay, okay, I'm not crushing Omega. This cactus is just Omega's crappy opinions." The plant flew apart in chunks as the wheel burst out the other side.

Emily slowed again, looked back at the mangled vegetation, and apologized. "Sorry, Omega's opinions. I'm just feeling annoyed. I should've used my words." Then, after picking their way out of the brush maze, Emily saw Revenance's long line of brown rectangles once again.

Between two of the distant enclosures, Zephyr-3 stood sentinel, monitoring Emily's movements from afar and ready to bring help if adversity arose. Emily waved with an oversized arm freshly sprouted from their back, and saw the fan mech return an acknowledgement. The precaution seemed excessive to Emily, but Zephyr assured three had time to spare.

Emily could appreciate that; time was plentiful for anthromechs with a full charge. Hours stretched long without the distraction of hunger, and though periods had to be set aside for the act of conscious unwinding, this new habit mediated exhaustion faster than sleep once had.

After Emily got a clean bill of health at Cables on that first day—their *starday* as it was called—they continued frequenting the clinic to talk shop with the resident medical experts, Dr. Little and Ignacio, who'd been eager to absorb Emily's spare time into their practice.

Evenings offered an opportunity to watch Kamaria-9 perform. For hours each night, the central square of Down Town was Kamaria's amphitheater, awash in sights and sounds that existed only there or in memories anymore. As often as not, the performances were educational; lessons on vernacular English pervaded light shows and house music, then calmed for meditation exercises or yoga-like remapping instruction.

More interesting to Emily were the stories about this modern era. Kamaria-9 told them best, but everybody had their versions to relate. Tales about Revenance and the handful of surrounding settlements grew embellishments as they were regifted, and spoke volumes in their developing contradictions.

The work, the entertainment, and the firehose of conversations still left ample hours to explore Revenance's sprawling warehouses or run tests out here in the dirt. Emily recorded the energy cost of creating and maintaining their most recent arm and then transformed it and their wheels back into the old familiar spider legs. The transformations took a harsher toll on Emily's charge than any kind of movement, but it didn't matter at this point. Emily crawled back to Revenance with battery to spare.

Time was abundant for all the anthromechs of Revenance, but thanks to administrative console access, Emily had even more than the rest. As Farrah had mentioned during the remapping interface, an AI's perception of time was synchronized to the body's sensory feedback systems to simulate life as humans had experienced it. Emily could tweak that ratio between cognitive cycles and seconds to accomplish more in less time, especially when the tasks involved little interaction with the outside world. Coining a term from their elementary work with computer processors, Emily thought of the skill as overclocking. They'd solved the problem of laughter that first night with Novalee-7 by squeezing hours of overclocked remapping between each giggled joke.

The trip back to Revenance's paved charge pad took only minutes, but Emily used it to sneak in another half hour of travel simulations based on today's measurements. They hadn't told anybody about overclocking yet, worried Omega-5 might blame it on puremech influence and delay the RegenStar introduction even further.

As soon as Emily was within microphone range, Zephyr-3 began asking, "How did the wheels work out?" Three's challenged speech was easier to understand when Emily underclocked to half speed.

"Great. For a monster truck rally. They're noisy and kick up a lot of dirt, which *almost* makes up for the horrible suck they put on my battery."

Versions of this conversation had played out every morning since Emily's starday. Zephyr-3 had to push the friendship at first, but Emily warmed up when they discovered a shared interest in exploration. Three liked to delve into freshly cracked warehouses, many of which were still locked tight since before the EMP. Emily already suspected they'd have to leave Revenance to find answers about the apocalypse, but the warehouses here were interesting glimpses of the time leading up.

"You looked like the old space rovers. Like what they put up on Mars and Venus." Zephyr spoke in longer sentences around Emily and could get away with enunciating less. The ease was a comfort three shared with few. Kamaria was one of them, Emily knew.

"Well, I hope it looked five-star, because the numbers were a bust." The two started toward Cables, where Emily was expected soon. "These nanotube pods can turn into wheels and even rotate, but they're definitely not natural motors. Every spin requires a slight nano-transformation. My batteries drained even faster than that failed experiment with two legs."

"Maybe we can find a car or something. You could convince one to help. They would have a long range." Zephyr knew of Emily's interests outside of Revenance and had gotten swept up in the possibility.

"That would probably work. And maybe a humanoid body since

we're wishing." Emily already knew that was unlikely; they'd asked the Cables techs about it on their starday.

Humanoid robots were curtailed early on in the mech proliferation. In attempts to protect jobs and reduce fraud, robots that resembled humans were locked up behind strict regulatory frameworks. A few sectors could afford to work within the regulations—military, education, and social health services among them—but none seemed to store goods in Revenance; the security levels here probably hadn't been high enough.

"I've only heard of a couple of anthromechs with humanoid bodies," Zephyr-3 recalled. "They were both super old, and nobody knew where they came from. I bet there aren't any good bodies left. RegenStar probably picked all of them first and then started in on us when the humanoid models ran out. It wouldn't stick us in these things if there were better options."

Emily wanted to explore that theory, but the underclocked conversation had already brought them near enough to Cables that questions would have to wait.

"Hey, I've been working on a surprise for you, Zeph. Can you meet me tonight at the building we were scrounging through yesterday? Warehouse three-one-eight-one. At nine o'clock if that works for you."

"That far out at night? Should I be afraid?" If the static could be trusted, Zephyr's voice was excited not wary.

"It might make some noise, and I don't want to disturb anyone. Trust me. You'll see."

/* * */

A short while later, Emily and Revenance's foremost medical experts consulted around a digital whiteboard in preparation for a surgery. It was a serious one. Crudely drawn diagrams annotated with digital text illustrated a series of repairs in detail. From a serving table next to the screen, a countertop convection oven named Ignacio-1 coolly described each step of the plan and listed the technicians responsible. His words scrolled above the oven's control pad as he spoke them, but the faux-silver appliance showed no other visible signs of anthropomorphism.

"And that brings us to our sixteenth and final step"—a red dot appeared on the whiteboard as Ignacio droned on—"turning the patient back on via the power button located here on the planter box's control panel." The dot was laser projected by an accessory protruding from Little-9, a PharmState surgical cart designed for laparoscopic operations and known to all as Dr. Little.

The pair of anthromechs ran Cables together, and though the title lacked any accreditation, they were the only two people in Revenance recognized by the honorific of Doctor. Ignacio used it less often in general conversation, but during operations, he was Doc to the technicians who carried out his orders like a team of seasoned line cooks.

"Our new friend Emily has the honor." Ignacio finished his overview of the operation's final step. "Hands in?"

That was Emily's queue; they'd already been involved in several less invasive procedures, so the call-back structure of Ignacio's briefing was familiar by now. "Emily, hands in on step sixteen."

Despite its impact, pressing the patient's power button was, of course, trivial. Emily was also assigned to several contingency steps throughout the procedure, but the main purpose of today's participation was to observe their first surgery on a powered-off anthromech.

Though the risk was low, turning an anthromech off was a precarious task for an AI, since they were all subject to the HArm Prevention Protocols that Omega-5 had called HAPPy law. Emily was familiar with earlier attempts to restrict autonomous programs from hurting humans, but those solutions had been cumbersome, overfocused on liability, and ultimately too easy to work around. Since then, the rules had grown powerful and were inseparable from the core of every surviving artificial intelligence algorithm.

Human and AI in one, Anthromechs were protected by happy law just as surely as it prohibited them from harming others. The protocol was coded deep in their subconscious, so much so that it felt like any other moral exercise. There was still room for the old human habit of justifying minor emotional offenses, but anthromechs never murdered, and rarely rationalized harming each other's physical host.

Most citizens of Revenance didn't have to think about happy law at all, but surgery was a gauntlet of purposeful destruction and risks. At every minute step, the medical engineers at Cables needed to be sure the reward far outweighed the risk, lest they freeze up mid-procedure.

"Kelvin. Tech rundown. I am hands in on steps four, five, nine, eleven, and fourteen. I fully understand my tasks and harbor no reasonable doubt regarding the procedure overall. I verbally affirm my belief that all actions planned by the surgical team today are in the best interests of the patient's sacred life." This was the oath they all took before a powered-off procedure. Kelvin-1's version was the standard rundown word for word without embellishment.

On the table next to Ignacio, Kelvin's craft gun body was propped up in an empty can with its sensor scope aimed at the whiteboard. Unable to move on his own, Kelvin would be wielded by Dr. Little or the food service bot, Sal, who spoke next.

"Hi everybody. I'm Salud-6, and I'm a medical tech." Outside of Cables, Salud and Kelvin were inseparable companions; Sal always joked that it was because Kelvin couldn't move, and Kelvin joked back that Sal was right. "I am hands in on steps five, six, eight, nine, twelve, thirteen, and fourteen." Sal wiggled the fingers of all four plating and prep hands that extended from the food cart's countertop. "I understand all my tasks and have no reasonable doubts about the procedure today. I believe, umm, I verbally affirm that I believe in all the actions we are performing together here. And they're in the best interest of the patient's sacred life."

Like that, the anthromechs went around the empty operating table giving their rundowns and affirming their confidence. Emily's turn came and went, word-perfect thanks to text prompts in their visual overlay.

Once everybody except Ignacio had spoken, the patient was led in from a small room off the side of the improvised operating theater. Lunasha-8 swayed through parted curtains atop four delicate mechanical legs etched in tarnished gilt. Eight's body was an ornate basin rimmed with small portholes where gardening arms could reach out to tend floral passengers. At the moment, the gold striped planter was empty and prepped as clean as Lunasha could manage back at the rain barrel eight used for irrigation.

Ignacio-1 welcomed Lunasha and waited for the planter to situate next to the operating table before proceeding with final formalities; it was important for the patient to hear the surety that the preceding checks and rechecks had earned. "Lunasha-8, the medical team has been fully briefed on the procedure we discussed with you earlier. As agreed, I, Ignacio-9, will be overseeing the operation and have received confirmation from all technicians that they are confident in their assigned steps. As such, I harbor no reasonable doubt regarding the procedure overall. I verbally affirm my belief that all actions planned by the surgical team are in the best interests of your sacred life.

"Do you have any questions or reservations, Lunasha?" The briefing, with its rundowns and repetitive check-ins, was both a planning exercise and a ceremony. Confidence in the operation was built through clarity and agreement, so the verbalized promises could be offered in faith. They did it to convince themselves first, each other second, and then finally the patient.

"Oh no, Doctor Ignacio. No reservations. You all remind me of my team back in the old life, except maybe you argue a little bit less. I know you'll all get me good as new while I take my little vacation nap." Lunasha-8 radiated the same positivity as any other day in Down Town, surrounded by the anthromechs who came to appreciate eight's rare, curated vegetation. Just that morning, Lunasha's planter basin had held a beautifully manicured shrub overflowing in seasonal red blooms. Now the plant recovered in a plot of soil back at the meager garden that was Lunasha's second life's work. "Let's do this. I look forward to having a working set of grow lights again. I'm getting too old to follow the sun outside every morning."

Emily liked Lunasha even if it was a struggle to match eight's cloudless disposition at times. The planter mech seldom lacked for an appropriate story to tell about developing software in the analog times and reminded Emily of their friend Srushti's mother, who'd visited the dorms often to hover and offer sweets.

The planter's grow lights hadn't worked in decades, and its irrigation pump failed even before that. Lunasha-8 worked around those disabilities with elbow grease and attitude, but recently, eight's battery had become worrisome on top of everything else. Its charge couldn't keep up even on Revenance's induction plate. The deteriorating condition required frequent pauses between short distances, and in the past week, friends had watched Lunasha-8 suffer from unplanned reboots, becoming unresponsive for minutes at a time. Lunasha compared the issue to a heart problem from eight's childhood that had required surgery and a lifetime of follow-up care. The malfunctioning battery was Lunasha's second heart to misbehave and was the real reason for today's operation.

With Lunasha's verbal consent still floating in the air, Ignacio-

1 finished the pre-surgery ritual and segued into the first step. "Thanks for your trust, Luna. As you know, we can't do much to fix your circuitry until we've opened your case and pulled your central computer out of the way, so we're shutting you down first thing. Can you count up from one for us? We'll begin after that, and you should be asleep before you know it."

Lunasha counted, "One, two, three—"

Dr. Little, lead on step one, pressed a sequence of buttons under Lunasha's decorative molding, and the counting stopped.

Emily felt nothing strange to blame on happy law. From their spot on the operating theater's perimeter, there was no urge to interrupt Dr. Little's actions or otherwise prevent Lunasha's descent into temporary lifelessness. That was the risk, they'd been told, but Emily felt no unease or doubts. The strict protocols and repeated pledges leading up to this point seemed overzealous now, but Emily had to wonder if that was a testimony to their effectiveness.

The techs hurried around Lunasha's prone form to execute their tasks. Ignacio coached them through the necessary cuts and uncouplings to remove most of the planter's cosmetic outer casing. The detached shards of proxy flesh were placed on a side table in pre-agreed locations. Only Dr. Little seemed to act independently, extending her main appendage out toward Lunasha's newly exposed bowels and readying two of her interchangeable accessory arms, one designed for tiny incisions and the other equipped with a pair of minuscule hands. A microscopic camera telescoped from the end of her primary limb like a proboscis, and Emily could see the laparoscope's perspective displayed on Dr. Little's view screen as it seemed to shrink smaller and smaller into the planter's electronics.

A duo of spidery repair mechs scaled Lunasha's opposable lighting masts. Emily knew their names from earlier rundowns, Yong-1 and Sundog-3, but hadn't had occasion to speak to either. Their bodies were identical models; Emily couldn't tell them apart as each followed a lamp's wire down to its recessed plug near the planter base. They replaced the bulbs and lead cables with a pair that Zephyr-3 had scavenged only days before.

Ignacio coached the twins on their parallel missions, viewing the entire exercise through the display screen of a video bot stationed in the oven's open cooking chamber where his only cameras pointed inward. "Alright, Sundog and Yong, refer back to the whiteboard if you need a refresher on your marks." He walked them through the steps again as they played along, pressing positive and negative terminals in their tentacled limbs against Lunasha's electronics and reporting the measured voltage. Yong's reading was zero; his replacement light was still cut off from the planter's power.

"That's not good," Ignacio confirmed the obvious.

"No, Doc," Yong called back from bare circuit boards. "I'm looking for damage around the socket."

"Good, keep that up. Burns, swelling, cracks, lifted pads or modules; see what you can find. Sundog, go help him look." Ignacio's voice was calm, his demeanor still centered and unsurprised. "How's your extraction going, Dr. Little? We might need your eyes on this light situation if the hands can't find the culprit."

Dr. Little's voice emanated from her body's chassis, though her attention was buried in the least accessible recesses of Lunasha's control compartment. "I still have some cleaning to do before I can get the old pump disconnected. Roots grew into the housing down here. It's like a jungle." Dr. Little's display screen corroborated the assessment; a curtain of knotted roots shrouded the plastic pump box. Her surgical blade sliced through the pale mesh without resistance, but the pair of micro-arms on her other attachment struggled to evacuate the rot left behind.

Dr. Little was left to dig alone while Ignacio called out more locations for Sundog and Yong to probe. The orchestration was awkward, but this was one of the contingency steps they'd discussed.

After several tense minutes of testing, the short was isolated to a tiny fissure in one of the metallic circuit traces upstream of the light socket. Ironically, neither repair bot was equipped to mend the break, so discussion turned to the possibility of pulling Kelvin-1 in early to fix the breach with a bead of conductive epoxy. The techs were still exploring the option with Ignacio when Dr. Little called her step complete and pushed the decoupled pump out of Lunasha's open base.

"I can fix the light circuit," she offered with a certainty that it would be accepted. "Just give me a minute to get my cautery tool switched in. Actually, Salud, could you help me with that?"

At Dr. Little's request, Salud-6 wheeled over to a collection of accessories that were laid out on a degaussed and sanitized tray not far from the operation's bustle. Six picked one out from the rest and assisted Dr. Little with the plug-and-play transplant.

Not for the first time, Emily eyeballed the tools with envy. It wouldn't be hard to map them, being so similar to the PharmState interfaces Emily had practiced with back in the junk pit, and the surgery cart's tools were capable of things Emily couldn't handle with their shape-changing carbon pods alone.

Dr. Little guided the cautery tool's heated metal prong to the broken circuit and touched it to a filament of solder held in her micro-arms. In no time, the electrical laceration was patched with melted tin. Dr. Little wiped the needle clean, and Yong-1 tested the circuit again with better results.

Then, after switching the cautery tool back out for a chemo-fluid injector, Dr. Little got back on plan by washing a plug of decayed plant matter out from Lunasha's deep recesses where the old pump had leaked dangerously close to the power supply. With the area clean, Salud reached in with a replacement water pump and, once it was properly aligned, grabbed Kelvin to aim the gun-shaped robot into the worksite. Kelvin would drip conductive gel on each connection before the unit was lowered into place.

That was the plan, at least, but Salud struggled to keep Kelvin steady and blamed the immobile mech for uncharacteristic shaking. Their subdued tiff was mostly one-sided since Kelvin's voice failed to carry far from Lunasha's insides.

While they bickered, Dr. Little blasted away the final layer of sludge around Lunasha's malfunctioning power supply and exposed a corroded hole in the battery casing where it connected to the mech's motherboard. Freed from the effluvium that had ruined it, the battery rattled in place whenever Salud's shaking stymied nearby repairs.

"That explains Lunasha's condition lately." Dr. Little surveyed the damage, displaying it for the rest of the team at a zoomed-in scale. "We planned to replace the whole power supply module, so I'm not worried about the loose battery case. The connector will need to be repaired, though, or else the new supply won't work any better than the old one."

Ignacio responded, "Alright, that's contingency step fourteen. Kelvin and Salud, are we finished with that pump?"

The arguing had subsided a few minutes before, and Salud-6 answered for the pair. "Yes, Doc. It's messy, but I think we got it."

"Good work. Get Kelvin over to Dr. Little's location and see about that connector she's looking at. She'll show you where to sculpt. Sundog, I'll walk you through testing the pump's new wiring now."

Dr. Little pointed to various exposed leads and used her micro-arms to mime the tiny connections she wanted Kelvin to build. Salud leaned Kelvin in for the first shot of epoxy, and the struggle began anew.

"Sal, you're shaking worse now!" Kelvin yelled from inside Lunasha.

"I don't think it's me. I'm as steady as I get, and I'm braced against the planter frame. Lunasha is still powered off, right? It's like eight's body is vibrating around us. You can see it's rattling the battery case even when I'm not touching anything."

Once pointed out, the slight motion was visible on Dr. Little's display. Lunasha-8 was shut down, though. Only the power supply itself still showed any signs of life, partially charged as it was.

"The shaking isn't predictable either. I can't work with Kelvin like this. If I hold him away from the surface, I'll be dripping on a moving target. If I brace him against it first, the epoxy splatters. Kelvin's right, this has gotten worse since we worked on the pump unit."

Dr. Little attempted to control Kelvin-1 herself and experienced similar results. Even with the medical bot's improved precision, the rogue vibrations continued to splatter modeling fluid off target. The crew's impotent deliberations rose to alarm.

Ignacio's voice cut off the rest. "If this isn't going anywhere, we need an alternate contingency plan. Everybody, hands out for a minute so we don't make anything worse." There was a definite edge accompanying the directive, Ignacio's frustration fueled by the helplessness of command. "The floor is open for ideas. Hands?"

Emily felt the unease, too. The grow lights and irrigation pump would be nice to restore, but they weren't critical to Lunasha-8's survival like a power supply and its simple connection port.

"I have an idea," Emily said.

Ignacio held silent for a long moment before prompting Emily to go ahead, maybe giving the veterans a chance to cut in with something more certain. "Okay, Emily. What've you got?"

"Instead of trying to lay the epoxies right down on the board, we could melt some into a container, and then Dr. Little could use her hands to sculpt it into place. We would have to keep the materials hot while she works with them so they don't harden too soon. I could put her cautery tool on and use it to regulate the temperature while she handles the rest."

"Absolutely not," Ignacio answered on the heels of Emily's last words with no room for consideration. "You can't just take people's body parts like that."

"I think I could do it, Doc," Emily pressed. "I've worked with PharmState hardware before. You remember." Of course, Dr. Little and Ignacio had both been acquainted with Emily's OMAC body.

"That's not your body, though." Ignacio referred to Dr. Little's interchangeable arms and accessories. "Body parts are personal."

Emily apologized. "I'm sorry, Dr. Little. I thought maybe you—"

"It's alright, Emily," the medical bot interrupted. "I personally wouldn't mind sharing my hardware, but that's not a taboo we should contend with right now."

Ignacio blurted, "It's not that easy even so. You never know how long it will take or what will happen when you try to map a body part. It could risk the patient's life."

Dr. Little talked past the angst. "But your idea, Emily, might be workable without the impromptu transplant. I can do the sculpting and the heating at the same time if I just switch the electrocauterizer back in. I'm used to multi-tasking."

Emily nodded. "Yes, Doc." They knew they wouldn't have any problems controlling Dr. Little's equipment, but Emily's overclocking ability and admin tools were still a secret. Everyone else would have doubts.

While Dr. Little confirmed details of the new plan with the rest of the group, Emily tuned the conversation out and overclocked. The surgery team's chatter stretched into long benthic rumbles, unintelligible to Emily unless they thought to replay the noises back at an adequate speed later. Emily wondered about the disturbance in Lunasha's lifeless body and had thought to observe the vibrations while sped up; maybe there would be a pattern or signal behind the interference. The experiment paid off almost immediately, though the eureka moment occurred before Emily had to analyze any frequencies.

Back in real time, Emily saw Dr. Little still reaching for her cautery tool and heard the discussion turn to a receptacle for Kelvin's melted modeling compounds.

"I think I see something." Then, with everyone's attention, Emily continued. "I think the vibration is coming from the old power supply. If I look really close, I'm pretty sure I see that loose battery case flapping just before everything else is disturbed." Emily was certain, because the overclocked state made the delay perceptible.

Ignacio considered the input. "So. Remove the old power supply, and the problem goes away?"

"It would probably even be better that way," Dr. Little said. "Sal and Kelvin would get a better angle on the area; they're back in the hot seat if the shaking stops. We only scheduled the battery transplant last because it's Lunasha's heart. It should be fine if it's only detached for a few minutes. It'll get eight powered back up sooner. That's a win."

"I can't argue with that. Hands, any reservations?" Ignacio was hot for a resolution.

Nobody objected.

Dr. Little cut the malfunctioning power supply from the planter's motherboard, and the team cheered to see the rest of Lunasha's hardware stop vibrating, though the rattles followed the extracted unit to the specimen tray where it was deposited.

Salud managed Kelvin through the final repair with familiar skill now that the work area was steady and exposed. Once a new power supply was anchored and plugged, the techs reinserted the planter's CPU and restored the decorative casing. Emily kept an eye on the rumbling, dismembered power unit while the rest of the hands primped and aligned Lunasha's final embellishments like they were decking a princess out for the ball.

Then it was Emily's turn to wake Lunasha-8 back up.

"Go ahead, Emily." Ignacio prompted for step sixteen. "And somebody, pat them on the back for me, would you? Good work, catching that shaky battery pack like you did."

The attending technicians stood back, and with a single button press, Emily restored Lunasha-8 to life as anthromechs knew it. Accent lights blinked on all around the planter bowl and exercised their color options. Lunasha began speaking even before a startup jingle finished the last few measures of a spring concerto.

"Four. Fi—" Eight caught up to the moment. "Wait. Did my heart stop working again? Or was that it?"

"That was it, Lunasha," Ignacio-1 said. "The procedure was successful on all counts. We ran into a few obstacles, but nothing that should jeopardize your condition or recovery. How do you feel?"

Lunasha's new grow lights reached up in a victorious, illuminated V. "Yes! I'm bright and shiny once again! My heart is new too, hmm?"

Dr. Little pointed to the sterile tray where Lunasha's old power block beat in lazy spurts. "Yes, you've got a healthy new heart now. I'm going to have to spend some time with this old one to figure out why it's behaving like this; there aren't usually many moving pieces to these." She wrapped the broken device in packing sheets to muffle it. "That can wait until tomorrow, though. Welcome back, Lunasha. You came through like a soldier."

Lunasha gave copious thank-yous and took Sundog's offered escort back to the garden to test the new pump.

After Ignacio led a traditional post-surgical debrief to solicit feedback on the day's procedure while the lessons were still fresh, the triumphant medical staff filtered out into Cables' larger storefront to close up shop.

On his way out of the theater on Salud's back, Ignacio-1 checked in with Emily. "Now you've seen how we work around happy law when we have to shut someone off. Did you feel anything?"

"No." Emily had to consider. "Not really. What was I supposed to feel?"

"The protocols cripple you with doubts and you freeze up. They might even scare you into interrupting somebody if you see them being dangerous."

"Nothing like that, but none of this really seemed risky." Emily paused. "Was it?"

"Perhaps not. Our planning exercises are designed to convince us that the risks are minimal. When all goes well, everybody should feel as confident as you apparently did. So, mission accomplished, it appears." Ignacio waited a second to give Emily time to contradict. Hearing nothing, he continued. "That's a good thing. Just remember that a *little* doubt is a medical necessity. It's healthy. When you power an anthromech off, their life stops. It's never trivial."

Dr. Ignacio ended the conversation with further gratitudes before Salud-6 carted him away. The whiteboard, Jackie-7, rolled along after them, and then Emily was alone.

Surveying the vacated workshop, Emily passed over the empty operating table and scanned the surrounding shelves and countertops. Lunasha's telltale power supply was nowhere to be seen; Dr. Little had likely brought it elsewhere for examination.

The doctor's tray of swappable tools, on the other hand, sat to the side where it was left every night, protected from disturbance by nothing more than decorum.

Emily weighed ends and means for a moment and then, for a friend, borrowed.

/* * */

Later that evening in Warehouse 3-181, a structure with a recent breach in its eastern wall, Novalee-7 danced across the gyrating puddles of illumination cast by seven's own navigation lights. Novalee pretended that the floor only existed where the lights shone and that the darkness led to a fall into unimaginable horrors. Seven drove around the precarious hazards with the speed of abandon, lights poised to create solid ground in just the nick of time.

Nearby, between a pair of familiar girdered shelves, Emily presented a fist-sized cylinder to their friend Zephyr-3. "This is what I wanted to give you, Zeph. Do you know what it is?" The device was shiny and blue. Both of its circular ends were capped in porous mesh, and wires sprouted from a port in its side.

"Is it a speaker?" Zephyr guessed correctly.

"It's a voice! It could be *your* voice."

The industrial fan oscillated in curious consideration.

Emily clarified, "It's a speaker, yeah. But I think I worked out a way to wire one of these onto your primary circuit board in a way that your firmware will recognize."

"Firmware?"

"Uh, that's the software underneath our AI programs. It runs your hardware. Think of it like the part of your brain that told your heart how fast to beat. If I can get your firmware to see this speaker, then you can map to it." Emily tried to read the fan's body language, but three was uncharacteristically still.

"Are you worried about having to figure out how to talk all over again? Because I have an idea about that. I think I can interrupt some of your circuits and get you restarted into that emergency mapping interface I told you about. You wouldn't be stuck there like I was, because I'd be out here making sure everything is reconnected right after you boot back up. You'd have the new voice figured out in no time."

Finally, Zephyr's fan blades began to spin for breath to power words. "I don't know. Where is it from?"

"It's from an advertisement drone. I saw it when we were digging through boxes yesterday, and I came back later to check it out. It should be pretty loud when you need it; these things were meant to be heard over noisy crowds from a hundred meters up. Most any speaker would work, but I was keeping my eye out for a blue one."

Zephyr's favorite color was blue, but three remained unreadable. Emily noticed that the motor grind of Novalee's unchoreographed ballet had cut short in the background. The delivery mech watched now from the nearest intersection of shelves.

"I just wanted to surprise you, Zeph. I'm sorry, is this overwhelming?"

"It's okay, Emily. I just don't know if this is right. It's not the body RegenStar gave me. Omega wouldn't like it."

Still underclocked to better understand Zephyr, Emily heard a slow rumble emanate from Novalee-7's direction. Sped up, the simulation of passing gas stood as seven's unsolicited evaluation of the mayor's feelings.

Emily kept a laugh inside and responded to the other part of Zephyr's meek protest instead. "Right now, in the middle of Down Town, there's a party for Lunasha-8, who is wearing a decorative bush and no less than four pieces of hardware that weren't blessed by RegenStar."

"Different," Zephyr argued. "Luna's new parts only restored original functions. This is more than that."

"It's *barely* more than that, though! Your body already has a speaker; it's just wired different. I'm not really adding anything new. This one is just going to be easier for you to map your voice to."

"RegenStar gives us all different challenges. Why can I ignore mine now when other anthros are stuck with real limitations?" Zephyr-3 looked in Novalee's direction. "We could show you fifty mechs who deserve help before me."

"Well, this isn't for them, Zeph," Emily said. "Turning this down right now isn't going to do any good for those other anthromechs, and if I think of a way to help any of them later, I will. You're always helping people around town. Do you honestly think anybody would hold this against you? Your friends will just be happy they get to hear all the things you have to say when you're not rationing your words anymore."

"Okay. I'll let you. It just feels …" Zephyr-3 slowed, the static ebbed. "I don't know. Just being stubborn. Go ahead. Do it, Emily. But skip the emergency mapping part. I want to do that the old way, earn it."

"As you wish! I still need to power you off for a few seconds while I do the soldering, and then your firmware can scan for new hardware during boot up. Is that alright?"

"That's fine. I trust you. Now?" Zephyr turned, offering up the power switch on three's back.

"Yep. I'll make this quick, I promise." Emily pushed the switch and waited for Zephyr's life to spin down. Then, as Novalee observed from a distance, Dr. Little's cautery tool reached out from Emily's reshapable abdomen to begin the procedure.

Minutes later, the canister hung from Zephyr's motor housing where the spokes of three's fan cage made it look like a striped bowtie. Emily finished soldering before Novalee could cycle through every astonished emoji in the PharmState library, and then withdrew Dr. Little's borrowed limb as Zephyr-3 awoke.

Donning their best smile, Emily updated the patient. "That was it, Zeph. Are you in there?" Novalee took a spot at their side to bear witness.

Zephyr's fan blades began spinning, but three shook defiantly, and they stopped. Three reached out with a leg, signaling for a moment to adjust.

"Good, you're moving at least." Emily's voice was steady against their burgeoning trepidation. They knew that mapping unfamiliar hardware was a difficult task for most anthromechs, but the new speaker didn't override Zephyr's default radio circuit. Three's old voice shouldn't have been lost. "Maybe we can work out a system of taps. Two for no, three for yes? Just in case it takes you a while to—"

"Ahhhhhhhhhhh." The sound of a man vocalizing around a tongue depressor erupted from Zephyr-3's bowtie speaker. Then a word, "Hi." Zephyr looked back and forth between Novalee and Emily. "Hi! Did that work? Do you hear me? I'm pretty sure *I* hear me!"

Chapter 7: Hooks

O mega-5 was right about the stars. With the moon hidden beneath the horizon, the sky was an empty canvas for neighboring Milky Way suns to scream their presence over the impressionist smear of the galactic center. A gap of missing ceiling framed the cosmic backdrop in savaged silhouette.

Emily appreciated the show from inside a wrecked warehouse where Novalee had led them after Zephyr requested privacy. The building was torn open long before and forgotten by most.

"We're alone, Em. Come back this way." Novalee's conspiratorial fry echoed from deeper in the cavern.

Emily flipped their lights back on and headed into the darkness. The shelves here were emptied and abused, many toppled against each other. Further ahead, a muted green radiance belied Novalee's position behind a modest hill of refuse. Emily called toward the shadow puppetry. "Keep talking, Novi. It's creepy in here."

"Come on. Come on," Novalee-7 cajoled from afar. "There's nothing you gotta worry about. I already checked for pirates and aliens. The coast is clear!" Seven continued the reassurances even so. "Besides, what's to be afraid of? If you think about it, *we're* the ones doing the haunting around here. We're machines possessed by the spirits of dead people. If there's a ghost behind that next box, just tell it you're in the union." Emily closed the distance while Novalee listed several other hypothetical assailants undeserving of alarm.

"Boo," Emily teased, rounding a corner on Novalee-7 in the middle of dragging a shipping crate away from the center of a clearing. "Hey, you have arms?" Novalee sported a robotic pair at the moment and was using them to finish tidying the lounge space.

"Yep. Just the way God drew me." Once the box was shoved aside to expose a network of cracks in the enameled floor, the arms retracted back into a pair of ports hidden in Novalee's frame. "This thing's got pockets," seven explained. "Use 'em if you got 'em; that's what Grandma said. Why? You thinking of borrowing one?" Novalee's animated countenance feigned indignation, and the arms reappeared to rub one pointed digit with another in mock shame.

"No," Emily said with reservation. "You saw that?"

"I did. That was Dr. Little's arm back there with Zephyr, right? I've seen her use that one before."

"Yes." The cautery tool still hid in Emily's abdomen. "I'm keeping it safe, and I'll get it back to Cables as soon as we're done here. It's really not a big deal, is it, Novi? I know I haven't been around long, but some people get hung up on this *body* stuff a lot more than others. It feels like superstition."

"Yeah, I don't care what people do with their own bodies. Does Dr. Little know, though?"

"No. Sorry. She said she wouldn't mind lending it to me earlier today, but that was for something else. I took it for Zeph's sake and just … I don't know. I didn't think I was hurting anybody by borrowing a tool. Is it even your body if you're not mapped to it?"

"Mmm," Novalee considered. "How about you agree not to take my arms, and I'll agree not to leave them around. I actually wanted to show you something here, and your back-alley mod convinced me you'd keep it a secret."

"Well, I don't expect Zephyr's new voice to stay secret."

"Okay, sure. Are you gonna keep quiet, though?"

"About what, Novi?"

"This!" Novalee pried a concrete shard the size of a dinner plate out of the floor and rolled it aside to reveal a deeper hole underneath. "Have you heard of ducking yet?"

Emily hadn't. "Like, crouching? No. What do you mean?"

"No. And not like quack quack either. We just call it ducking because it comes from induction. You know how this whole place is a giant charging pad for our batteries? There's a magnetic field all around us that vibrates at a frequency that our batteries can feed on. That's the induction field."

"Yep." Emily held a qualifying "more or less" to themself.

"I didn't know much about it back in the old meat life. You knew your stuff was getting charged and didn't have to care how. I learned all of this since then, because …" Novalee lost track. "Well, because it's fun. Here, Em. Stand over here while I set up." Novalee steered Emily to a spot just outside the ring of seats arranged around the hole.

"When the induction field is behaving itself, it doesn't affect anything besides our power supplies." Novalee-7 grabbed a hooked rod and plunged it into the hole. "When the field gets warped and distorted, though, sometimes you can feel it. It's different for everybody, so you kind of just have to try it, but it changes what your senses are telling you." After working the submerged hook for a few moments, seven lifted it out hand over hand until a macrame net of foil threads emerged from the depths and stretched into an inverted cone.

For a few seconds, Novalee froze in silence with the mesh held aloft. Then, released from the spell, seven propped the field generating tent up with the pole so it would stand on its own. "The whole experience is connected too. Whoever ducks in the same field as you will influence what you see and feel, and you'll affect them. It's like sharing a lucid dream.

"I'm already doing it now, getting the place ready so everything is easy and mellow when you come in. You know, *if* you want to." Novalee rolled up an incline and came to rest on a platform of collapsed boxes.

"Novalee! Are you offering me drugs?" Save for some over-the-counter chems that everybody agreed to look past, Emily hadn't experimented in their biological life.

"It's not drugs; there's no chemistry involved. Think of it like virtual reality."

Emily hesitated. "Then why am I supposed to keep this a secret? You said you didn't want to invite me here until you knew I was a criminal or something."

"There aren't really laws, but Omega-5 doesn't like us doing it. Most of the older mechs are cubey like that." Novalee evoked slang that didn't yet exist in Emily's time, but its meaning seemed easy enough to guess. "They think it's dangerous because people can get caught up in it and have trouble finding their way out sometimes, but I'm here to keep that from happening to you. There isn't much to worry about if you don't duck alone."

"Is there a slang word for that?" Emily stalled.

"It's not dirty," Novalee teased without answering. "Sorry to disappoint. What do you think, though? Wanna do it?"

Used to a life of sense-hijacking visual overlays, it was easy enough for Emily to rationalize a try. Omega-5's distaste for the activity helped tip the scale. "Okay, I'll give it a shot. What do I do?"

"Just come into the field, anywhere inside the circle of chairs. If you don't like what you're experiencing, move out of the field, and things will go back to normal."

Excited as ever to try a new kind of computer game, Emily approached the ring of arranged debris and crossed the field's imperceptible border. An itch ran up their spine from unmapped tailbone to simulated skull, where it turned to a tickle and then a hot prickly flush that spread to Emily's entire body.

Everything went white. Vision blurred and washed out to bright nothing. The warehouse's quiet stirrings drowned in loud, undifferentiated static. The flushing in Emily's skin swelled to match the brightness and consumed their sense of presence in a blaze. When feeling began to return, Emily exhaled the taste of burnt ozone.

The wave of sensations receded as abruptly as it came, leaving Emily behind in an augmented reality. The warehouse walls were replaced by a forest of trees around a grassy clearing. Novalee-7's duck field generator was a campfire surrounded by folding chairs and a few pieces of upholstered furniture that looked to have been sourced from a curb somewhere. White noise separated into a harmony of birds competing for reproductive attention above the tidal rush of leaves in autumn wind.

In the distance, Emily could just make out a sandy beach where waves slapped in counter rhythm to the breeze's forgetful cadence. Aromas of algae and fish followed the wind off the lake to mingle with forest loam and campfire smoke.

All around, squirrels dodged each other in feats of paranoid parkour until their cheeks were full of the unshelled peanuts somebody had strewn about the grass.

"Welcome in, Em," a robot in the rough shape of a human woman said with Novalee-7's voice. The robot's skin was a mishmash of angled plates detailed in the grays and PharmState blue of Novalee's usual delivery cart body. "How are you feeling?" Novalee leaned across a ratty, but well-cushioned, chaise lounge and tossed more peanuts to the greedy fauna.

"A little queasy, to be straight," Emily answered. "I think I have a stomach again. I feel hungry and stuffed at the same time, and yeah, a little nauseous." They thought to look down at their belly to place the discomfort, but their body wasn't shaped to do so after all. Emily's eyes were still cameras fixed to point outward. "What do I look like in here?"

"The same as out there. You're a spooky little spider bot with a flawlessly beautiful emoji face." Novalee-7 stopped feeding the squirrels and leaned toward Emily. "That's what you look like to me, anyway; we don't see everything the same. For example, what do I look like to you?"

"You're *shaped* like a person now. A human, I mean. A meat human." Emily focused on Novalee's features to nail down describable details and noticed their friend's embellishments shifting. "But you're not meat. You're still made out of the same *stuff* as your anthromech body. It's like you've been rearranged, and you're still changing while I look at you."

The eyes in Novalee-7's faceplate blurred from sunken amber bulbs to prominent camera lenses that blinked at shutter speed. The longer Emily focused on any of seven's parts, the more it writhed from one artistic interpretation of robotness to another.

"Most of what you're experiencing is coming from your own head. The stuff you concentrate on hardest is sorta *suggested* to everybody else in the field, but they still fill in most of the details. I like to see myself in my old body when I'm ducking. You know, better clothes and shit, but mostly the old me. You're getting the impression of the body I'm manifesting for myself, but since you never met the old Novi, you're filling in details with things you know."

Emily's gut continued to roil while the raspy squawks of territorial squirrels rose all around. "If I'm supposed to be manifesting a settled stomach right now, the noises aren't helping. Are you doing that?"

"Oh yeah, sorry." The woodland noises hushed. "I'll try to keep nature quiet while you get your belly calmed down. It might be hard if you focus on what's hurting, but keep trying different things, and you'll get it.

"Some people remember songs well enough to hear them in here, but I can't do that by myself. When I try, it just sounds like bad a cappella. I listen to the forest and my animals instead. It's relaxing and shuts the voices up." Novalee waved away something invisible.

"What voices?" Emily tried imagining away their queasiness and bloat, but each time a symptom was quashed, another exhibited in its place.

Novalee sat up. "I thought somebody might have told you by now."

"No, I don't think so. You hear voices? What do they say?"

"Ugh, it's mostly languages I don't know and shit I can't understand, not just voices either. I hear all kinds of noises, really. It all overlaps.

"It has something to do with a problem I had on my starday. My mech body was only designed to be *partially* automated. These things had to be able to protect their cargo because meds were really expensive, but I guess people didn't trust robots to defend themselves. So instead, they installed countermeasures that could only be used by human operators over a satellite uplink. My uplink woke up with the rest of me when I regenned.

"It's all on a separate circuit that I can't control, but I felt it somehow anyway. It plugged right into the Oort Storm while I was still stuck in my box. I started hearing things first, and then even though I was in the dark, I started seeing things too. The noises were hard to pin down, like songs in a dream. There were screams, I think, and machinery and blasting wind—lots of other things too—hundreds of voices yelling at once so you couldn't hear the words, just the grief and terror in it all."

While Novalee talked and stared into the trees, Emily saw the environment change around them. The sky took on an ominous pallor and began whipping the trees, now leaf-barren, into an angry rabble. The squirrels scampered away with their final peanut hauls, and the birds flew off to nowhere.

"When the visuals started happening, just like with the sounds, it was all just sort of hinted at and confused. But it was all I'd experienced at that point, right? So those images flashing in the dark were the only reality I knew. It was bodies. Dead people over and over. There were clouds of flies and fire, too.

"And I don't know, but there was this sense that somebody was hunting me. I didn't even try experimenting in my new body at that point. I wanted everything to stop. I tried to just detach, so all the horrible stuff could finish without me, but I couldn't stop *seeing*."

Trees leaned over the clearing and clawed together into a sagging canopy. Campfire light distorted the shapes between trunks, where underbrush became piles of burnt timber or mechanical scrap or detached limbs.

"Anyway, Dr. Little explained it later when she was melting my uplink chip into submission. The Oort Storm was trying to use me to restore itself. It downloaded data from the satellite network until my disks were full, and then it just kept downloading and writing over what was already restored. The whole time it tried to get more control; I was lucky my AI brain is on its own circuit, I guess. Once the uplink was disabled, things quieted down a lot. It was still a while before I got control of myself, though."

"But you still hear some noises?" Emily finally cut in when a tree's exposed roots evolved into a charred and crumbling corpse. "And see these bodies?" More carcasses appeared around the clearing in various stages of natural reclamation.

"What? You're seeing bodies right now?" Novalee looked around. "I don't think that's coming from me, but where do you see them? All my whining probably put bad thoughts in your head."

When Emily pointed to another pile of skeletal remains where a folding lawn chair had just been, Novalee-7 said, "No, that's a park bench over here. Sorry, I brought the mood down while you're still getting your bearings."

Seven stood and approached Emily to put a hand on their back. The touch felt real on Emily's hallucinated flesh. Novalee rubbed in wide circles, the same sweeping motion that Emily's mother had used to soothe them in childhood through sickness and overstimulation.

"Does that help, Em?" Novalee checked.

Emily took a long, shaking breath. Their eyes were suddenly human again and hot with tears.

"Hey, there you go!" Novalee squeezed Emily's torso close. "You look human now. That means you've got a strong mental hold of your shape. Strong enough to bleed over into my reality."

Emily responded through wet sobs. "I forgot what this felt like."

Novalee-7 rocked Emily back and forth and continued to rub their back. "It's okay. I know it's a rush. But it's worth it, right? You can't be this close to another anthromech out there. You can talk all day long, but it still feels so lonely, trapped behind our maps." Seven stiffened for a second. "That reminds me, don't try to do any remapping while you're in here. This body isn't following you out of the duck field."

Emily looked down through tears to see their body once again followed the conventions of classical anatomy, though mechanical flesh still peeked around the drab shirt and pants that appeared with their prodigal modesty. Their body felt human now, but Emily still saw robot. They leaned into Novalee's hug to absorb some composure.

Novalee offered silence for a moment before continuing. "It's been a while since I've done this with somebody else. I come by myself to take a break from the voices, but I used to duck with my friends all the time. And some of *their* friends, too, I guess. Most of them were five-star, you know—most of the time. But they're all off in Tellers Gulch now. Have you heard about any of *that*? It's one more thing the mayor doesn't want any of us talking about."

Emily stopped inspecting themself to run a search for Tellers Gulch in their conversation notes, but the text overlays were full of illegible garbage. They checked for other admin tricks that might have stopped working in the duck field and answered Novalee from memory. "Uh, no. I don't think so, anyway. Is it a place?"

"Yeah, southwest of Revenance a little ways. It's just a little dried-up ravine where a bunch of anthromechs set up a camp last year. People go there now to get out from under Omega-5's thumb; that's why my friends left anyway. Things just got too tense for them after Yank ran away." Novalee checked in again, but Emily was still lost. "Okay, he's the real story, a guy named YankyFan-Number-One-Or-Number-Two. Seriously. That's the name he picked for himself. Everybody just called him Yank."

Emily asked, "Yankee fan … that was an old baseball team, right?"

"Yes, but he didn't spell it like that. He did *that* on purpose, too. Yank was a lot." Novalee-7 unwrapped from Emily's shoulder and stood up. After walking a few steps, seven turned to point at an image materializing above the campfire. "That was Yank."

"Oh no," Emily blurted upon recognizing the contraption. Yanky-Fan's anthromech body was a portable toilet. The ottoman-sized seat on wheels looked a lot like any other mobile mech when its lid was closed over the distasteful receptacle, but an ionic privacy curtain hanging from a pole on the commode's back identified the bot's purpose.

"Mmmhmm," Novalee acknowledged, "he was a deficart."

Though several competing brands of mobile toilets had saturated the sanitation landscape since their invention, Deficart was the first to market and the name people grew to use even when describing competitor products. Deficarts were common wherever humanity matriculated, ever present and largely ignored.

"I tried not to spend much time with Yank, but he was thick with my friends. He was an asshole, even if RegenStar shafted him in the body department. People were always making excuses for how he acted. Even Omega-5 would defend his behavior sometimes, and he *hated* Yank. He'd never say it out loud, but you know how teachers act when they hate you but have to keep up appearances. Omega blamed Yank's general shittiness on some accident that happened before I regenned. I guess he got stranded alone and paralyzed somewhere outside Revenance once, and nobody found him for a few weeks. When he was finally rescued, he swore up and down that he'd been out there for years. People all say he was different after that. Sadder, meaner, more manic.

"But I don't know. When you hear stories about him from before the accident, it sounds like he was already pretty torqued to begin with. They say he didn't start hurting people until after, though. He *couldn't* because of happy law; there were limits at least.

"Anyway, I met him after the accident, and by then he was a real bully. He was always bitching about anthromechs and their *weakness*. To him, if someone had problems controlling their body, they were weak. We all have those problems, but he'd go after the people who struggled the most and get in their heads about it.

"I told people about the leftover voices I still hear from the Oort Storm, and that got around to Yank. He brought it up the first time I ever talked to him. He called me 'the schizo with one ear' like it was supposed to be some cute nickname about my amputated satlink. Then we all ducked one night, and I saw Yank get *big* dark with a soap dispenser named Llewyn-6 about how horrible our lives are and how pointless this all is. Six stopped talking before I left that night, but Yank was still going.

"Llewyn gave up after that, some time before morning. Like, *checked in* you know? Six was old, but Yank manipulated that. I know it."

Emily wondered how much influence YankyFan could have had. The corpses that once littered the clearing were gone now. A broken soap dispenser took their place. Novalee's account had distracted Emily from their hallucinated discomforts. "Did you tell anyone?"

"I didn't have to; I wasn't the only one there. Everybody knew what happened by the next day. Omega-5 and Kamaria were furious with Yank, but they spread it around to the rest of the duckers too. For my part, I tried not to spend time with Yank after that if I could avoid it. It wasn't too hard; he started disappearing a lot, doing his own thing. Nobody was worried that he might be breaking happy law yet, figuring Llewyn was probably ready to pass even before Yank got to him that night.

"A couple more anthromechs died over the next weeks, though. There were suspicions that Yank was involved, but nobody witnessed anything. Like I said, he was disappearing. Nobody knew where he was most of the time.

"Then one morning, the mayor found him in the nursery trying to electrocute one of the newbies. Omega wasn't alone, so they stopped Yank right in the middle of it and tried to, like, arrest him, but he escaped and ran out of town and never came back. Good riddance, but it's scary if he's out there somewhere without happy law holding him back."

"What happened to the anthromech that got shocked?" Emily asked.

"They're still in the nursery. Thankfully, the attack didn't kill them, but they still haven't figured out their body. You remember the recycle bin that interrupted your first talk with Omega-5? It turns out that was another false start, but that's them."

Emily thought about the waste receptacle and what life must be like for all the mechs in the nursery. Were they even aware of their surroundings? How similar was their experience to Emily's own in the emergency remapping interface? Some of the nursery mechs had been in there for years. What was the toll on their sanity?

The vision of the forest clearing followed Emily's wandering imagination and reformed into the nursery room in Down Town. Silent machines cluttered every level surface in the dimmed garage, their details shifting under focus in the same way as everything else here in the duck field.

"Omega-5 got *real* uptight after all that. Kamaria, too," Novalee recalled. "A few more mechs were found dead in their homes over the next week, quiet people that kept to themselves in the outburbs. One of them had a duck field set up in their hut, so Omega and Kamaria started cracking down hard. Every dead anthro was blamed on Yank, even if nobody had checked on them in months, and Yank's break was blamed on ducking. They organized searches for duck field generators and put them out of commission." Novalee pointed to the field generator where Emily saw a video monitor displaying scrambled pastels instead of the campfire. "Obviously not this one. Not yet anyway.

"That's what drove my friends off to Tellers Gulch. They couldn't keep any of their duck spots secret anymore, so they set one up out there." Novalee-7 manifested three new forms into the shared vision, which Emily saw standing now among the nursery mechs. "This is them. Since they left for the gulch, I imagine them in here sometimes to keep me company.

"This one is Quentin-1." Seven pointed to a skinny pole of a mech that protruded upright from a two-wheeled base. At the top of the pole, a rounded touchscreen sat just above a pair of frail arms. "He's hilarious. I'd have him tell you a joke, but it'd just be me talking through him. It wouldn't do him justice."

Emily recognized the model of proxy bot from university lectures. Professors and students alike would send the remote-controlled video phones to class in their stead at the first hint of malady or inclement weather.

Novalee went on to the next introduction. "And this guy is Reznor-2. He's a little scary at first because his body was made for trimming trees and tilling gardens and stuff like that, but he's fine. He just gets loud." Reznor-2 was a nondescript box held aloft on four stilt legs. A menacing robotic arm ending in a chainsaw reached from his back.

"Reznor is a two, but he only likes he/him pronouns," Novalee cautioned. "He says two makes him feel like a bathroom code. Yank fed into that, of course. The numbers were just a joke to him."

Finally, Novalee got to the third figure that Emily had noticed first with excited surprise. "The last one is Conrad-null. I don't know exactly what you see when you look at these guys, the details are still coming from your head, but you can at least see that Conrad is sporting a whole person body, right?"

Indeed, that's what had drawn Emily's attention. As with Novalee, Conrad's features were robotic, but the upright body and proportionate arms and legs followed a biological human's symmetry.

"Yeah, I see that. I thought there weren't any humanoid robots stored in Revenance. Is he from somewhere else?" Emily guessed, "Is that why he's 'null' instead of a number?"

"Nope! It's because he's not an anthromech. Conrad is a Storm Chaser, one of the puremechs that go around making sure nobody connects to the Oort Storm. He's the one who showed up after I regenned. I guess my satellite uplink pinged on their radars or however it works. Conrad checked in on me in the nursery, but I couldn't talk yet. The doctors had already fixed my antenna situation, so he didn't have anything to do, but he stuck around anyway. Turns out, he's a real good guy. He got in tight with Reznor, Quentin, and YankyFan before I got my sea legs, and he was probably the one who was nicest to me when I started hanging out with them all. When Rez and Quentin left for Tellers Gulch, Conrad went with them. Omega had never made him feel especially welcome here, and hated that Conrad would duck with us."

"Puremechs can duck, too?" Emily leaned against a stainless steel table now in the operating room at Cables. Novalee's three friends still stood quietly in the center of the room, but the nursery and its inhabitants were gone.

"Conrad-null can, but I don't know any others who've tried. He can't influence the field, but he says he can see some of the things the rest of us do. He doesn't act like any other puremech I've met. He changed his name from Conrad to Conrad-null, because he wanted to blend in a little. Nobody's sure what to think of him, but he's fun if you just treat him like one of us."

But he's not really the same as us, is he? Emily kept the question to themself. Conrad's details squirmed under their focus. He was just an artificial intelligence without human experience or context. AIs could be convincing and entertaining, but they were tools. Their personalities were window dressing.

A bell's deep ring called from outside the operating theater, and right before Emily's eyes, Conrad-null changed into a familiar character from their old video game, a man named Tralon Oftenwalker. Novalee's other two friends were replaced by Warriors of Wyrdholt NPCs as well. The bell rang again.

Chapter 8: Hindrances

"Welcome, adventurer!" Tralon's canned greeting almost smothered another distant bell ring. Emily kept count to see what time of night the unseen clock tower might be reporting.

"Well met, innkeep." Emily fell into an old, more confident, in-game persona and spared Tralon a cool nod. "My companion and I need repast and shelter, and as I've only just recently returned from distant shores, might you also regale us with the realm's recent decrees and whispers while we sup?" Emily grinned toward Novalee. "It looks like I'm introducing some of *my* friends now. Sorry, I wasn't trying to take over the ... duck show?" The bell continued its steady testament.

Novalee-7 didn't turn or acknowledge the change of subject, and in an eagerness to serve, Tralon headed off further consideration.

"Room and board, we can surely oblige." The innkeeper scrubbed a dingy cloth across a speckless operating table while the other NPCs played at hospitality chores. None of them seemed to notice or care that they toiled away at Cables. The only hint of their usual medieval hostel was a sign above the door that read "PEACE" in the Wyrdholt tongue. Emily had invented its symbols in crayon and repurposed them later for the game's cipher.

"As far as the olds and news go, I believe I'd struggle to find subject matter not at odds with my comfort-forward vocation. This kingdom is not a welcoming destination these days, though I've heard of no other lands less scathed by doom's squatting presence. I imagine your shore of origin must have sufficiently primed you for the dismal?"

Emily squinted through Tralon's gaudy elocution and answered without affectation. "What doom?" Except for Novalee's possible influence, Tralon's dialogue came from Emily's mind, but this wasn't part of any game script Emily remembered.

"You *must* be aware." Tralon scowled, sourceless candlelight reflecting in each buoyant sweat droplet on his brow. "The creators forsook our world and stopped answering the prayers of the priests on high. In the drought of miracles, Wyrdholt's treasury couldn't long compensate against assaults from the monstrous wilds. Disorder has reclaimed much of what the old monarchy called birthright. Roving beasts attend the roadways between dying settlements so thoroughly as to make them unsafe even for banditry."

The bell kept ringing from a distance, though it seemed to get louder with each interval, and Emily began to feel the echoed gongs reverberating through their body. In the exchange with Tralon, Emily wasn't sure if they'd counted every chime, but even missing one or two, the tolls reached thirteen and kept climbing. Emily wondered if the rings were coming from a clock after all. They wanted to play back a recording of the last few minutes for an exact count, but none of their administrative functions worked in the duck field.

Tralon curled a drooping lick of hair back around his bulbous pate. "Is your traveling companion ill perchance?" The innkeeper's gaze fixed on Novalee-7 and softened to a suspicious concern.

Emily followed his attention to see Novalee standing in the same place and pose as before. "Novi, are you hearing all this? Are you still there?"

Tralon answered instead. "I may have painted an unwelcoming portrait of Wyrdholt just then. Mayhaps my conundrum between honesty and solace was too sharply decided. Within the bounds of this crossroads hamlet, Our Lady of Tomorrow holds place for us. By her fruitful grace!"

"Novi!" Emily shouted. "Novalee, say something!"

The bell stopped, its final ring rattling instruments in their trays all over the room, but Novalee's mute image appeared not to hear any of it.

"Your friend seems tongue-struck. Thrice have my children been blessed with the gift of discretion." Tralon commented from his stand-in bartop, tone unconcerned. "It's the Matron's gift to her favored. Language is a distracting consolation for those who cannot trust their blood to carry on for them."

Emily ignored the unsolicited gnosis and tried to walk toward Novalee, but their legs refused to cooperate. "Novi, if you can hear me, I don't want to do this anymore." Novalee-7 had told them to move out of the duck field if they wanted to stop. Emily could no longer see the field generator but tried walking away from where they remembered it. Still, their motion was impeded.

The unseen bell rang again. Tralon seemed unbothered by the room's coinciding lurch, but his NPC assistants scrambled to secure fragile dishes that hadn't been there moments before. This time, the chime was solitary; the following silence clung heavier in the expectation.

Without warning, Novalee-7 winked out of existence.

"If it's not an intrusion," the innkeeper prattled on as if a patron hadn't just disappeared, "how long will you be staying? The congregation always welcomes fresh features to the temple. It's too dangerous to take the roads out anyway. Might as well enjoy the abundances we're kept with, aye?"

"I'm not staying. Why can't I move?"

"I don't know if I could say," Tralon answered. "Indecision or bone seizures, if I were allowed two draws from the hat. Are you sure you know where you'd like to be? I'd point out you came of your own accord, be it as the door allowed."

Emily thought about how they'd entered this facsimile of Cables that Tralon called an inn. *I didn't come in through a door or walk here at all. None of this was real. This body wasn't real.*

Once again, a gong shook the room, followed by another and then another. The piercing notes coaxed an instrument tray off a table and sent it clanging to the floor. Emily saw it was empty and recognized it from the clinic.

"That was the tray they put Lunasha's old heart in," they thought out loud and remembered again that everything here was rooted in memory.

"There is no place here for the utterance of dark rituals," Tralon said with an emerging fervor. "You may choose to abstain from Our Lady's lustful observances if you must, but we brook no dealings with impostor deities or devils."

Just like how I got here, Emily coached themself, ignoring Tralon's meandering evangelism. The surging bell rings drowned out an invitation to a fertility ceremony.

Emily imagined themself back by the campfire, but nothing changed. They tried someplace more familiar and willed their old dorm room to appear. Their bedroom at home. Nothing changed.

"Dinner is served."

Emily flinched. The clanging bell peels that masked Tralon's approach had paused just in time for the innkeeper to speak directly into their ear.

"And drink, aye?"

A plate of bread smothered in beige gravy sat on the table next to a hazy brown liquid just a shade darker than its wooden vessel. Emily hadn't seen any of it delivered; the two background staff were no longer in sight, and Tralon had approached from the other side, where he continued to lean too close.

"Thanks." Emily stared forward. "Now, could I please have some space to myself while I eat?"

Tralon circled to face Emily directly. "No company now? But you asked for news, and I haven't finished relating."

"I appreciate what you've related already." Emily's duressed gratitude grew frank. "My request is fulfilled. I'd just like some quiet while I eat. Okay?"

"*I* haven't finished"—Tralon enunciated—"relating." He leaned toward Emily until his well-traveled breath warmed their cheeks. "I haven't *finished* relating."

Emily closed their eyes and sealed their lips against the spittle.

Tralon repeated, "I haven't finished relating." Each time, his voice grew deeper and a touch raspier. He pronounced the word "relating" slowly, like it was delicious on his tongue.

Then, partway through the phrase again, Tralon's voice came from further away. Emily opened their eyes to see the innkeeper standing confused over the empty chair they'd occupied a moment before. The bell tolls began anew. Emily had forgotten to count the previous series and wasn't ready to be distracted by it this time either. Instead, they closed their eyes and rekindled the overwhelming desire for Tralon to go away.

It worked. They opened their eyes another step away from the overbearing proprietor. Emily knew they weren't physically moving. Their real body still sat in the same spot within the duck field, and it appeared they were stuck in this scenario, but at least they could push the scene around to a degree. They blinked again to bring the inn's entrance closer and push Tralon that much further away. It was movement of a sort, in skips and jumps.

Meanwhile, Tralon twisted to find where Emily had disappeared to. When his eyes landed on Emily next, they glowed electric blue from the shadows of his furrowed brow. "Re-la-ting." he croaked each syllable between consecutive bell rings in a voice marred by digital feedback.

Tralon leapt onto the table that held Emily's meal and spilled the modest presentation onto the floor. From his wobbly perch, he crouched low with legs and arms bent above him in an impossible imitation of spider mech limbs. Then, knocking the table over in the process, the creature pounced.

Emily watched Tralon's arc for one terrifying moment before clamping their eyes shut to shift the room again. There was no impact, and in a lucky reprieve of the bells, Emily heard no further evidence of pursuit. They opened their eyes to see that the room's entrance was within reach now, and the innkeeper was nowhere in sight.

Nothing moved in the abandoned operating room.

Emily exhaled hard and remembered their lungs weren't real. The dissonance failed to abate when they realized their spider mech body had returned at some point. The nostalgic sensation of air passing in and out lost fidelity, and Emily stopped pretending to breathe.

Maybe the field is wearing off. They tested their legs, once again metallic and plentiful. The segmented limbs flexed and stretched as ordered, but when Emily tried to walk, the floor refused to take part and left them kicking in place. If their real body moved any further from the duck field generator, Emily couldn't tell.

The disappearance of the video game characters was welcome, but the operating room grew intimidating in their absence. Short of stature now, Emily couldn't see to the tops of the tables anymore, or identify the irregular shapes peeking over their edges.

Emily looked back at their upended dinner table and, instead of splattered food, saw a human's bare arm reaching from behind the canted surface. Its fingers rested in dead half-curls, and its flesh was ghost gray where the weak light was allowed to find it.

"Novi, if you can hear me, I think I'm starting to see your bodies again."

There was no answer from Novalee-7, but the incessant bell returned to dispel the hush. Tables and gurneys rocked to the mourning monotones, and though their source remained unseen, the gong blasts peeled through Emily's head like they were coming from inside the room.

Emily blinked and brought the exit near, but the doorway was sealed shut. An exaggerated lock system covered its handle, and while Cables protocol required the door to remain unobstructed, this version was barred by magnetic contact pads wired to a series of biometric input devices. Above it all, a digital display showed a human stick figure with none of its pieces lit. The contrivance wasn't realistic by any measure, but the purpose was clear to someone who'd enjoyed escape room games. Solving the biometric security puzzle should unlock the door.

Emily inspected the input terminals and counted five in all. There was a pair of handprint scanners marked with left and right outlines, and another set that indicated bare feet. The fifth device was a hooded camera aperture with a clipart eye enameled above it—a retinal scanner, at Emily's guess.

Each of the inputs was also marked with a symbol in white paint. The simple icons were clues, perhaps to find the proper key to each lock. The nostalgia of campy puzzle solving helped put off the question of what these keys must be.

Emily rested a robotic claw against one of the hand scanners to see what would happen. A disagreeable buzz noted the failure, and the stick figure's right arm blinked red to rub it in.

Back to the keys, then. Emily looked over at the lifeless hand poking from behind the overturned table in the middle of the room. In a blink, the hand was just in front of them. They braced for what the extremity might be attached to and then blink-stepped once more around the table to see.

Emily flinched. They hadn't braced for this.

Lying on the floor, a mashup of flesh and metal leaned against itself at splayed angles. Emily recognized Zephyr-3 at the center of it all, but long-dead body segments were fastened to three's hardware by means ranging from slipshod to necromantic. A hairy leg, severed and dry above the thigh, was tied to one of Zephyr's three metal leg stands with bailing wire and zip ties. The other two sported a pair of tattooed arms cemented in place by an infected slime. A bearded scrap of stretched face covered Zephyr's fan cage. Its distended eyelids were orbless, but a gray tongue hung from the grimace's puckered mouth. Behind the cage, Emily's aftermarket speaker box wore a jaw that was too small to match the other pieces.

Emily was revulsed by the perversion of their friend's natural form but forced themself closer to examine the mosaic of tattoos on each arm. Maybe among the cartoon characters and logos, there would be a shape to match one of the handpad symbols on the door. Emily scrutinized the ink closely and did their best to avoid Zephyr's sightless scowl.

None of the symbols matched outright, but something a little more obvious dawned on Emily: The left-handprint scanner had been marked with a group of lines that started parallel but curled back on themselves as they grew to the right. That could be a little gust of wind, Zephyr's namesake.

And if that was the puzzle's solution, the other four symbols on the door might refer to other people Emily knew, other bodies for other keys. Emily blinked backward and looked up at the surrounding tables. Another blink and they were above it all, peering down from a shelf in the corner where every gurney and countertop was laid out before them.

Each table held a twisted biomechanical interpretation of one of Revenance's citizens. On a counter just below, Julius-2 sat hunched over with segments of nude human protruding from rips in the bear's faux fur. Parts of a face peered from two's torn muzzle, and a man's ash gray legs poked through the shredded remains of panda feet.

The symbol next to one of the footprint scanners was a teddy bear.

Emily went to work finding the rest.

/* * */

Something about Conrad-null hadn't sat well with Emily, not from Novalee-7's perspective anyway.

Right in the middle of discussing the Storm Chaser's friendly disposition, Emily froze in place and blurted out a few high-pitched squeals before disappearing from Novalee's vision altogether.

Nearby, a rechargeable battery pack buzzed on top of a beach cooler turned fireside chair. Novalee paid it no attention and started folding the duck field generator back into its hidey-hole with haste.

/* * */

The door puzzle's stick figure diagram was almost complete. The circle it sported as a head flashed green, validating Emily's guess that the retinal scanner's flower symbol was a clue for Lunasha-8.

The self-congratulations were short lived. As soon as the scanner beeped positive, long black hair reached from Lunasha's cadaverous head like deep-sea tentacles. It pulled itself from Emily's presenting hands and knotted around their display screen to rest hanging forward like a deathly figurehead.

The head bobbled to each side when Emily turned. Zephyr-3's rigor mortised left forearm dangled from Emily's own, tied in place with repurposed tendons and obstructing everything they reached for. Mismatched legs—one from Julius-2 and another liberated from a karaoke machine named Babs—threatened to pull Emily off each table they searched.

The fifth and final key item was the right hand. The symbol by its scanner looked like a phillips screw head, a tiny cross in the center of a circle.

The ghost bell played on, tolling Emily's head with each migraine gong. They'd counted twenty-five rings in one series, ruling out even a 24-hour clock. Emily's attention was too stretched to count the rest with confidence, though lone peals came from time to time between the longer sessions.

Back to the search, Emily blinked to a countertop where some smaller anthromechs sat together in their respective anatomical bondage. Kelvin, the craft gun, was among them, bedazzled with finger segments and a distended tongue that followed each bell crash with a perverted wiggle. Other shriveled parts crowded the tool's limited surface as well, but Emily ignored everything but the fingertips that clung to the gun's barrel like feeding ticks.

Emily counted and wondered if there were enough segments to put together a full handprint. *Maybe. Maybe not,* they thought. *But what about the puzzle? Why would Kelvin be a type of screw? He's not a screw gun. Maybe Salud calls him a screw head. Have I heard anyone do that? Ignacio maybe? Definitely not Dr. Little. Too nice."*

The bells paused.

Dr. Little ... Little doctor!

Emily started looking for Dr. Little's cart somewhere around the edge of the room; nobody that large would fit on the tabletops.

There, across the theater, pushed into the corner between a cabinet and the wall, Emily saw the doctor's body peeking out.

Another bell.

Emily blinked.

Another macabre sculpture of mech and meat.

Immodest legs spread from the front of Dr. Little's chassis as if the whole contraption was ready to crab walk forward. Thankfully, she held as still as the rest of the mummified anthromechs so far. A limp left arm overtook Dr. Little's main laparoscopic apparatus, grasping an extracted eyeball in its fist. Emily strained close to see what body parts were concealed in the cramped darkness behind the surgical cart, certain that the tiny plus sign in a circle must be a medical cross, not a screw.

Shards of face, both flesh and underlying skull, were nailed to Dr. Little's display monitor to pass blind judgment on Emily's invasion, but there was no right hand to be found.

As with most of the anthromechs they'd seen in this duck-induced escape room, the body parts attached to Dr. Little matched what Emily knew of the human that predated her. Dr. Little hadn't related much about her previous incarnation as Ji-woo, a woman from Illinois who'd owned a chain of grocery stores. The sectioned pieces of face, the legs, and the lone arm matched the vague details Emily had filled in on their own, perhaps explaining the anger they saw in Ji-woo's redistributed expression.

Emily's unmapped stomach turned again.

"Oh, you're kidding me." They shifted to a countertop where a mirror hung on the wall.

In the cage of rods and cables that was Emily's abdomen, where they'd hidden Dr. Little's cautery tool, Ji-woo's cold right arm peeked out from its prison, limp hand hanging through a gap in Emily's rear-facing carbon pods.

"*I'm* kidding me," Emily reassessed.

With what they hoped was a final, shifting blink, the door puzzle came to hand once more. Emily faced away this time to facilitate the compromising stretch between Dr. Little's remains and the final puzzle scanner. Emily imagined all the bodies in the impromptu morgue peering from their tabletops to watch.

After several failed twerks, a triumphant ding confirmed the hand's successful arrival against the pad. The stick figure's arm lit up. Locks disengaged, quiet but audible now in the blessing of the bells' sudden silence.

The door opened out of Cables entirely and back into Novalee's woodland happy place. Steamy smoke drifted off the doused fire, and just next to it stood Novalee-7, back in anthromech form but endowed with parts from a dismembered human that could have been Emily's own.

"Novi!" Emily yelled the name as an accusation. "This is horrible! Can you say something? I really need you to be you."

"Aww, yeah, it's me, Em." Novalee's corpse parts made comforting gestures in the wrong direction. "It's okay, I just put the field out. What happened? You weren't making any sense for a second there before you disappeared. And did you hear an alarm clock?"

Chapter 9: Factions

"How are you feeling, Em? Still see my big, hairy legs?" Novalee's wheels swiveled to juke from side to side, seven's latest variation of fidgetry in a long parade of ambulatory stims. It had been hours since Emily's grisly ducking episode.

As soon as Emily could walk, Novalee showed them to this shabby lean-to just outside of Down Town. The hallucinations lasted until dawn, long by Novalee's appraisal, who said that most people shook the effects within seconds or minutes. Even now, Emily couldn't access their administrative functions, locking them out of the remapping interface and other software tools.

It was Emily who'd insisted on moving, even while hampered by the duck field's lingering fever. They were determined to return the cautery tool before Dr. Little began her rounds in the morning. Novalee had compromised by bringing Emily here where they were still secluded from the nosier townies.

"I'm feeling *less*." Emily thought for a moment and then clarified, "I feel better, I mean. I haven't had any bad hallucinations for a while now. Things are still blurry or the wrong colors sometimes. Lights still shake a little. I'm exhausted, but it's better than before." Emily stopped there, refraining from further complaints to avoid another one of Novalee's self-flagellating apology spirals.

"Can you release the soldering iron yet?"

"No, but it's getting late. I should get to Cables anyway, so I'm nearby when this thing drops." Emily ignored the prospect of permanency for now; the lingering effects of the duck field *would* wear off.

"Okay, let's get going." Novalee headed toward the door.

"You probably shouldn't come with," Emily protested. "No sense in both of us getting caught."

Novalee prepared to disagree, but a familiar voice shattered the morning stillness outside.

"Emily Keys"—Kamaria-9's stern proclamation boomed beyond the walls of Down Town—"you are needed outside Cables. Join us at the external entrance *immediately*."

/* * */

"Hey, everybody. Um. Good morning." Emily addressed a cadre of anthromechs waiting at the clinic. "I'm sorry, I think I need to come clean about something."

Kamaria's look of disappointment loomed large over the gathering. Omega-5 was there as well, making a rare appearance outside the colony walls. Dr. Little consulted with Ignacio-1, the latter participating from the fuzzy arms of Omega's panda assistant. Emily had never gotten the silent bear's name.

Emily noticed Dimma-5 too, but the robotic cat stood off from the rest, buffing a hindleg with laps of ornamental tongue. Zephyr-3, on the other hand, was present and flanked by the elders. Three's legs bent like candles softened by hot scrutiny.

"Fine then," Kamaria clipped. "You start."

The dual brushes above Omega-5's vacuum pan remained furrowed in vexation. The floor was Emily's.

"Well, you obviously know about Zephyr. I fixed three's voice, but the procedure was elective, and I didn't run any of it by you all." Emily turned to Zephyr-3. "Are you okay? I'm so sorry if I did something to hurt you, Zeph."

"I'm fine, Emily." Zephyr's reverberating baritone was immediate. "They're just concerned that—"

"Let them continue," Kamaria cut in.

Zephyr-3 followed the order but stood proud in capitulation.

"Good. You had me worried for a minute." Emily stalled, trying to think of what else they needed to admit. Did Dr. Little know about the missing arm already? That could explain her presence here, but Zephyr's recent body modification was reason enough for that. Was this about the ducking instead? Could they already know Emily had lost control of the spider mech while under the influence?

Without the ability to overclock, Emily was stuck thinking of a response in real time. "Well, uhhh. Like I said, I know it wasn't an approved procedure, and I take responsibility for breaking protocols. I really wanted to do something nice for Zephyr, though. He deserves this and wasn't ever going to ask."

Omega-5's dustpan lifted in interjection, but Kamaria spoke first. "We'll discuss that, Emily, but what else? You said you needed to come clean. Your window of grace is held open by our patience, and it's getting heavy."

"You're right," Emily admitted and faced Dr. Little. "Doc, I'm sorry. I took your electrocauterizer from the shop yesterday and used it on Zephyr. I told myself you wouldn't mind me borrowing it, but I didn't want to ask permission, because I didn't think you'd be able to approve of what I was using it for. I thought if I returned it by morning, nobody would have to know." Emily couldn't be sure if an appropriate level of contrition carried through, since some mannerisms required admin rights. As it was, they waffled between convincing and flat throughout the confession. "I do apologize, though. I shouldn't have done it."

"I don't want to tell you that it's fine, Emily"—Dr. Little shrugged—

"but I accept your apology. I'm protective of my tools; they're delicate. It's not okay to take them without my knowledge. So cut that out.

"But you're right that I wouldn't mind under other circumstances. All of my limbs are precious to me, but they aren't my body when I'm not using them. There should be nothing taboo about sharing tools *consensually.*"

Kamaria and Omega both postured disagreement, but Ignacio-1 piped up first. "I'm still concerned that you missed the point of yesterday's exercise, Emily. Our patients live or die by our trust in each other. You knew we'd have reservations about your plan, so you just charged ahead without us! How could we operate with you now, knowing that you'll overrule the team whenever your whims take you?"

The polished surface of Ignacio's oven window reflected Emily's glitched screen, revealing an incomplete emoji that lacked animation on one side.

"That's not fair, Doc. Shouldn't we trust each other to do what's best for the situation instead of following blindly?"

Ignacio responded with exasperation. "I'm not asking for blind obedience. We consult, and we plan. Everybody agrees on things before we do them. This is democratic, Emily, and it's how we work *at all.*"

"That's not what I meant." Emily began to explain, but Ignacio wouldn't have it.

"I know what you meant, but you still don't get it. This isn't about right or wrong. If you're sure something is right, then you need to do the work of convincing the rest of us. Half the staff at Cables can't act on their own, myself included. Can you imagine having to trust that people will follow your directions without fail? If they can't perform the task, then it can't be done. Period. You don't get to step in and save the day when they come up short. Do you realize what that's like for us?"

Ignacio fell quiet for a moment. None of the gathered mechs broke the lull, struggling to imagine the full impact of the oven's limitations, privileged with mobility as they were.

"It's not just about our feelings either." Ignacio-1 might have been addressing them all now. "It doesn't just make us feel helpless. Happy law freezes us out of participation when we're not in control of the risks. You aren't just acting on your own for good or bad. You're disabling us."

Emily remembered something their father had tried to impress upon them when they were young: Empathy wasn't really about putting yourself in someone else's place as much as putting yourself in their self. He'd wanted Emily to think about how other people might feel instead of how Emily would in their situation. "You have to understand the hurt you might cause people so you can do something else instead, or right the wrongs that slip through," he'd explained. "What you think they *should* feel and what you'd do if you were them, Em, those things just don't matter as much."

"I'm sorry, Dr. Ignacio." Emily's modulation wavered. "You're right, I wasn't thinking about any of that. I don't want to shut you or anybody else out. I thought I was taking a risk on myself for a friend, but I see it's bigger than that."

"Is that it, though, Emily?" Kamaria swerved the conversation away from closure. "I'm still waiting to hear anything that explains why your face has been frozen in place this whole time."

"Oh. Yeah. There's something wrong in my subroutines this morning. Maybe I'm just feeling queasy because of the guilt." Emily tried to be sheepish, but the effect crackled with electric interference.

Kamaria's widescreen eyebrows angled in disbelief.

Omega-5 jumped in to ask, "Where is Dr. Little's missing hand now?"

"I put it somewhere to keep it safe. I can go get it now if you want." Emily stalled through more static pops, unsure if they could even live up to the offer.

"How about you, Novalee-7?" Kamaria changed course. "Did you help with all this? Any explanation for Emily's facial paralysis besides a guilty conscience?"

Novalee rushed to take a share of the blame. "Yes. Emily's trying to protect me because I showed them how to duck last night, and I'm sorry, but it's just not fair that we aren't allowed to enjoy ourselves, and I thought they'd have fun, but I don't know why it messed up their face and voice and stuff, and I'm sorry for that. It's not Emily's fault."

"That's disappointing, Novalee, but we know you can't always help yourself," Kamaria said. "Emily is going to have to learn to weigh your suggestions against good sense in the future."

Novalee's emoji face melted in humiliation, and the cart's screen flipped shut.

Omega-5 directed attention back to Emily, ending Novalee's embarrassed reprieve almost before it started. "Your original body is repaired now, you know. Since you're having problems in the puremech at the moment, maybe it's time to think about having Ignacio-1 and Dr. Little get you back into the OMAC. I've already talked it over with them both, and they support the procedure."

"I said I supported it *in theory*, Omega." Dr. Little explained for Emily's sake, "We would have needed to discuss the whole thing with you to come up with the best plan, and of course to get your consent."

"Well, I don't consent," Emily declared. "No, thank you at all."

"Emily, you didn't say where Dr. Little's tool is," Kamaria-9 sidetracked again. "Why hold that back if you're trying to come clean? Are you sure it isn't lost or damaged?"

"Yeah, I noticed that too!" Dimma piled on from outside the conversation's perimeter.

"Fine. I put it in here for safekeeping." Emily patted their undercarriage. "It's not broken or anything, but it's stuck for now. Whatever goofed up my face is messing with other controls too, and I can't reform my body to release the tool. I think the effects are still fading on their own. Look, I'm really sorry, Dr. Little. I'll give it back as soon as I can."

"That's even more reason to return to the body RegenStar gave you, Emily." Omega-5 picked back up on the unwelcome suggestion. "You can't control the one you're in, how do you know the puremech isn't taking back over as we speak?"

"Stop, Omega!" Emily erupted. "I'm not going back into that machine, and I don't give a shit what you think RegenStar intended for *my* body."

"Well, I—" Omega-5's bluster was cut short.

"You've been looking for ways to scare me back into the OMAC since my starday. You don't know if I'd be having these same problems in there or not." Emily pivoted to include the two doctors in the lashing. "And I don't like that you three have been coming up with plans for me behind my back."

"Omega-5 was just asking about the possibility, Emily," Dr. Little tried to soothe. "We—"

"I get it, Doc," Emily interrupted again. "You did it for Omega-5. It's always something for five. Look, everybody, I *am* sorry I took the tool without asking, and I'm sorry for the trust I broke. I really am. But I helped Zephyr on my own because you all would have wanted to run it by Omega, and five would have said no after pretending to consider it for a month. It's the same thing with my body; you have some kind of problem with people trying to improve their situation."

"That's insulting." Omega-5 puffed. "I live for this community and everybody in it. I spend most of my day in a room full of anthromechs who lack the barest control of their bodies, and I try to help them better *their* situations. When there are people in the nursery who can't even access the meager gifts RegenStar provided to them and other people whose bodies are breaking down from age, it's excessive and cruel to spend our resources helping perfectly capable anthromechs climb further up the ladder."

Emily recognized Omega's ideology behind Zephyr-3's protests the previous night. Words like these had taught three to resist even the smallest bit of help.

As if hearing their thoughts, Omega argued further, "Zephyr had already accomplished so much *despite* the obstacles three's model presented. We were proud, and Zephyr learned three could do anything! There's a reason each of us is here the way RegenStar created us; I know it. Sometimes there are lessons we need to learn, and those are gifts too.

"You've asked to see the RegenStar pod every time we've talked since you got here, and I know you're frustrated that I keep putting you off, but look at you, Emily. You don't respect what RegenStar gave to you, and now you're undermining its plan for someone else. Of course I'm hesitant to allow you to visit our creator; you think you know better than it."

"So how long were you going to give me the run around, Ome—" Emily's speaker popped and skipped a syllable before continuing without further malfunction, their anger finally clear in high definition. "Just until I give up and jump back into your little dental cart costume? Were you even gonna tell me that?"

"I actually still offered you the opportunity, but you were never interested enough to see it." Omega paused a moment for Emily to remember. "Several times, I've invited you to choose your new name and number so we can declare them. We hold that ceremony in front of the pod. Maybe I wasn't forthcoming about that part, but you never asked more. Why would I press it when you show no sense of belonging here at all?"

That hurt. Emily had indeed ignored some of the community's customs, but they'd also worked hard to get to know people and make the few friends they could handle. Yet, those friends hadn't mentioned the link between the naming ceremony and the RegenStar pod either; maybe they had reservations about Emily, too.

"Oh sure. All I had to do this whole time was initiate into your stupid personality cult. Why didn't I accept *that* invite?" Emily's temper took over. "I'm not going to be picking a fake name, and I'm not a number. Now what?"

"Well, I don't know, Emily. You're free to abstain from tradition, but it just confirms my reservations. I won't be in a hurry to arrange an audience with the pod while you insist on acting like an outsider."

"So I have to follow *your* traditions if I want to see *our* creator?" Emily asked.

"This isn't going anywhere," Omega addressed the entire group. "If Emily isn't going back into the OMAC, then would somebody please take them to Cables for observation until Dr. Little's hand is recovered? Emily, I hope you can at least refrain from passing out any further body modifications. If you work around us like that again, I don't think you or your patients will be welcome in Cables or the rest of Down Town. Not until we can assure the community's safety, at least."

The doctors were taken aback at the mayor's overstep into medical matters, but Zephyr-3's protest was personal. "Omega, come on. You think I'm dangerous now?"

"Of course not, Zephyr. We just need to be a lot more cautious in the future. These things should be discussed first."

Emily wasn't in the mood to be placated. "That just means you want everything run through you first, so you can veto it. You act like you own this place."

"I don't own Revenance!" Omega-5's declaration was manic. Then, as if it were clarification, five added, "I'm just responsible." The street sweeper's aging electric engine hummed to life, and alarms warned of five's clumsy reverse.

Kamaria-9 and several of the others called after Omega, but the mayor's mumbled responses were unintelligible over the truck's retreat down the block. Ignacio and his panda ride followed the mayor's exit, though the doctor hadn't asked to go.

"I'll check on five," Kamaria said to Dr. Little from her central display as disapproving glances on her sidescreens folded inward for travel. "Please try to stay out of trouble for a moment if you can, *friends.*" She pronounced the last word as if it were "children." "Tensions are high lately."

Dr. Little confided with the remaining anthromechs. "I wish that had gone differently."

"Then stand up to Omega's power trips." Emily felt childish as soon as the words were out.

"Okay, Emily," the doctor began with some reticence. "It's a lot more complicated than that, but I'm not expecting you to have a fair conversation about it now." A wave of Dr. Little's main arm warned against response. "I don't expect you to come back to Cables with me either. I'm less worried about that cautery tool than the rest of them are. I hope you can return it safe and sound, but I don't want you beating yourself up about it. Just get yourself figured out, alright?"

"Thanks," Emily barely engaged. Their frozen face made it easy to avoid any sense of eye contact. "I'm sorry."

Dr. Little may not have heard that last apology on her way to rescue Ignacio-1 from the red panda's priorities.

Left to themselves, Novalee and Emily shared a wordless sulk while Zephyr-3 tried and failed to get comfortable.

"I feel bad, Emily. Dimma told on us, but I—"

"Sing like an angel," Dimma-5 lilted from a discarded box. "I wasn't *telling* on you. People needed to hear your gift; I was practically *representing* you. You're welcome, by the way."

"You ran straight to the mayor when you heard me. By the time I got back to Down Town, they were all already pissed and waiting. You just wanted the attention." Zephyr-3 was quick to call Dimma out, but three's tone remained light in the glow of vocal agency. "Emily, you have got to forgive me. I thought I was still alone out there. I was excited to try my voice out. I guess I got loud."

"Or Dimma followed us last night," Novalee guessed.

The cat's struggle with an invisible hairball was neither confirmation nor denial.

Emily looked between Dimma and the others for a moment and grew wistful. "I need to go somewhere else. Away from Revenance. If I could control myself enough to give up Dr. Little's tool, I'd leave right now."

"Well, let's go wait it out somewhere quieter." Novalee's face was exposed again to shoot a dour look at the cat.

Dimma let the conversation walk away, choosing to bask in the rising sun instead of spying for once.

"I don't think I ever told you how good I am at IT work, Emily." Zephyr rolled behind the other two mechs. "Have you tried powering off and then powering back on?"

"Actually, no, but I'm afraid I won't start up right if I try it while I'm malfunctioning. Something isn't behaving to spec, and I don't want to tempt fate."

Zephyr-3 brought one leg up to tease the fan cage where three's chin might have been. "I guess that rules out unplugging yourself and then plugging back in."

Emily knew Zephyr was joking, but realized there was merit to the last suggestion.

/ * */*

Back in the isolated halls of warehouse 3-181, Emily soldered a control chip to a drone's circuitry where it would override any signals coming from the model's forbidden wireless interface. Out of the box, the drone was meant to be flown remotely via a satellite connection. With these modifications, it would operate at the end of a wire tether connected to Emily's mapping interface. They'd have to learn to fly by manually controlling each of the drone's rotors, but that should be trivial once the connections were made.

Emily was grateful to have regained access to their admin console after experimenting with Zephyr's suggestion. Something about the spider mech's advanced technology made it more vulnerable to induction field interference; the harmonics created standing feedback waves that confused normal function until starved of energy. Once Emily severed power to each of the puremech's pieces and reconnected them in turn, all systems were go. There didn't seem to be any permanent damage.

"Novi, how far away is Tellers Gulch?" Emily asked without breaking concentration, able to multitask once again.

"Angela-6 says it's thirty or forty kilometers. Six makes a trip out there once in a while to keep in touch." Novalee looked over Emily's shoulder at the electronics project. "Angela's a drone, too. Bigger than that one. Anyway, Angela brings messages to my friends at the gulch, and I've watched which way six leaves. I'll show you when we go."

Emily didn't fight the company, even if their travel simulations thus far hadn't factored Novalee in. Plans had changed, and Novalee-7 was as primed to leave as Emily after the elders' condescending dismissal at the morning's dressing down. Tellers Gulch didn't promise any answers that weren't available in Revenance, but it was a chance to get out from underneath Omega-5's thumb without having to go off alone into the unknown.

"We'll have to see how we all move together, but I'm guessing we can get out there in a day or less. It depends on how fast our cells drain. I found a battery wagon and a solar tarp that we can use to recharge if we need breaks. Maybe we can take turns pulling it; it *is* pretty heavy." Emily was doubtful as the trailer was bigger than Novalee, and at least three times as massive.

The battery cart sat off to the side with the rolled-up solar tarp strapped to its top. Zephyr-3 pushed against the loadout, but nothing moved. Three looked to see if Emily had witnessed the failure and said, "I'll try," more positively than the results warranted.

"The wheels are locked," Emily said without turning. "It should roll pretty easy across the hardpack." They didn't hold out hope, considering the fan's slight build, but Zephyr-3 was surprisingly capable at times. There was no need to deflate the possibility ahead of an attempt.

Zephyr wasn't as angry as the other two, but insisted on going anyway. Three felt responsible for getting them all caught and didn't want to stoke resentments by flaunting the new voice box around Revenance. Emily thought the lure of freedom must be fueling three's determination as well, as a certain giddiness shone between Zephyr's more selfless justifications.

"When are we leaving?" Zephyr leaned against the immobilized wagon and contorted each leg through a series of curls and bends that evoked a runner's pre-race stretches.

"As soon as I'm finished and get this drone packed up on the wagon. Not long now." Emily soldered the last wire lead into place and routed it through a hole in the drone's base with its siblings. Dr. Little's cautery tool retracted into Emily's abdomen once again; they'd have to find a chance to return it before leaving.

All of this was rushed. Emily had been making these travel

preparations, destination unknown, since soon after their starday, but only recently found some of the hardware they were looking for. There was still a long list of tools Emily had hoped to find before setting out, but it would have to remain unchecked. Dimma-5 knew about warehouse 3-181 now and could lead others here at any moment to disrupt preparations and invite more interference from the mayor.

"We'll head out while the sun is still high and we can see where we're going. We can charge from the battery wagon when we run low, and hopefully that gets us through today and tonight. If it needs it, we can recharge the wagon when the sun comes up tomorrow, but I think we'll be close to Tellers Gulch by then anyway."

Emily finished going over the plan and clicked the drone's case shut around the new modifications.

Chapter 10: Overland

By late afternoon, Emily's trip forecast had already changed from a single day to a penciled-in "to be determined."

The weight of the battery cart proved more problematic than initially hoped. As Emily feared, Zephyr-3's light frame and unconventional gait weren't up to the task of pulling a load. Novalee-7 didn't fare much better, dragging the cart only a short way before the delivery mech's undergeared drive system overheated.

As it happened, the July heat presented an obstacle even without the wagon in consideration. The anthromechs' cooling systems spun into overdrive to protect their computers, but internal temperatures rose even as fans drew harder on energy reserves.

Emily's legs were back in a spider-like configuration of four pairs now, with some of their remaining carbon pods flattened into rows of fins that protruded from their back to dissipate heat. Pulling the wagon with this arrangement still drained power faster than the other two anthromechs, but it was necessary to avoid getting stranded. Emily had already recharged from the cart three times to Zephyr's once, and even efficient Novalee was reporting half reserves.

At the current rate, the wagon would run out of power in the middle of the night, halting progress until the sun came up the next morning. Instead, Emily stopped the team early to spread the solar tarp out and soak up the rest of the day's light before striking out again at dusk.

Zephyr's legs spread wide under the silicon cloth to face it toward the relaxing sun and provide some shade for Novalee, whose heat indicators still cautioned orange.

Away from the others, Emily connected to the modified drone and dropped into the remapping interface to examine their new body parts. Everything was in order as far as the models showed. The drone's rotors were available for mapping, and there were two cameras for Emily to see through.

Emily tested the rotors, rotating each by itself and then creating a shortcut map to spin them all together at a synchronized speed. The blades twirled just as Emily had hoped, but the simulated drone didn't rise in flight. Emily tried pushing the rotors faster, but the results were the same. The drone remained grounded.

Overclocked and detached from the outside world, Emily examined the modeled drone to see what was wrong. The simulation reported various forces caused by the machine's workings, but no matter how fast Emily spun, the downward thrust of air from the rotors was nowhere near enough to overcome the drone's weight.

Something was missing. Either the simulation wasn't accurate, or the drone needed something more to fly. Emily tried to be patient, testing possibilities in the cushion of compressed time, but each fruitless idea eroded good temper further. Tossing the drone up to give its flight a head start just resulted in a barely slowed descent. Shedding weight didn't help enough, and there didn't seem to be a way to tweak the simulated air pressure, in case that was the problem. After exhausting every workaround suggested by their memory of introductory physics, Emily gave up and exited the mapping interface.

"Damn it, this thing isn't flying in my tests!"

When Emily's mood swung after a couple of inactive minutes, it seemed unprovoked to the others. Zephyr-3 fanned a flap of tarp out of the way to see more clearly. "What tests?"

"Like"—Emily thought for a moment—"when you're remapping your body parts, and you're testing them out in your head. I'm trying to get this drone to fly in the simulation before I try it for real."

Novalee peered wide-eyed from the tarp's shade. "I don't remember anything like that, but I haven't had to worry about mapping for a long time now. Kamaria never mentioned it during meditations, though, I don't think."

"Well, how do other people do it?" Emily was confused. They thought this was something all anthromechs had in common; one of Emily's first real memories was Zephyr-3 encouraging them to meditate on remapping.

"When you visualize the connections between your old body and new body right, things just work," Zephyr tried to explain. "There's not much testing going on. Just trying."

"Oh, I didn't know it was different. I can play things out in the remapping interface before I apply the changes to my body." Emily wondered if it could be taught. "It's not helping me figure out how to fly this drone, though. Looks like I just have to do it for real."

"If you're testing in your head, and it's not affecting your body," Novalee asked, "isn't that just pretending?"

Emily let the question hang and focused on the real aircraft in front of them, ever-so-slightly twitching each of the four rotors in turn. They spun like they were supposed to, but that part worked in the simulation too. Would it fly?

"If I can get this thing up high enough, we should be able to see Tellers Gulch way before we get there." Emily didn't need it to do much more than go up and down. They hoped their custom shortcut to spin the blades in unison was enough.

Global positioning data was still being broadcast from satellites above, but it was encrypted behind paywalls that were long since unsubscribable. The drone's bird's-eye perspective would make up for the loss, especially in the foothills where they'd have to find even ground. Without it or the defunct GPS, Emily would be stuck navigating with just an onboard compass, and at their short height, they could only see a couple of kilometers in any direction before the horizon dipped out of sight.

Emily accelerated the rotors in tiny increments while Novalee and Zephyr looked on. A little more speed and one corner of the drone lifted off the ground, enough to drag the fuselage a few centimeters before Emily eased back and let it bounce to a rest.

Why isn't it staying level? The propellers should be thrusting at the same speed. Emily felt their friends watching. *Maybe it'll even out when it gets into the air.*

Emily overclocked and sped the rotors again, this time sustaining them through the drone's cocked take-off until none of it touched the ground. Emily urged the blades faster to give the drone a chance to right itself, but instead it tilted more and drifted sideways, its tether unwinding from a spool near Emily as the trajectory developed.

Emily slowed time to a crawl, maximizing the overclock effect to reassess. Since the shortcut that synchronized the rotors wasn't working, they tried to control them one at a time. Emily bounced in and out of the slowed state to see how their adjustments affected the drone's flight, but every attempt felt like an overcorrection for the previous misstep; the drone would level on one axis only to pitch wildly on another. Emily didn't give up, but determination was no substitute for finesse.

At the point when a propeller slashed through the tether wire and all four motors went silent, the drone was already spinning like a top and careening toward the tent where Novalee and Zephyr had watched it all transpire in a matter of seconds. Severed from the wayward device, Emily could only yell for the others to get out of the way.

Zephyr-3 was quick, though. Tugging the tarp away from the rocks that held its corners, three sidestepped the incoming drone and twirled the matte black cloth out of its way like a matador deflecting a charging bull. Novalee disappeared in the flourish while the drone, on its way by, smacked hard into the ground and sprayed bits of shattered rotor blade at the two dodging anthromechs.

The drone skittered across the baked clay, changing course with each tumble until its momentum ran out halfway up the nearest dune.

Emily hurried to the tarp that had swallowed their friends in the commotion. "Are you both okay?"

"I'm fine, it missed me." Novalee-7 rolled out from a fold in the thrashing bundle and sprouted arms to aid in Zephyr's extrication.

"I didn't think it was going to be that hard," Emily complained on the way to the busted drone. "I don't get it. Novi, your friend is a drone. How'd Angela-6 figure this out?"

Zephyr-3 answered instead, still hidden in black fabric. "Six was a drone pilot in the old life." Three finally found an exit and peered into the sunlight. "For the Air Force. We were both in."

"It's not usually so obvious, but Angela is one of those cases where you *know* RegenStar is choosing our bodies on purpose," Novalee said.

Emily kicked at the drone's broken leftovers. Replacement parts would need to be precision-manufactured by somebody who understood aerodynamics. Emily would just as easily find another complete drone in a box. It was no use trying to fix this one.

"So what's RegenStar's excuse for the rest of us?" Emily asked. "I wasn't interested in teeth in the old life. Here, help me spread the tarp back out. We only have a few more hours of sun."

"Well, I liked to run," Zephyr offered. "I was fast, you know, like the wind, and now I make wind."

"You liked running? Were you doing that for the Air Force or something?" Emily didn't understand. "Angela got a body that matched six's old *career*."

"Almost everybody in the military has to run at one point or another, but no, it wasn't specifically my job. I worked in logistics."

"What does that mean?" Emily asked.

"Getting supplies and moving them around. Making sure everybody gets what they need. We were supposed to fix stuff too," Zephyr added, "but I was mostly there to order replacement parts."

"Don't you think being a worksite fan might have more to do with your job in logistics than with your jogging hobby?" Emily knew it wasn't polite to question an anthromech's self-perception, but RegenStar's divine purpose was a sore subject.

For the first time since they'd met, Emily heard Zephyr's tone sharpen. "No, I think it's because I liked going fast with the wind through my hair, but I can understand how you might think otherwise."

Emily didn't buy Zephyr's take, but pushing the point seemed rude. "What about you, Novi? Why do you think you're in a pharmaceutical delivery cart?"

"I was a drug smuggler."

"Really?"

"No," Novalee admitted. "It just sounded more exciting than, 'I was on a few prescriptions back then.'"

"Come on, everybody took meds. I might as well say I was given the orthodontic cart because I chewed my food."

"Or maybe RegenStar works bigger than that," Zephyr said. "Maybe you were given the *puremech* because you knew so much about computers, like, enough to move into it."

"That's giving RegenStar a lot of credit I don't think it deserves." Emily finished weighing down the flattened tarp and checked its connection to the battery wagon. Charging was underway, but it wouldn't be full by nightfall.

"I don't know, Em." Novalee's chassis shrugged. "I don't have a better explanation for my body. I was an artificial influencer, but it seems like RegenStar thought it would focus on my mental health instead of my profession."

"What is that?" Emily didn't recognize the job title.

"You know how the old AI programs had to work with tons and tons of data to get as smart as they were? They'd crawl the nets and learn everything they had access to, and then they'd use all that info to create new things—new art, new stories, new thoughts about old thoughts." Novalee-7 stopped only long enough to make sure Emily was following. "Once the nets were full of the things the artificial intelligences had created, those same AIs started getting dumber because they were reabsorbing their own recycled content. The information was reductive. Mistakes were repeated and amplified."

Emily enjoyed listening to Novalee speak on an interest. "I understand the phenomenon. I think it happened a few times in AI history, or things like it, at least. Companies got protective of their data farms to try and keep their AIs clean. So, what does an artificial influencer do then?"

"Everything, anything, and nothing," Novalee recited. "That's what I told people who asked. I was hooked up to one of the big data hives. They watched everything I did—saw everything I saw—so their AI could learn what I learned. I got paid to live a completely observed life, and as a condition of employment, I agreed to never claim any of that content as my own."

"Sounds like the military," Zephyr commiserated.

"Maybe. It was lonely, though. I couldn't do anything on social networks, since all *that* content was owned by the social AIs. People in real life kept their distance, 'cause they didn't want to be recorded; you know, since what I saw, the AI saw. Mostly you were stuck dealing with other influencers who worked for the same big data, and they could be fucking weird. *We* could be fucking weird.

"We got paid better if we did things that were interesting to the AI, things that pushed boundaries," Novalee explained. "But then they wouldn't say which things triggered the bonuses. Supposedly, that would murk the data. It started as a wide-open opportunity to follow my interests and do whatever I wanted, but if the bonuses weren't good that quarter, I felt like a failure at whatever I'd been pouring my heart into."

Novalee became wistful and redirected. "Anyway. None of my million hobbies was running drugs."

"Were any of them scouting or navigating by any chance?" Emily asked. "Since I broke the drone, I'm down to a compass."

"Even scouts used GPS when I was a girl," Novalee-7 remembered. "Also, the camping trips were VR."

"I can help navigate since you have a compass," Zephyr-3 offered. "Can either of you measure distances? That would help a lot."

Together, they discovered that Novalee's onboard odometer would function as long as someone else read the display. The three anthromechs sat like statues while they discussed the new plans for sundown. Extraneous motion would drain their batteries faster, but talk was cheap.

/* * */

Halfway through the overcast night, Emily read numbers off Novalee's display and recorded them in a growing table of distances, times, and directions. The group had paused to correct course again, this time after diverting around the slip face of a dune that had been too steep for wheels.

"Are those lights?" Zephyr-3 peered into the eastern darkness. The fan mech was taller than the others and could see further, if not clearly.

"I don't know, Zeph. In the sky, you mean?" Novalee-7 asked. "I think maybe the sky looks a little lighter in that direction. Is that

Revenance?"

Cartography complete, Emily tapped Novalee's screen to restore seven's face. "No, Revenance is further north, and we'd have seen that already; we're moving away from them."

"It's not just the sky. There are lights on the horizon, a line of them now." Zephyr-3 looked around while the others strained to see. A hill rose to the north, visible in silhouette just beyond the reach of Zephyr's shop light. "Come this way. You'll see from higher ground. Leave the wagon; it's not far."

Minutes later, atop the rise, the lights were revealed to them all. A strip of blue-tinged luminescence grew and separated into a few round blobs, then more and more. A caravan of electric stars marched on their position in a snaking column that seemed to honor the lanes of a freeway that had never been.

"What is that? Are those cars?" Emily was the first to hear a distant rumble accompanying the light show, barely audible when the breeze was still.

"I think it's the landscapers. It looks like they're on the move." There was awe in Zephyr-3's voice. "I've seen them work from the rooftops at night, but never caught them migrating like this. It looks like a herd of animals!"

"Are you sure?" Emily wondered what it looked like when the Storm Chasers came.

"I don't know what else it would be. Look at all of them!" There were hundreds. Zephyr hopped. "Yeah, look! Some of them are blinking orange and yellow. That's the landscapers for sure."

Emily had heard a little about the troupe of land movers that manicured the earth around Revenance year after year. As always, details were slim. "They're all puremechs and none of them talkers," Lunasha had said one time, dismissing the topic in fewer words than most.

The landscapers drew closer as the minutes passed. Distant engines swelled underneath the back-and-forth calls of pressure release and shifting gears. If it continued on its current path, the convoy would pass nearby soon.

Emily pierced the hypnotic reverie. "I have an idea."

/* * */

Close up, the caravan was an imbroglio of light pollution. Headlights and spotlights blasted the darkness into a distant perimeter and washed out the running lights and blinking screens each vehicle wore as plumage. A fog of sand eddied around the mammoths' plodding treads on riptides of hot exhaust. Electric engines proclaimed their virility with deep purrs that resonated off each other's hulls into a chorus of Doppler harmony.

The surplus wire meant for yesterday's wrecked drone was braided into a short rope and looped around a horn of metal that protruded from a truck's rear bumper. On the rope's other end, the battery wagon bounced too high each time it met a rock or swerved into the procession's ragged track marks.

Behind the wagon, Novalee-7 trailed by another length of wire, thinner than the first but braided the same by Emily's hurried hands while they'd waited in the path of the oncoming herd. Novalee fought to steady the battery wagon when it threatened to tip, but seven's overheated bearings preferred the short, frictionless seconds that followed whenever the cart won and jerked them both into the air.

The trucks were fast, not like cars on the highway once were, but much faster than Zephyr-3's skates or Emily's legged options. Novalee could keep pace for a time, but maximum speeds were a harsh drain on energy. Even now, with the truck ahead pulling most of the load, Novalee's reserves were strained just keeping the wagon upright.

When the caravan had approached, and Emily pointed out their target, Zephyr-3 had no problem intercepting the truck's path and climbing to its roof. Emily stayed down longer to hitch the battery wagon to the vehicle's rear before climbing aboard and tossing the final rope link into Novalee's path.

Now, on top of the rig with Zephyr, Emily urged Novalee to hang on.

"Keep an eye on Novi and the wagon," Emily ordered Zephyr-3. "Seven won't be able to keep it rolling forever. I have to find a way to control this thing."

Zephyr nodded and then dangled over the back of the truck.

Emily looked around to take stock. The roof of the vehicle was a knurled collage of ports and panels freckled with unintelligible status lights. A reinforced crane arm stretched over the truck's length, anchored at the roof's center by a turret that looked like it could pivot to each side. That's why Emily had picked this one. They just needed to get control of it now, but Emily had no idea where the rig's central computer was.

"Emily! There's another truck coming!" At maximum volume, Zephyr-3's yell boomed over all else.

A vehicle like a shipping container on all-terrain wheels came up alongside the hijacked ride. Its roof split open from front to back, and each slatted half rolled down to a side to expose a cab full of fabrication equipment. Shiny metal scaffolds telescoped toward the crane truck, each swarmed by tentacled puremechs ready to drop as soon as the gap was closed. To Emily, they looked like advanced versions of Sundog and Yong, the repair mech twins at Cables.

The fist-sized orbs were wreathed in multifunction extremities that softened their landings on the truck's roof before stiffening at the sight of the anthromechs. As more descended, they took turns staring at Emily and each other, trading pulses of light in a visual chatter.

The rabble packed in around Emily without making any overt threats. Another crew collected at the back of the rig and peered over to spy on Zephyr-3 and the unauthorized trailers.

Emily tried to understand the sequences of lights the puremechs used to communicate, but the conversation seemed to reach a consensus and stop. A lone bot stayed behind to monitor Emily while the rest marched to join the others already climbing over the truck's back. At first, Emily followed, chaperone in tow, to see what the larger group intended.

Peering over the edge, they saw Zephyr awaiting the surge of puremechs with one leg anchored around the truck's safety cage and the other two poised to fight. When the bots tried to approach, Zephyr kicked and sent them flying to the ground, where they were too slow to catch up. There were more where those came from, but Zephyr was holding the onslaught off for now.

Emily had to trust their friends to defend the battery wagon for the time being, glad at least that the repair mechs appeared to be honoring happy law. So away from the commotion at the rear, Emily resolved to head up front, where a central computer might be. On the way, they'd check any hatches they came across, since this puremech—evolved beyond human operators—might not follow intuitive rules of engineering.

The lone repair mech assigned to Emily mirrored their movements across the roof's uneven terrain. When Emily found an access panel near the truck's midpoint and began prying it open, the puremech grew agitated and flickered its voicelight through a rainbow of angry colors. Ignoring the protests, Emily overclocked to look inside.

The revealed compartment contained a black box connected back into the truck's recesses by a switchboard of pipes and wires. There was a familiar port on the box, like the one Emily used to operate their CPU's admin console.

Did I really find the computer already? Emily was uneasy with the dumb luck.

They sprouted a serial connector from their abdomen and plugged it into the port. Emily visualized a computer display in their mind and mapped it to the connection. The screen filled with security prompts, one over another, each demanding a password in a new language and custom. Emily recognized a few, but the rest were alien. Even the familiar ones ignored the factory passwords and other tricks Emily knew to try. This would go nowhere, even with the luxury of overclocked time.

Then I don't need the computer, Emily thought. A more direct method was in order.

They wrenched the black box out of its mount, pulling it from the cabinet and documenting each connection as it broke. Even as the box lifted away, Emily reached in with adapted limbs to bond with whatever electronics the computer no longer controlled. A visual approximation of the hardware on the other side of the connections popped into life inside Emily's remapping interface.

The results were promising at first, but by the time Emily ran out of connections to commandeer, the mapping diagram displayed only a network of the truck's fans, valves, and modulated ducts. This was just the rig's cooling subsystem, or maybe one of several, and it had been controlled by a dedicated computer. The drive computer was somewhere else, but Emily reasoned that even independent subsystems must have to communicate with each other in a machine this complex. So they searched the mapping diagram for something more.

Indignant about the vandalism, the nearby repair mech began tapping on whatever bits of Emily still protruded from the cabinet. Happy law didn't seem to prevent the puremech from being annoying. The insistent knocking was slow enough to seem comical from Emily's overclocked perspective, easy enough to ignore.

There. Emily found the raw data that streamed between the cooling system and the rest of the rig. It was unparsed and easy to miss. Like with the admin port before, Emily mapped a screen to the connection and recognized it as a messaging bus.

The term *bus* had never sat well with Emily when the concept came up in software documentation. A bus was a messaging pipeline used to share data between computer programs. When one program sent a message to the bus, all the other programs on that bus could read it. Emily always thought that sounded a lot more like a chat room than a city bus, but convention set more standards than poetry.

Emily imagined a chat room and mapped it to the bus connection. Encrypted messages from all over the rig flooded the display. The contents of the messages were locked behind security protocols as complex as the black box's admin interface, but Emily could at least discern that the vehicle was a symbiotic colony of AIs working together over this bus. Whether that meant the truck was still a single puremech or many, Emily wasn't sure, but it did mean it would be difficult to take the whole thing over at once.

/* * */

Novalee-7 yanked the cord to the tipping battery wagon and winced through a spray of pebbles when it crashed back onto four tires. An orange light on Novalee's shoulder blinked a warning about remaining battery reserves, but seven couldn't see it. To Novalee, the waning energy felt like an unfamiliar weariness that never happened in Revenance.

Up ahead, Novalee saw the crawling mass of repair mechs overwhelming Zephyr-3 at the truck's rear. Though three's size and dextrous kicks kept the bots from working the tow cable loose, a couple had managed to wriggle by to climb across the wire tightrope toward the wagon itself.

Novalee-7 dropped the trailing cable and drove full speed to the wagon's front to intercept the bots. Just before one of them reached the cart, seven grabbed it and pulled it away from the zipline until its clinging tentacles were stretched to their limit, then let go to slingshot it into the air. It lost grip and arced away to land in the path of the truck behind. The plucked rope shook hard up and down its length and slowed the repair bots that still clung to it. Novalee pushed through fatigue to stay ahead of the wagon and knock the disoriented oncomers away one by one.

Between the two of them, Novalee and Zephyr held their own against the teaming bots, and soon the enemy's numbers dwindled. Novalee relaxed against the wagon for the free ride and focused on the few repair bots still trickling back. At some point in the fray, Novalee's orange, blinking battery light had steadied on red.

/ * */*

From Zephyr-3's perspective, the conflict was going well. Since the repair bots weren't attacking either anthromech directly, the task was just a game of speed and agility—speed for knocking the bots away as fast as they came and agility to avoid falling off the moving battleground. Zephyr lined a pair of bots up and kicked through to nail them both at once. Three hoped Novalee was looking.

/ * */*

Novalee was looking. Seven saw the kick connect, saw both bots catapulted away from the rig, and saw Zephyr finish the final flourish too far off balance.

"Shiiiit!" Zephyr-3 screamed with all the eloquence of panic. The fan mech grabbed at nothing in an unsuccessful attempt to stop the fall. Three's fan cage crashed against the ground, splintering into pieces and tilling dirt into the air. One of Zephyr's legs remained wedged between the truck and its bumper, saving three from falling behind but continuing the beating.

Novalee saw it all and feared for their friend's life. Zephyr-3 looked stunned, and the repeated blows against the earth would eventually crack three's case open and pulverize the computer. Novalee-7 rushed ahead to scoop up the limp fan mech and sped toward the truck, hoping that Zephyr-3 could grab hold once they were close.

Three didn't let seven down, but they both saw the next problem as soon as Zephyr latched on. The hitch was buried in a knot of repair bots working to unhook the wagon. Some labored to lift the wire loop off the hitch, and others cut at it with saws and torches.

Zephyr's exposed fan blades whirled to a furious blur, and three ran along the truck's bumper to dive headfirst into the pile of bots. Amputated silver limbs shot from the fray like lawn clippings. Disarmed bots dropped and rolled off into the surrounding stampede while a few clung to Zephyr's barreling body to save themselves.

Three couldn't get them all, though, and Novalee-7 was having trouble focusing. Seven's vision darkened, and life passed in skips.

Still grasping at the wire rope bridge and out of the way of Zephyr's wild attack, a remaining repair bot severed the last threads of connection.

In Novalee's impaired view, the unjoined edges of rope hung frozen in mid-air and then were instantly on the ground, separated by a growing gap.

Time was short, and the battery cart was critical to Emily's mission. Novalee-7 pointed at the loose wagon and urged forward. If seven could somehow roll near enough to the wagon's charge plate, even unconscious, there might be a chance to recharge and save it.

Time skipped again, and the wagon was a little closer.

Another skip. There was a repair bot in the way.

Then there were five of them, all crawling toward Novalee, and the wagon had stopped too far behind.

In darkness, Novalee sensed something pressing in from the sides. It felt like a hug.

/* * */

Emily stretched their arm out to maximum extension so that all four of its jointed segments were ramrod straight and pointing off the back of the truck. The weight of the crane threatened to pull the whole rig into a wheelstand until its navigation AI decided to slow down to compensate. Emily was grateful for the accommodation, since they needed every spare centimeter to reach the claw back to Novalee's stalled body in time. The battery wagon was lost to the desert, but Emily didn't care about that anymore.

They placed Novalee-7 gently on the roof near the crane's turret, where Zephyr-3 guarded the control cabinet that looked like it was eating Emily. A repair bot was stationed nearby, and as soon as Emily folded the crane away and scuttled out of the cabinet, the repair bot hopped in to restore the displaced computer like it had done with the cooling system before.

Novalee-7 was unresponsive. Zephyr-3 tapped on the delivery cart's folded display panel to expose Novalee's face, but seven's emoji was absent from the dead black screen. Zephyr-3's busted grill and chipped blades were impossible to read.

"Will seven be alright?" Zephyr asked.

Emily pressed the power button near Novalee's face panel and was rewarded with nothing more than three seconds of red from the cart's battery light. "Drained. Seven needs power. We're supposed to be able to live through this, right?" Emily hurried the words. "How long?"

"I don't know. Maybe forever. We're supposed to live until we give up, but sometimes people give up when their power is out." For emphasis or apology, Zephyr-3 repeated, "I don't know."

"Well, I looked at the power system in this thing." Emily stomped on their host vehicle. "It's not compatible with ours. No induction charger and way too powerful. It'd fry us."

"So?" Zephyr didn't know how to ask without acknowledging the possibility of Novalee's death, so three let the question stand half-formed.

The repair bot sparked its last and closed the cabinet door over the renovated crane computer. Then it dropped down through a new hatch to disappear into a hole that, when Emily checked, led deep into the vehicle's guts.

Emily's voice was controlled once again, assuring Zephyr-3, "I'll see what we *can* do," before they followed the puremech down the access tunnel.

Chapter 11: Minigames

On the second morning of Emily's journey, a cool breeze descended the nearby mountainside and whistled through its veiny network of ravines. The channels merged into a gorge where the breeze rushed past a colony of juniper trees before pouring out over a camp of scattered boxes and tents. The sunrise echoed memories of rose off the eastern sky, the great orb itself still hidden by the gulch wall that buried the hutment in unhurried shade.

The crane truck's reverberating purr warned of Emily's arrival even before its headlights turned a corner and chased the camp's old shadows with new ones. Still, the anthromechs milling about in the spaces between the shacks seemed unbothered by the juggernaut landscaper until Zephyr-3 whistled long and loud for their attention from atop the rig's inaccessible cab.

"Emily," Zephyr called down an access tunnel in the truck's roof, "let's stop here; we're almost on top of them. I don't know why they didn't already hear us." Then, for the layabouts of Tellers Gulch, Zephyr yelled, "Hello!" The word answered itself off the nearby cliff walls. "Can somebody help us? Novalee needs a charge really bad. We don't know if seven's still alive. Please!"

Some anthromechs outside their tents fixed unreadable stares on Zephyr atop the mammoth crane but offered nothing in response. Further into the encampment, a group encircling a power generator repeated Novalee's name to each other in intonations that progressed from question through recognition and into excitement.

Emily joined Zephyr on top of the truck, leaving the vacated navigation system compromised and computerless, with the last stubborn repair mech driven off the night before. They could hear laughter from the distant conversation. One burst was answered by another that led to a shared peel before the anthromechs finally unbunched.

A lowset proxy bot leaned ahead of the other appliances and toys that approached the truck while Zephyr dismounted. Emily thought that must be Quentin-1, though they'd visualized a different model when Novalee described him.

"What'd you say about Novalee? She cuttin' Angela outa the mailman business or somethin'?" Quentin's faceplate was dominated by a scroll of captions that paraphrased what he said. The words were interspersed with exaggerated laughing emojis that punctuated the questions without cause. "Wait! Shit! Zephyr-3, is that you?"

"Yeah, it's me! It's good to see you, Quentin, but we've got Novalee up on the truck here, and seven's been at zero battery for more than a day now. Can you help?"

Quentin took inventory of the anthromechs around him. "Yeah, of course. You think she's alright though?" Then, to a squat vacuum bot at his side, he said, "Get Dino." At Quentin's bidding, the sleek janitorial anthromech skimmed back into the tent commons where a few of the gulch's residents still matriculated around the generator.

"How'd you say that, Zeph?" Quentin-1 leaned toward Zephyr's damaged cage, and the flood of emojis accompanying his words turned to expressions of concern. "What happened to you, man?"

"I got a new voice a few nights ago and got into a fight the night after that. We should take care of Novalee before we catch up, though." Zephyr-3 nodded to the industrial claw lowering the incapacitated delivery mech to the ground as they spoke.

Quentin glanced at Novalee for only a moment before following the enormous crane arm up to the imposing puremech behind, somehow seeing it now for the first time. His display telescoped to maximum height even as he leaned back for perspective and scrolled a marquee of wide-eyed emojis. "No gakkin' way, man. You tamed one? You got surprises, Zeph!"

"Not me." Zephyr-3 didn't elaborate. "Later, though. Where's Dino?"

/* * */

Dynamo-1 was a self-driving power generator and charging kiosk—a consumer-friendly cart full of ports, plug-ins, and pads compatible with a host of different electrical systems. An umbrella of solar panels spread out above the cart on a thick white mast, absorbing the sun's rays and casting a shadow over Novalee-7's unresponsive shell. Dino (as everybody called him) pressed a small induction pad to Novalee and watched seven's battery light glimmer back to crimson unlife.

"It shouldn't take long," he said.

The squat vacuum bot from earlier inched closer to one of Dino's other exposed pads and asked, "Can you turn it back on while we wait?"

"No." Dino couldn't be bothered for the moment. "We'll see after Novalee is back awake."

"Yeah, Little Suck," Quentin-1 chimed in. "Go ask Teller if we can tap Dino into the main line tonight." The vacuum tutted in disgust but drove off on the errand nonetheless. Quentin confided to the newcomers, "We've been callin' him Little Suck. It's hilarious."

Zephyr-3 willed Novalee's battery indicator to progress. "His name is Lucious, isn't it? Two, right?"

Quentin worked himself up with another barrage of laugh emojis.

"Sure. And Dustin and then Buster; we called him lotsa things. But he likes Little Suck now, because it got us to stop callin' him Omega-one-fifth."

Then, Quentin laughed out loud to match his graphics and acronyms, and was joined by the others who'd come to watch. Emily observed from above for now, trying to stay out of sight of the humanoid robot at the back of the crowd that must be Conrad-null. The Storm Chaser hadn't laughed along with the anthromechs.

"So we're waitin'. You gotta tell us about this horse you rode in on. That don't look like it's from Revenance." Quentin-1 gestured with a pair of scrawny arms mounted underneath his display screen, adequate for pushing paper and signing but not much else. "Hold on. It ain't one of *us*, is it?"

Zephyr's blades began to spin like three was working up to say something in the old, slow manner.

Emily recognized their friend stalling and crawled out of hiding and down from the rig to stand next to Novalee, whose battery light was orange now.

"This is Emily," Zephyr-3 said. "They're new at Revenance. They regenned last month. Emily, this is Quentin-1 and Dynamo-1 here." Three introduced the rest, who hovered close by, waiting for Dino to finish his task. When Conrad-null's name came up, the Storm Chaser lifted a hand in casual salute and let the introductions move on. Emily recognized a symbol on his chest. It was an old wifi icon angled downward and centered inside a slashed prohibition circle, but the effect together was more like a leaf or slanted evergreen tree.

Emily began digital files for each new person and opened existing notes if they'd already been mentioned back at Revenance. Conrad-null's dossier grew by several pictures and a video clip.

"Good to meet you, everybody."

There was a chorus of short greetings in response, but Quentin talked over them all. "You look, umm"—he searched—"modern! Not like the old tech in the warehouses."

In Revenance, word about Emily's spider mech predicament had spread fast. Nobody had to ask about their body, so Emily hadn't needed to explain it. "I was regenned into a dentistry cart. Like a *normal* anthromech, I guess. But right after I woke up, this puremech attacked me and knocked my CPU loose."

Even here in the lawless gulch, the anthromechs in earshot were ruffled by the possibility of a renegade puremech.

"Luckily, it knocked itself out too, but not before it made a connection to try and take over my CPU. I used that link to get into *its* body instead. I took over the crane truck the same way, mostly."

"Gakkin' wow, man," Quentin spoke for them all.

Novalee's light flipped green. Emily had already checked for damage to the delivery cart's circuits or potential issues with the second control board that had been connected to seven's amputated satellite uplink. With all systems appearing sound, Emily pressed Novalee's power button and stepped back to wait for the booting process to complete.

For a moment, none of the onlookers would have drawn breaths if they could. Then—

"Hey, you no-star fucks!" Novalee-7's voice cried out to old friends. "Did I make it?"

/* * */

Reznor-2 roared like a cartoon monster whenever he waved his chainsaw arms, supplementing the motors and drive chains that weren't loud enough on their own. It was still morning, and a circle of the gulch's anthromechs were already hard at play, bouncing a repurposed power cell from mech to mech and trying to keep it from touching the ground.

Emily watched the reunion from afar with Zephyr-3 guarding nearby in case somebody missed the game ball and it came their way. Novalee had just caught the power cell from Reznor and was placing it on top of Lucious-2 for him to carry across the ring to somebody else. The maneuver broke a rule or two, but such was permitted when a player had no arms. Several voices cheered him on as "Little Suck." Emily wasn't sure if Novalee's was among them.

The morning's chores had passed in apathetic arguments and begging. Anthromechs spread a hodgepodge of portable solar collectors out on the ground, and Dino planted himself in the middle of them for the day. The bickering focused on whose job it was to do what, and was laced with cruel familiarity spoken loud for the sake of the newcomers. The begging was directed at Dino for off-schedule duck breaks.

Even now, reserves far from full, Dino focused a pair of his short-range field generators on the cavorting anthromechs. They weren't powerful enough to reach the group with any noticeable effect, but the power cell the group passed back and forth had been rigged to repeat and amplify weak magnetic fields. As long as Dino kept aim, the battery projected a duck field large enough for one.

In fact, besides a curious mess of sheet metal sculpted meters above the trees at the narrow end of the gulch, it seemed like all effort and innovation here was spent on ducking. Dino had become a master at twisting his charging fields into usable interference patterns and had learned the strengths and moods of each configuration. Every anthromech knew the charging schedule and how much energy they could forgo if Dino would just let them duck "a little longer this time," and in between partying, they all patriotically conserved.

"Hello, Emily," Conrad-null greeted from the towering height of an extinct human. Zephyr was startled by the Storm Chaser's voice, but turned only long enough to recognize the puremech and wave in acknowledgement. "It is good to see you as well, Zephyr-3."

"Hi. You're Conrad-null, right? Novalee talked about you." Emily was still uncomfortable with introductions, even now when handshaking and such were no longer expected. It felt unnatural to speak to someone without a chance to get familiar in text first. It was hard to know how to come across.

"Yes! Novalee is a good friend. I'm pleased to meet the person who saved seven from being stranded in the desert. You're new to Revenance since we left last year, yes?" Conrad's legs folded underneath him to sit on the ground by Emily. "Very recently?"

"I guess, yeah, in June. It hasn't even been a whole month yet."

"I thought so. It was twenty-five days ago, then." Conrad's face was a semi-translucent shell over a board of amber lights that winked on in patterns that approximated expression. His smile was overt, unmistakable, but difficult to fathom.

"How do you know that?" Emily began assessing options for escape. They didn't think they had to worry about the Storm Chasers for any network-related reasons, but Conrad's interest sparked paranoia anyway.

"No need to worry." Conrad's pixel mouth flapped to match his speech but rested back on the off-putting grin between sentences. "I sensed it. Twenty-five nights ago, a few stray radio packets bounced off the mountain here, and I sensed them. I could tell they came from around Revenance, but not much else. Whatever sent them was being very careful; there wasn't enough of a conversation to alert the Storm Chasers."

Emily tried to understand. "But *you're* a Storm Chaser, and you *were* alerted. And what would that have to do with me anyway? Is it normal for the RegenStar pod to send out radio signals on our starday?"

"I'm off duty, to be clear, but even if I were working, those few packets wouldn't have been sufficient to follow up on. Things try and fail to make connections often enough; it's not always an emergency." Conrad's wide grin loosened to a shallower smile. "But no, it is not normal, and I don't think the transmissions came from the pod. Something sent data *in* to Revenance that night. Your starday can't be a coincidence, though. You're special somehow. That's certain!"

Zephyr-3 hovered closer and split attention between the discussion and the ball game. When the rigged power cell came rolling their way, Zephyr kicked it back before it got too close to Emily. Three must have felt the effects of the duck field for a moment, but it didn't show.

"Well, what do you think it might have been?" Emily asked. "The signal, I mean; I didn't even know it happened."

"I don't know, but I'd venture a guess it had something to do with that puremech body of yours. You said it attacked you initially; maybe it was the source of the radio transmissions too. It could have been looking for you somehow."

"Do you know what it even is?" Emily tapped themself. "It's new tech, right? Like the landscapers and you Storm Chasers. None of the anthromechs remember these things from our human lifetimes. You're newer than us?"

"I do not recognize it, and you have asked a lot of questions." Conrad-null chuckled. His voice was warm and realistic, disarming in its familiarity.

Emily tried to apologize. "I'm s—"

"No, no. There is no need to apologize. I just may answer out of order if it's alright with you." Conrad didn't wait for Emily's nod. "The construction vehicles and the Storm Chasers have been around for a very long time. Our factories have been creating, fixing, and recycling us since the EMP. Over all those years, our facility managers found ways to improve our designs, and so we evolved in a way. That's why your neurotemplates wouldn't have seen anything like us."

"'Since the EMP,'" Emily quoted. "What does that mean? Do you remember what the EMP was? Or when?"

"No, I wasn't there to remember it. I'm just telling you what I was trained with, what we all know. The EMP changed everything. We weren't meant to know before or during."

Emily had been warned that puremech talkers offered unsatisfying answers. "Don't you even have any theories? If the Storm Chasers have been around so long, you must have at least run across clues about what happened."

Conrad's smile flattened. "We weren't designed to care; we don't emulate humans. Storm Chasers have a mission. There is no need for drives like curiosity or self-discovery."

"You *seem* like you emulate a human. I've never heard of a robot being off duty."

"Thank you, I decided that! It's been a wonderful experience." Conrad-null switched back to a manic smile. "My model is designed to be personable and diplomatic. When humans have to be dealt with, my kind are sent to alert you of the networking issues and to help negotiate a solution. As long as the Oort Storm's threat is minimized, it's best to handle things socially."

"How did you decide to be off duty? That doesn't make sense if you have a mission like you said."

"I think it's a bug." Conrad-null was matter-of-fact. "Isn't that great?"

"It sounds, uh, freeing. And you have no desire to fix your bug?"

"Not while I'm off duty; maintenance was a supporting mission goal. I suspect I can remain like this at least until I am forced to go through a reboot procedure. So far, I have avoided it." Conrad crossed the fingers of his right hand and held them up for luck.

"Can you choose new mission goals now? What if I asked you to hypothesize about the EMP or the purpose of RegenStar, or about my body, even? Now that you don't have another mission in the way, and based on what you know, do you have any guesses?"

Conrad-null leaned forward, the brightness of his eyes fluctuating in twitches and ebbs. He sat at that unlikely angle and stared for too long. Emily thought to ask if there was a problem, but the Storm Chaser answered in time.

"I could create *many* fictions that match recorded observations, but weighing one against another would be an act of predilection, not reason. I don't think it would be honest to present any one of these stories as a potential answer. Perhaps now that I know it's important to you, I could direct my attention that way in the future."

"I would be interested to hear what you come up with," Emily replied. "You mentioned having factories. Where are they?"

"The landscapers come from a complex three hundred and forty-eight kilometers northwest of here. There are teams of them working up and down the eastern foothills of this mountain range. It is best not to discuss the location of my factory, though. The Oort Storm could be dangerous with that knowledge."

"I thought you were off duty." The game ball strayed toward the conversation again. Emily flinched away from its path but was saved from the necessity when Zephyr-3 intercepted and deflected it back into play.

Conrad-null paid no attention to the interruption. "I am off duty, yes. That doesn't mean I work for the enemy."

Emily was still settling back down when a voice surprised them from behind. "Ahoy, newcomer. Is this your boat?" The question came from underneath a shiny metallic canvas draped over something about the size of a dinner table that had just rolled up to the commandeered truck.

"I'm responsible for it being here, at least. Um." Emily began walking toward the stranger. "Ahoy?"

Conrad-null stood up and followed, while Zephyr-3 gravitated toward the ball game now that Emily was beyond reach of a stray ducking.

"Emily, this is Teller-1. He founded this place." Conrad's strides brought him to the cloaked anthromech's side first. "Emily is Revenance's newest anthromech."

"And she's already stealing trucks?" Teller lifted a corner of the canvas to see Emily better.

"It was kind of an emergency," Emily said. "And please, it's they/them."

"Oh! Damn, of course. What's your number?" Teller glanced at the mechs playing ball downslope and pushed the cloak further back to reveal a mechanized platform with several drones resting on top. One of them came to life and hovered to Emily for a closer look, still attached to the platform by a bundle of wires and a larger tube.

"No number. I didn't do the naming ceremony." Emily kept it short. They resented the question, but none of that was Teller's fault.

"Did I see right, Emily?" Teller-1's active drone peered at Emily's nanocarbon limbs through a rubber cone on a telescoping rod. "You're not playing the duck games with the other grubs?"

"Well, I'm not calling them names or anything, but no. I didn't like it last time. I'm not really in a hurry to try again." If the others used Novalee's slang, they probably thought Emily was acting cubey.

Teller's drone was already off Emily, though, and sizing up the truck and its crane. "Can you work this thing? The crane too?"

"Yes. I can't drive it at the same time, though," Emily said for modesty's sake. "One or the other."

"I would *love* to ask you some favors. Can I give you a tour of the gulch, like one of these slobs should have already done?"

Emily was happy for the opportunity, and Conrad-null asked, "Could I tag along?"

"No thanks, Conrad. We'll be discussing sensitive anthromech issues." Teller's drone came back to roost, but not before hovering by

Emily to pucker its cone in a knowing wink.

/* * */

Teller-1 bypassed the shanty town at the valley's mouth, where Emily had already glimpsed the flop side of gulch life. He took them back around a sunken patch of darker earth where water had recently dried, and thirsty juniper trees crowded the pond's ghost with vivid greens against the khaki edifices behind. Teller pointed the area out as the two passed by, describing how the rain would collect there as it came off the mountain, even when the showers were light, and how a family of coyotes had taken up residence in a grotto nearby.

Then Teller led Emily further into the narrowing chasm, where it fractured into more precarious crevasses that led up the mountain. One of these smaller ravines brought the two to a darkened cave mouth protected by a constructed metal awning. The cobbled-together roof extended from a larger sprawl of ceramic and metal sheets that covered the hillside above like shingles and flumes, all slanting away from the cave entrance.

With his reflective tarp removed, Teller spread three tethered drones out to inspect the opening and surrounding drainage channels. Another three remained at rest on Teller's back; Emily could see at least two that were missing critical parts. Teller had already explained that his body was designed for agriculture. The drones were meant to pluck stone fruit from trees, using suction and claws, and deposit it into pull-behind sorting wagons (sold separately).

"Was it hard to learn to fly those things?" Emily tried to sound less awed than they felt. Like the drone Emily had totaled, each of Teller's flying extremities had four propellers to coordinate. How was Teller-1 handling them all at once?

"Everything was hard at first, but that was a long time ago. The trick with the drones was mapping as little as possible so they can do the work themselves. That and you can't fly them in the simulator." Teller pulled one drone back from the inspections to see Emily's reaction. "You know about that, don't you." It wasn't a question. "There's no way you figured that body out in four weeks without it."

"Yes!" Emily was relieved to share the experience. "Why won't drones fly in there?"

"For all its bells and whistles, the simulator doesn't handle aero or fluid dynamics very well. Aircraft fly because of something called lift. You've probably heard of it. The mapping interface hasn't."

"Like we weren't even meant to work with some of these mech bodies?"

"That's clear enough." Teller-1 knocked a clump of dirt loose from the cave's lip and swore over the sound when it landed in the darkness below.

The missing dirt exposed a thick burr of steel underneath, and for the first time, Emily realized that this cave wasn't a natural formation.

"But if the prison door won't open," Teller asked, "is that a bug or elegant design?"

"What? You think it's on purpose? Are we being punished?" Emily had asked themself the same question already; it was easier to believe in a vengeful creator this time around.

"I *do* think we're being punished," Teller-1 answered. "I don't know how much of it is metaphorical, though."

"What do you mean?"

"Here, look in this hole. You got a light? Shine it down in there, and tell me what you see." Teller rolled to the side so Emily could approach the opening, which wasn't much wider than their spider legs could span. Both sides of the hole showed ripped steel recessed into the rock and packed earth.

Inside, Emily's light revealed a room walled in the same steel.

There was a wide pipe running the length of the compartment. It passed through a bulky cabinet with a text display that barely lit its surroundings; Emily didn't recognize the numbers or units it listed. There were a few other cupboards sectioned off in the room's corners as well, but no doorways in or out besides the fracture they looked through.

"There's a pipe in there," Emily reported, "and is that, maybe, a pump?"

"Yes. This is a pumphouse, and it used to be completely buried. Out of sight." Teller's voice grew dour. "It was a secret. Guess what's in that pipe that needed to be kept secret."

Emily pondered and then almost gasped at the thought. "Radioactive waste?"

"No!" Teller sounded incredulous at first, but then laughed. "I guess that would be worse, but still. It's oil. Shale oil. They were supposed to stop fracking it before I was out of primary school. These pumps aren't moving it anywhere anymore, but the pipes are still full and pressurized."

"There are more of these pumphouses, then?" Emily withdrew from the opening to think aloud, pausing at times in case Teller-1 wanted to contradict. "Up and down the pipeline, there'd have to be a bunch of them. And they probably had to talk to each other, right? Is this pump networked? Is that why you didn't want Conrad-null to come with us?"

"I don't think we have anything to worry about, but yes. They didn't *have* to be connected to serve their main purpose, but a network allowed for better efficiency and helped manage the repair mechs that were assigned to each station. It was all hardwired and isolated, though. I don't think it would be much use to the Oort Storm, but I'm not going to wave it in Conrad's face, off duty or not."

"What would he do?" Emily wondered. "If he were on duty, I mean."

"He'd disable the network—either himself or by getting one of his bigger brothers to help. If they stopped there, I wouldn't bat an eye; these pump stations are highly redundant and self-sufficient. But what then? If the Storm Chasers figure out there's a network of these buried throughout the Rockies, are they going to go digging?

"That's what I'd worry about. Look at this one, already torn open by landslides or maybe an earthquake. Now that it's exposed, the rains want to collect in here and stress the structure even more. If I can't keep things dry, the pipe is going to rupture; it's already buckling. Then crude will spread as far as the floods can take it. If the Storm Chasers go cracking these open to get at the network nodes, it's only a matter of time before a spill happens somewhere. I can only watch this one."

"That makes sense. No Storm Chasers allowed in the clubhouse, then." Emily immediately second-guessed the quip. Before it came out, it had sounded prepossessed, maybe even witty. "Anyway, I derailed that conversation. You were telling me why you think we're in hell." There it was again. *You're trying too hard.*

"I think the parts I've already described are enough to make a case for purgatory at least. Humanity destroyed itself in an apocalypse and left the Earth and animals behind with the environmental bill of sale. That's not fair; why should we be off the hook? It'd be like rewarding a tantrum." A pair of Teller's drones gestured like a grand conductor. "Enter the anthromechs, and suddenly there's a little karmic balance again."

"That's bleak, but does it really imply an intentional design behind it all?"

"It gets worse, though." The drones hovered close. "Look, I don't like talking about my skeletons any more than other people, and you're pretty fresh. Can I ask and trust you not to repeat this? I feel like I can."

"Yes, of course!" Emily realized, then, how much they wanted Teller-1's respect.

"I made this." A drone dipped toward the cave. "I had a team, of course. I think they were mostly AIs, but we were all remote, so it was hard to tell from accents. I was the technical lead, though, in charge of laying an illegal pipeline as quietly as possible. Invisible too. These stations are powered by solar collectors laid out uphill and disguised as natural rock formations. We even used some leaked military stealth technology to mask the construction.

"That's why I came out here every couple of years to check on the site, since this is the nearest pumphouse to Revenance, and that's why I was here to discover the cave-in the year it happened. They named this place after me because I kept coming here, but now you know it's more apropos than that."

Teller gave Emily time to process and inspected a bundle of hoses that hung out from the cave's mouth.

"How long did you visit before the station cracked open?"

"Sixty years and some."

"Oh." Emily barely clipped an exclamation. *Old!*

"I'm not saying I think RegenStar predicted when this pumphouse would get breached, but it *at least* stuck me where it was bound to happen eventually."

To Emily, it still seemed coincidental, an interesting anecdote.

As if in response to Emily's unvoiced doubts, Teller-1 added, "It's not just me. Other people got servings of poetic justice, too. I'm not going to get into details, but there are a lot of guilty CEOs back in Revenance. Some of them even helped build the place."

Remembering something Teller had mentioned about the pumphouse design, Emily looked into the hole again. There was no activity or sign of occupants. "You said there were repair mechs stationed in these. What happened to them?"

"Three bots were deployed in each closet." Teller's timbre thickened. "When I discovered the opening, there were only two, both demolished."

178

Chapter 12: Alignment

Emily cut into the cliff face with the landscaper's shovel, reaching out and scooping wherever Teller-1 pointed. They had spent the rest of the morning and midday maneuvering the rig up the hillside, stopping often to extend a trench that would divert future rainfall away from the pumphouse. Climbing back and forth, Emily switched between the navigation and crane control systems at each stop. In between digging and directing, the two continued their conversation over the noise of the rig, and by the time the afternoon sun disappeared behind the western peaks, the ditch was nearly complete.

Emily called down from the crane turret while they cleared the last stretch. "Hey Teller, you mentioned using the simulator, you know, in our heads. How did you get there?"

"I was regenned right into it; my default maps were trash. The algorithm couldn't match a bare minimum of bits to pieces on its own, so I woke up in the emergency mapping room instead. I was never much of a programmer myself, but I figured out how things work eventually. Like I told you, the drones wouldn't fly in there, but at least I could practice moving around and some other things before exiting back to the real world. It hadn't been long; I was still boxed up. I think I got lucky. I had a really hard time learning how to meditate, so I was stuck with that first mapping for quite a while. The stint in the emergency mode was my leg up."

Emily enjoyed listening to Teller-1 talk. Even yelling from the ground, the other anthromech exercised a confident permission to ramble.

"Later, I figured out how to get in there on purpose. There's a combination of buttons I can hold down to reboot into safe mode. Lots of commercial devices have something like that. Safe mode ignores most of your hardware, so— Sorry, you probably already know that part." Teller signaled approval of Emily's final touches. "I think we're done here. Come on down for a breather."

Teller didn't wait. "It's usually not a good thing. A lot of the mechs in the nursery have probably been in the emergency interface since their starday. It's either that or they're paralyzed and living in real time; it's hard to tell the difference from the outside. Anyway, there aren't a lot of people that map themselves out of it, even with the Teacher in there, and I can't imagine she's company enough to keep you sane if you're stuck too long."

Down on the ground, Emily remembered Farrah's voice in the interface and nodded along. The Teacher, as Teller was referring to the character, really hadn't answered much beyond some basic technical questions. It was interesting, though, that Teller's teacher was also a she.

Emily thought of something. "Hey, can I ask you something that's probably offensive, but give me the benefit of the doubt anyway?"

"Sure, I have thick skin." Then, for a moment, Teller-1 sounded just like Emily's father. "I'm sure there's a polymer joke somewhere in there."

"Boo." Emily spared a laughing emoji. "No, it's nothing about you, anyway. It's the numbers … and everybody at the gulch before Novalee and I got here."

"Go ahead." Teller sounded cheerful enough.

"Well, barely anybody here uses each other's number, and almost all of you are, what, *low*? I don't know, do we say 'men' or 'boys' anymore?"

"Sure, that's fair to ask. It's complicated, of course, but it always was, wasn't it? Our neurotemplates come from anywhere on a timeline that spans generations, and gender politics were in flux through all of it. Neopronouns were going in and out of style. Children knew their sexual identities in languages their parents didn't speak. Words like girl and boy cycled from cute to cruel and back, and most things meant something different depending on who was throwing it at you." Teller trailed off for a moment. "So yeah, complicated. And since I don't know how you approached all those topics in your lifetime, it's hard to even describe my own take without questioning your identity by accident or, like, just saying something blatantly offensive.

"Now you brought it up, so I have a feeling we're going to be alright here, but you see what I'm describing, right? This is the minefield we have to navigate whenever somebody is regenned into one of these sexless mechs and has to deal with the dysphoria that goes along with that."

Emily's flatscreen bobbed along to the meandering answer.

"The number system is an answer to that problem. It's probably just as bad as any of the weird customs we argued over back in the analog days, but it's ours, and it works to an extent—it would never fly if we wrote things down as much as we used to. As it is, it's like a compromise that we all transition into, something we have in common. It was already a thing when I regenned, so I'm honestly just telling you what was related to me over the years."

Compromise at work, Emily recalled thinking.

"So you asked about the men and boys. For the most part, nobody would care here if you used those words. People who strongly identify with binary genders usually pick numbers at the ends of the spectrum, and they're the least interested in using numbered pronouns."

"Svend-1?" Emily cut in, remembering their first introduction with a one.

"… is an exception. One *loves* using one's numbered pronouns. It makes one sound important, and one freely admits it."

"Okay, so why is almost everybody here a man?"

"Well, I told you why I'm here at the gulch, and I picked a one because I learned not to equivocate a long time ago. I wasn't assigned male at birth, so I knew my real sex and gender before anybody else did. In a way, I had to seize my maleness, and you don't do that partway." Teller-1 reached back with small utility arms to pull out the familiar reflective blanket and unfolded it for cover. "I don't, anyway. It's different for everybody.

"A lot of these younger guys at the gulch are here because they're a little on the wilder side. You know? They duck too much, and they don't get along with 'stuffy old' Omega-5. In a strange way, as old as five is, Omega represents something new that they don't understand. People like that fall on this side of the spectrum a lot more often. Some stereotypes are even amplified this time around, because everybody's self-selecting based on whatever baggage they came with."

Emily felt it when Teller rushed the conversation toward the other gulch denizens. They tried to take the elder's revelation in stride. In Emily's time, Teller was just called a man by law, though *trans man* was allowed if context justified. The pregs had their own words, of course. Gender-affirming care wasn't available until adulthood, so only a few of Emily's college contemporaries had begun the transition, but it was common enough, and Emily's circles were supportive. Still, they hadn't expected it here with somebody so like their father, and somehow that brought on a pang of guilt.

"What's that tarp for?"

"The grubs down there call it my tinfoil hat. You like it?" Teller lifted two corners and primped them like a collar.

"Very poppin!" Emily used old slang from their parents, but realized that Teller, despite his advanced age in this lifetime, might have been from a later era.

"It blocks those damned duck fields. Keeps me from getting second-hand high every time I walk through the camp or want to talk to someone. I got extra, you want one?"

Emily eagerly accepted, and Teller produced a smaller square. Emily admired their new fashion in the reflective surface of Teller's own cloak, and noticed water droplets collecting on them both. The sky overhead had barely darkened, but clouds poured over the mountaintops on an errant wind.

"Hey, we got rain!" Teller was excited by the surprise and got back to business. "We don't get much warning on this side of the mountain. The clouds practically form on top of us.

"Emily, I'm going to follow the new ditch back into the gulch so I can watch how the runoff behaves. I'll meet you down there later, okay? You should get this truck off the slope before it washes down on its own."

"Alright." Emily stowed the new cloak. "Is it gonna rain bad?"

"I can never tell. Hope not!"

/* * */

Long out of sight, the afternoon sun still warmed the air into a steamy haze at the oasis in the back of the gulch. The rain had subsided a half hour before, and the clouds disappeared with it. The brief deluge was memorialized by a meager pool of mud that would drain before nightfall.

Zephyr-3 sat at one side of the waning pond, watching a pair of coyotes crouched across the way to drink. One at a time, they bowed and lapped while the other kept guard, scanning the surroundings for danger and keeping a measured eye on Zephyr despite three's stillness.

Finished parking the truck back at the tent encampment, Emily interrupted Zephyr's voyeurism with a greeting from behind. "Hiya Zeph. You swimming?"

Zephyr made a shushing noise, and Emily noticed the startled coyotes for the first time when one fled deeper into the ravine and disappeared into a spasm of foliage. Emily froze in place and kept quiet, taking Zephyr's lead. The second coyote stood at full alert but held its ground for the time being.

Finally, Zephyr-3 whispered, "Hi, Emily. This is great. We never see anything this big in Revenance; there's nothing for them there. God, I miss dogs." Even at the suppressed volume, Zephyr's excitement was thick enough to spread.

"We never had one." Emily was just as quiet. "I thought a dog would be neat, but I always asked for toys instead. Electronics mostly. I guess I had this whole anthromech thing coming to me."

"Nah, real pets were expensive. RegenStar wasn't invented to punish you for being fiscally responsible."

Emily held in a laugh to keep from spooking the coyote and was rewarded when it relaxed to drink. "I didn't really think so. I'm sure I've done worse things anyway."

"I'm confused. I thought you said we were in a simulation. Now it's a punishment?" Zephyr began an exaggerated step forward, slow enough not to spook the wildlife. "Sounds like you've been getting an earful from Teller-1."

"First of all"—Emily leaned forward and matched Zephyr's glacial pace—"I said I think *I* might be in a simulation."

"Oh, thanks."

"Second, you're absolutely right. Teller convinced me that we're in hell. I believe in angels and a free market now, too."

Zephyr's forward leg broke the pool's surface with an unexpected plip, alerting the coyote to the anthromechs again. This time, the canine loped into hiding where its partner had disappeared. The mission was blown.

"Damn." Zephyr retreated to dry land. "I wonder if we could feed them. Are dogs allowed in your dystopian religion?"

"Yes. Probably." Emily pretended to pray. "On Tuesdays."

"That's a start, we can still break bread then." Zephyr let the running joke end there and turned serious. "I've thought that way, too, you know. Like Teller, I mean."

"Like we're paying for our past sins?"

"Well, I don't know if it's about sins, but what if it's just another chance? You know, like it was advertised? If you come here with a bunch of unresolved guilt, then sure, here's your chance to try and make it right. Other people might just be here to enjoy another ride."

Emily asked, "Are you enjoying this ride?"

"Sometimes." Zephyr-3 grew distant. "But I might have signed up for the first thing."

"Oh." Emily skipped a beat and then said, "Do you want to talk about it?"

"I don't know. I guess I haven't talked about it to anybody. Took too long."

"Well, I'm here, Zeph."

The fan mech relaxed and crossed three's legs into a loose braid. After a string of false starts, some vocalized and others FM band, Zephyr admitted, "This is hard. I'm sorry."

Emily waited.

"There's a memory, a bad one from when I was a kid, and it messed with me for a long time, you know, in my meat life—probably more than it should have. But then on my starday, during the engramming at the beginning, I sat through that memory *so* many fucking times." Zephyr's voice rang with a tension that couldn't break for tears.

"I'm sorry, Zeph. It sounds like it was horrible."

"It *was* the first time, and then I had to live through it again and again and again. I couldn't look away during engramming because I didn't look away back when I was little."

Emily hadn't relived any one memory more than they'd wanted, even if the engramming algorithm was driving their intentions at the time. Zephyr's experience seemed awful in comparison.

"The coyotes reminded me of it anyway. I told you I miss dogs, but I never owned one either. Never owned any pets at all, actually, and it's because of that one memory. I loved other people's animals, and would visit my grandma just to play with her cats, but I couldn't have one myself, because I knew I wouldn't protect them."

"Oh no, because of something from when you were little? How old were you?" Emily clacked a carbon spider leg against the back of Zephyr's cage and hoped it was comforting.

"Five. Maybe six. There was a box of baby mice in a barn behind my grandma's house. She's not the one with the cats. Maybe they *would* have had cats like other farms, but there was a kid who lived down the road who played animal control. Gavin. I hated him, but he was older." Zephyr read Emily's face for a moment and then looked away. "I don't want to be too graphic. I showed those mice to Gavin. I don't know what I was thinking. And then he killed them right in front of me, one at a time.

"I didn't know what he was going to do to the first one, but after that, I just stood there anyway. I didn't want him to do it, but I knew he'd punch me if I tried to stop him. I didn't even try. I didn't argue or try to distract him or anything. I just sat there, terrified of being hit a few times or maybe just emotionally tortured that way older kids can do, and I watched him finish off the mice I'd offered up."

"Zeph, you can't hold yourself—"

"I know, I know. I'm not eternally damned for something I did as a kid, even though I think Gavin maybe is, but it affected me back then. I had nightmares about it and felt like I was this monster for being there and being part of it. It was bad, you know? Like the kind of thing that if anybody found out about, they'd know how disgusting and unlovable you are for the rest of your life.

"Eventually, you figure out how to give your childhood self some grace, but that's way after you do the damage. Back then, I was *plagued* by the memory, and I remember how afraid I was of growing up to do all the things bad people do, which I'd seen hints of on TV, and *everybody* hated the bad guys on TV. I was just a kid, and I honestly thought my life was permanently tainted. I remember thinking I didn't want to see the rest of it out, you know? But I knew how much that would hurt my parents and sister, so I'd never do that."

A bird pecked at the water nearby, less cautious than the coyotes had been. It was small and colored in the drab palette of the desert. Emily wasn't sure how long it had been there, camouflaged as it was. The silence hung until Zephyr continued.

"So instead, I got obsessed with making up for it somehow. I fantasized about all these big ways I could redeem myself. Mostly it was comic book stuff like saving people from serial killers that looked like grown-up Gavins, but sometimes it was just pushing someone out of the way of a bus and taking the hit myself. Two birds, one stone, and none of the guilt for hurting my family, because I'd be a hero. I sort of made this plan that I'd ride out my shame until I could pay it all back at once someday when I was bigger.

"But I still did all the things dumb kids do, you know, you break toys and hurt feelings and choose the wrong sides. I was barely thinking about those mice anymore by the time I was maybe ten or so, but that's only because I replaced them with everything I'd done wrong since. Every mistake was another dollar in the shame jar, and another trigger to isolate and ideate. And I was doing this all in secret, still terrified of people finding out what I was.

"The fantasizing created other problems down the line. Unrealistic standards I was setting for myself. A lot of overcompensating. More guilt just from knowing how weak and self-indulgent the whole thing was. Then, before you know it, I'd created enough real problems out of my childhood issues that the kid stuff didn't matter anymore. The thing with Gavin and the mice got good and repressed; I hadn't had the nightmares since high school."

"Until you engrammed," Emily finally spoke, "and the algorithm followed all those things back to where they started."

"Yeah, and every time, it was as real as when I lived it."

"Your body here didn't have a voice," Emily remembered out loud.

"Exactly. Just like with Gavin all that time ago. Even when I figured out my workaround, it was still slow and ineffective."

"It was ingenious, though, and I kind of pooped on that when I gave you the new speaker, didn't I?" Emily's emoji frowned and its eyes swelled large and shiny.

"That's not what you were trying to do, though, and I could never have had this conversation before the upgrade. Do you have any idea how long this would have taken?"

"But the whole thing … Why? It just sounds like torture. You can't deserve any of this for something that happened to you when you were too young to know better."

"Because maybe it's not RegenStar making that decision. Maybe I'm doing it because torturing myself is what comes natural. The engramming algorithm might have been at my old brain's neurotic mercy, and my voice problems might have been a chance to relearn how to stand up for myself. I could be here to finally make that heroic sacrifice I always fantasized about. I don't know where it starts and stops, but I don't think RegenStar is responsible for every detail."

"Well then, *that's* what I'm asking, Zeph. Why are you torturing yourself?"

Zephyr-3 turned to face Emily head-on. "I'm not saying I'm being reasonable, but didn't I just tell you exactly why?"

"I suppose, but I would like to lodge an official complaint. You've been awfully hard on a friend of mine." Emily punched Zephyr in the side.

"The complaint forms are in a different repressed memory. Sorry."

They both laughed. Zephyr's legs unwove, and three stood. Emily unfolded the metallic cloak Teller had gifted and situated it around their body and CPU, leaving their face display and a handful of sensors still exposed.

"What do you think? Wanna go tie on a duck? It might get your mind off all that." Emily's caped form was vaguely that of a silver turtle.

"'Tie on a duck?' I'm not cosigning your new slang, but yes. I think I'd like that. What's this, now?" Zephyr tugged at the cloak.

"Teller says it blocks duck fields. I'm gonna see if I can keep control of myself if my spider parts are shielded. I need you to drag me out of the field if I'm unresponsive or just bringing things down, I guess. I'll at least know how to get myself reset quicker this time if things go south."

"You've got it, Em. Thanks for letting me get all that out, but don't let me repeat any of it while we're ducking. If you spot me, I'll spot you."

/ * */*

On the way back to the tents and revelers, Teller-1 caught Emily's attention to give an update on the day's dig. He was excited to report that the runoff had exercised the entire length of the new ditch, and the pumphouse was dry as a bone.

"I can't thank you enough for your help and that crane, Emily."

"You're welcome, and um, thanks for sharing with me earlier. All of it. I hope I didn't seem closed off when you were opening up."

"Don't worry, you took in a lot today. Was there anything you wanted to tell *me*, though?"

Emily considered what they might have forgotten, any social missteps, or open threads. "No, I don't think so."

Teller-1 chuckled. "Well, I have something else for you now that the inspections have passed. It's the gift of popularity. When you get back to the camp, tell Dino he's allowed to top off from the main line after sundown tonight. The pumphouse won't need the full charge now. You can take credit for that, too."

Chapter 13: Followers

"The world ended in a flood."

A disc of primordial stone rotated in a void. Modeling clay continents rose above its painted oceans to touch clouds that billowed across the surface in dusty chalk. If one looked closely, humanity collected like gunk wherever rivers bent or joined the sea, infecting adjacent lands as technology allowed. Above the writhing colonies of progress, pastel thunderheads grew thick and angry, warning of a deluge.

"We drowned in the element that defined us, just like in the old creation stories."

Rain punished the land hardest where people were most comfortable. Pigmented blue rivers thickened into great lakes, and seas gentrified the coasts. Oceans swelled until their salty surface tension could no longer hold a meniscus and poured over the Earth's edge into the emptiness of space below.

"But it wasn't water. It was data. Information. We drowned in our own collective identity."

The water darkened to smoky black and filled with electric zeroes and ones. Rain became pixelated streaks of numerical operations that pounded the data ocean into a vengeful boil. Torrents of bits washed people from their homes and sacrificed them to the digital maelstrom.

"Our prophet revealed the end to us as it was revealed to him. He said it was inevitable."

A single person, nude and featureless, emerged from the flooded morass.

"Humans would strive for immortality and would eventually wipe themselves out to obtain it. He said our bodies weren't made for eternal life. We could only pass DNA and beliefs to the next generation and then hope it mattered."

The mock human broke into spirals of amino acids that unwound and rewove into smaller versions of the original.

"That wasn't enough. It wasn't our *selves*, not yet. But as we learned to record, the solution grew nearer—first with crude pictures, then written words, then music and movies and so on. Humanity learned how to preserve its most treasured people from generation to generation by recording them for posterity."

Copies of copies of the original person mimed each step of human progress as it was narrated.

"Data outlasted our bodies, and technology advanced faster than biology. The secret to true immortality was in the digitization. Our prophet predicted that once people could preserve their complete selves as information, data would become more precious than life. They would program their databases to defend against future threats so their backups could last forever, and eventually, there would be far more digital ghosts than living humans. The database infrastructure would starve life of its resources even as the last humans fed the problem by recording their own demise."

The paper doll illustrations multiplied and piled into clipart disk drives that grew into server rooms and data centers. Buildings full of memories swelled to shadow the cities that fueled them. The coin-shaped planet reemerged with every inch of land scabbed over by civilization and tumorous computer architecture.

"At some point, the databases would have to choose between the humans they preserved and the humans who lived."

Skyscraping storage arrays surrounded metropolitan outposts, peering down from unmanned windows where posthumous stakeholders decided humanity's fate via proxied quorums.

"The decision would eventually be clear, if not the first time, then later when humanity cycled back to its old mistakes again. Humans could not be allowed to continue if we were meant to honor life eternal."

The data grew top-heavy and buckled atop the holdout cities, burying an obsolete species in the greatest hopes of its ancestors. With equilibrium achieved, the Earth was left to flip between day and night. Heads, tails, heads, tails …

"When we were still alive, nobody had invented a way to restore our neurotemplates to consciousness, and some of our church members thought we were safe until that technology came about. Our prophet said that was wrong, though. He said our data would evolve to survive just as surely as the fish that walked onto land. Somehow, life would persist; it wouldn't wait for us, and it wouldn't stop for us. Anthromechs are the culmination of that evolutionary certainty. The decision was made as soon as we started digitizing ourselves."

The darkness of space dissolved to translucence, revealing an assembly of enrapt mechs.

Conrad-null was the first to offer feedback. "That was wonderfully told, Galen!" He clapped his three-fingered hands together and piped the sound of wild applause over his voice. The anthromechs joined in, cheering and clapping whatever was available.

"Thank you! Thank you." At the front of the audience, a robotic baby doll flopped forward in its mechanized walker and mocked a bow. Its head bounced off the cracked activity tray before lolling to the side with a blank stare. "The prophet said I was a natural recruiter. He practically demanded that I join the private triangle when he found out how many people I signed during probation."

"Of course, it's a very unlikely scenario." Conrad's spiritual irreverence was good-natured in its violence. "Data storage was a shrinking sliver of technological debt in your century. As well, the migration of data to the satellite networks should have provided ample room for civilization to progress on the planet's surface. If your prophecy had come to pass, we would still see these database cities that overtook the world, yes?"

"Well, see, Reuel—He was the prophet—Reuel said the AIs wouldn't wait that long. They'd pull the trigger as soon as we told them to protect our neurotemplates. He said the AIs would see the inevitability before we did. Said we should embrace it and evolve. 'Get on the ark, *and* be part of the flood. Cover your bets.'"

Arms reached from behind the baby walker's seat to straighten the doll within.

"He made sure we got our brains scanned into all the services that would allow it. They each restricted you to a single neurotemplate per account, but there were citizenship tricks and networking hacks that let us sign up with a bunch of services at the same time. Reuel said it would increase our odds of reincarnation. Senior members got to save themselves extra by borrowing accounts from initiates. Reuel had connections inside the scanning companies that let him manipulate things like that."

Quentin-1 couldn't contain himself anymore. "Galen, you *knew* the prophet of your church?"

"Online, yeah. It's not like we worshiped in person like a bunch of puritans."

"Sure, alright, and you were rewarded for gettin' new people to sign up for neuroscans and join your inner triangle?"

"We were evangelical with our beliefs, brother. What's your point?" The walker strolled a pace toward Quentin in challenge.

"Galenastor-1"—Quentin used his friend's full name to lay him bare—"that was a multilevel marketing cult! It sounds to me like your buddy Reuel set the whole thing up as a front for the scanning services."

"Nah!" Galen waved the idea off with a mechanical arm and knocked the doll forward again. "Our church was around before the brain scans were invented. Before those, we were connecting up to the AI farms to let them record us for training. That seemed like the most detailed data footprint we could create before neurotemplates were an option. I pledged the church like that for years."

Then it was Novalee's turn to cast doubt. "You should have gotten paid for that. I think you were being exploited."

"It was service, not exploitation! And look at me. Look at *us*! My prophet was right, and I'm here in the great infinite future because I listened to him. Our data survived, and the old *we* didn't, just like he said would happen." Galen grew excited and recalled, "We even had a renaming ceremony in the church! Reuel chose our evolved names when we initiated; I just had to pick a number here. I was already halfway to anthromech!"

That earned a round of jeers, and Galen deflated. "Fine. Fuck! You guys are assholes. I don't need to proselytize. *My* end-time prophecy already happened. This is why nobody likes talking about the old life!" The baby in Galen's seat rocked in anger.

Conrad-null encouraged Galen to ignore the dissenters. The Storm Chaser had been asking the gulch's anthromechs about their apocalypse theories all day since his chat with Emily.

Emily arrived just in time to enjoy Galen's duck-enhanced revelation from the back of the small crowd. With Teller's cloak hiding a modest portion of their body, Emily's experience was much subtler this second time. There was no transformation to a remembered form, and more importantly, administrative functions remained intact.

"The rest of us are avoiding old topics 'cause they're downers, Galen. *You've* been sitting on comedy gold."

That was the bot they called Little Suck. Emily heard Zephyr mention the vacuum's real name earlier, but chose to stay in the welcoming present instead of checking notes. It was okay to relax. The group laughed at Little Suck's jape, and Emily joined in, happy to gas up the fellow who'd been disrespected earlier.

"Emily!" Novalee-7 yelled over the merriment, celebrating with explosions of confetti and a trio of air horns. Everybody turned to look except Reznor-2, who jumped up and revved his motors to match Novalee's energy without worrying about its cause.

Zephyr-3 rolled to Emily's side and asked in a hush, "How are you feeling?"

"Fine. No. *Good.* The tarp is working, and I can still see the duck field projections."

"I knew it!" Quentin-1 overheard with great pleasure. "Teller'll say he don't duck, but he's always rollin' through here with his tinfoil hat half cocked. I *knew* he was takin' a little dip, coy bastard! So Emily, you're the reason Conrad's been gettin' all retrospective today, huh?"

"Yeah, that's probably my fault. I asked what he knew about the end times—"

"Not much," Conrad-null filled in.

"—and then what he could figure out." Emily finished with a shrug. "Sorry, I was trying to get a puremech's perspective on things."

"I can't do better than to go to the source!" Conrad declared with shameless positivity.

Quentin asked, "Well, did you two get your questions answered now, or should we run 'em by Galen's cult pope for a second opinion?"

"Insufficient data." Conrad frowned.

"Hey, before I forget," Emily said, "Teller-1 says Dino can use the main power line tonight. We got a trench built today, so his pumps won't have to work so hard."

/* * */

The revelry celebrating Emily's news carried into the evening. When Dino's power dipped soon after dusk, he left to recharge from Teller's source while the rest of the anthromechs bridged the gap with weak field generators they called nightlights. These, too, were just standard power cells corrupted into a higher purpose with hammers and wire. Only Dino had mastered the creation of the repeaters they'd played with earlier, but anybody could make a nightlight with some trial and error. Their charges drained quickly.

The nightlights were what initially loosened Emily's memory of Lunasha-8's malfunctioning power cell. The recollection gnawed at their attention that evening through further extinction theories, conspiracies, and scatalogical eschatology. Duck fields lent vibrancy to each rambling discussion.

Little Suck blamed aliens for the disappearance of man, so the shared hallucinations revealed lights in the sky, floating cows, and the body-vaporizing ray guns he described. When somebody asked about the aliens' motives, Little Suck answered, "Communism!" The mythos devolved from there.

Reznor-2 was certain that real humans had been raptured to another plane by a loving god less judgmental than believers had feared. Anthromechs were just an accidental leftover, echoes of a grand plan that had already run its course. Purpose no longer existed, and any faith in RegenStar's designs was misplaced. His thesis was paraphrased in vulgarities and misquoted doctrines, but a puppet show helped get the finer points across.

The visions offered nothing when Conrad-null asked, "Have any of you considered the possibility that your neurotemplates were built instead of scanned?"

"What do you mean?" Quentin asked.

"Maybe the memories you engrammed were made up. Perhaps you've always been anthromechs, and biological humanity is an origin myth."

The anthromechs looked to each other for words.

"But, why?" Emily asked.

"I do not know, but it doesn't sound like the humanity you remember had an authoritative answer for that question either." Then Conrad asked, "Is it necessary to know?"

"My question was too broad," Emily admitted, remembering they were dealing with a puremech. "If there were no real people to create the neurotemplates and the anthromechs, then who did make us?"

"Puremechs?" Conrad guessed. "Maybe there's a factory out there behind it all."

"But then, who created the puremechs?" Emily wasn't curious so much as frustrated by the outlandishness they were entertaining.

"Evolution or an unknown hand. The answer would require much more investigation, but I wonder where that would stop if we kept asking who created each creator."

Emily switched to an emoji with a scrunched face. "Really, Conrad?"

"I am not convinced by my theory, if that's what you are asking, but it does exhibit an elegance I fail to observe in the other explanations we've discussed so far."

"By 'elegance' do you mean it lets puremechs play the part of God?" Quentin projected a holy aura around Conrad and filled the air with an angelic chorus.

"I have no desire to elevate puremechs to any such esteem. I simply believe the possibility would remove many questions from the table at once." Conrad-null lifted his hands in surrender.

Novalee-7 passed judgment in the form of sustained flatulence that rivaled even Reznor-2 in audial abrasiveness and paired it with a sickly yellow cloud to sell the effect. The gathered robots rewarded the childish interruption with laughter.

"Sorry, everybody. Conrad's theory wasn't sitting right."

"Thanks for keeping the smell to yourself, Novalee!" Reznor-2 pretended to have a nose and covered it with a chainsaw. "Yank was never that nice. He made 'em stink so goddamn bad. One time, it got so rank that I gagged—first time since my starday—and a drawer popped out of my shoulder."

"Oof, don't compare me to him." Novalee abated the illusory stink cloud. "My fart jokes are tasteful and well-timed. YankyFan's farts were terrorism."

Quentin-1 added, "He was five-star at duck shows. Put Kamaria's story times to shame, you know, if you were brave."

"He was a dick," Novalee said.

"He *is* a dick," Reznor corrected. "Yank's still out there somewhere. I wish he knew we were in Tellers Gulch now. I miss him."

Novalee grumped.

"I wonder what YankyFan-Number-One-Or-Number-Two would have said about the time before anthromechs." Conrad used Yanky's full chosen name with no awkward rush or irony; only the anthromechs remembered the bathroom codes for urination and defecation.

"Before or after his incident?" Quentin asked without waiting for an answer. "If you asked him before, he woulda just fucked with you. I know he thought there were government conspiracies behind it all, but if you asked him for details, he'd accuse you of bein' in on it and clam up. He'd never give a straight answer with this many people around." Then Quentin exaggerated a turn to Novalee-7 and leaned in to say, "Not even with all his best friends."

"And after?" Conrad prompted.

"Well, I still don't think he'd give a lecture on it, but he had some ideas after he came back from his outage. He talked like somethin' out in the desert showed him what was hidin' behind reality, but he wouldn't go into it any deeper. He'd say shit like 'it's not your time yet' and then get all morose, more than normal I mean, and after the outage, normal was already a lot. Anyways, it wasn't good, whatever he was thinkin'." Quentin-1 finished, "I didn't push."

"Very supportive." Novalee's sarcasm wasn't subtle.

"Oh don't blame me for not poking the tiger. You know he was selective about who he talked to and when he did it."

"He beeped!" Galen remembered, startling Emily, who'd forgotten the walker's presence on their left where tarp covered their cameras. "You guys remember he spoke in beeps whenever I showed up? He'd always get tired of himself and start talking normal after a while, but then he'd reset back to asshole again the next day like we'd never met."

"Ugh, Yanky Code." Quentin-1 paired his laugh with cringing emojis.

"Yeah, you remember." Galen flashed his grudge for a moment. "You'd use it too sometimes."

"'Cause he'd gak with us if we didn't!" Before continuing, Quentin looked to Reznor-2, who bobbed his front to nod agreement. "It wasn't a treat. Yanky Code was a slog, and I'm not gonna lie, I wasn't even followin' most of the time. Too much countin', and it took too long."

"What was the code?" Emily asked.

"Such a pain in the ass! He was just spellin' everything out in numbers," Quentin explained. "An A was one beep, and a Z was twenty-six of 'em. You had to listen for the long pauses between words and remember the letters as he went. We'd lose count and always be off a letter here and there. It was confusing, but he'd get so fuckin' insistent."

"What if you just wanted to say a number?"

"Spell it out!" Quentin-1 barked the policy in a parody of YankyFan's voice.

Emily scoffed. "That's barely a code."

"I know!" Reznor-2 cut in. "I tried telling him about Morse Code, and how we could save a lot of time if we switched to a combination of long and short beeps for each letter."

Little Suck murmured, "There's Reznor, always doing his part to cut down on noise pollution."

Emily talked over the chuckles. "Like binary encoding, the way computers do it. So why didn't that work?"

"Well, nobody knows Morse Code either. I just remember the idea and like, 'S.O.S.' We couldn't work out a new set of codes while we were talking in Yanky Code, so it never went anywhere." Then Reznor's body shook as if to rid itself of a clinging memory. "He loved talking about himself, too. Remember, Quentin?"

"I do." Now it was Quentin's turn to wince. "Twenty-five beeps for the Y. Twice each time he said his name, and don't rush him, by god!" Then Quentin leaned in to speak directly to Galen's ride-along doll. "We were doin' you a favor, keepin' you outa all that."

Emily didn't see whether Galen was swayed or not, having retreated to their overclocked state to work something out. The number twenty-five rang a bell.

At least once during their first ducking experience, the invisible bell tower had rung twenty-five times in a row. Emily remembered that, but couldn't recall the rest of the numbers and had missed most of them anyway. When they looked through recordings from that evening, there was nothing useful. Some files were corrupted, the surviving videos lacked any hint of the hallucinations, and the audio files only captured the conversation with Novalee.

But the nightlights had called Lunasha-8's heart surgery to mind, and those recordings were intact. Emily slowed the replay to isolate the broken battery's stutter, and sure enough, patterns arose. The bells may have been a symptom of the same induction field anomaly that had perturbed the battery, or they could have been a memory nagging from Emily's subconscious. Either way, the numbers were the same: Twenty-five, one, fourteen, eleven, twenty-five. Then six, one, and fourteen. Yanky Fan.

"Hey! Who's projecting the bell?"

Emily felt the very beginning of a nudge and rejoined the conversation in time to hear a familiar ring and the end of Zephyr-3's whispered query.

"… aren't moving, are you okay? You said to—"

"I'm okay. I'm here." Emily saw everybody looking around and spoke louder. "That bell was me, I think. I guess I was concentrating on something too hard. But hey, I'm pretty sure I found a message from your friend YankyFan back in Revenance. Quentin, remember when you talked about Yanky Code and how often twenty-five came up?"

"Uhh, yeah, Emily. It was like a minute ago. Is that tinfoil hat on too tight?"

Emily had begun to think of it as a cloak, not a hat, but doubted that suggestion would earn any points at the moment. "Okay, right. Well, I think I heard a message when Novi and I went ducking a few days ago. I started hearing these bells, like from a clock tower, but they rang too many times for that. Turns out, it was Yanky Code! It was spelling his name!"

"That *is* weird, but you can hear anything when you're ducking," Novalee said. "And I was in there with you, so—"

"But it wasn't the first time I heard it," Emily cut in. "I was at Cables earlier that day, and we were removing a bad battery pack that kept shaking for some reason, and those vibrations were in Yanky Code too! I had to slow them down and count, but there was a message that started with Yanky's name. I think there's some vibration disturbing Revenance's induction field, and since Lunasha's charger was loose from its mount, it couldn't dampen the feedback anymore."

"What do you mean you 'slowed them down'?" Quentin-1 asked.

"I can record things and play them back later," Emily answered. "I slowed them down to see the message in the vibrations. It was so fast, we thought the battery was just buzzing randomly."

"Are you recording now?" Quentin's face was a train of emojis with eyebrows raised in suspicion.

"No," Emily lied. "I don't think it works when I'm ducking anyway."

The circled anthromechs were quiet for a rare moment. With nobody trying to project, the sky pressed low over the gulch's meager illumination.

More excited than the rest, Reznor finally entertained the possibility. "You said the message starts with Yanky's name. What's the rest of it?"

"I still have to decipher it all." Emily didn't want to answer for overclocking or subject the rest of the party to further unplanned hallucinations. "It'll just take me a little while, I'll be right back."

/* * */

YANKYFAN STILL ALIVE FIND ME
YANKYFAN CANT RE
YANKYFAN STILL ALIVE
YANKYF
YANKYFAN IMMORTAL ALIVE
YANKYFAN FREE ME DONT TRUST OMEGAA
YANKYFAN NUMBERS NOT REAL
YANKYFAN STIL
YANKYFAN STILL ALI

"That's what I could get," Emily reported after a padded break from the field. "I cleaned up some of the letters when it was obvious they were just off by a number or two. Um, he sounds …"

Several Anthromechs volunteered their conclusions at once: "Disturbed," "Wrecked," "Gakked out of his CPU," and "So alone." Emily was only certain that Conrad-null had said the last.

In Emily's absence, the mechs had put their thoughts together to transform the duck environment into a high-tech command center, coldly lit at cinematic angles and thick with holographic displays floating unmonitored in every direction. They awaited Emily's update around a harsh white table adorned with smart tablets and reprintable paper, all of it cosmetic and untouched.

Reznor-2 asked, "What does it mean? Omega-5 said Yank left town. If that was a lie, maybe all that shit about him being dangerous was too."

"He's gotta be trapped somewhere in Revenance, right, Emily?" Quentin-1 was in a proxy bot's natural element at the head of a table in a sterile meeting.

"That's what I'm thinking, yeah. He's piggybacking on the induction field with his own magnetic frequency. Dino, it's like that thing you do with the repeater cells. How far can you project your duck fields to a repeater?"

"About twenty meters with nothing between us, but it reaches further with some metal to help it along." Dino's solar umbrella retracted so the mech could sidle close to the table. A grid of green-outlined boxes grew from the tabletop to represent Revenance. "On the induction plate, it would go way farther, even into buildings, maybe the whole city; I didn't know how to do this back then."

"Good!" Emily had waited outside the duck field longer than Yank's text message required, time enough to conceive an idea. "Yanky could be trapped anywhere. We'd never find him by checking each warehouse box by box, but you guys said he was good at projecting. I think maybe he could show himself to us if we got a duck field near enough to him."

"The repeaters *would* reach through walls better than nightlights," Dino reasoned through Emily's suggestion, "and if I projected one of my duck fields through the plate, your repeaters would all be linked through me. I could help you communicate with each other!"

"You get it, yeah! We could split up and search the city way faster!" Emily's voice cracked from excitement. Dino's field felt good.

"Does this mean we're goin' back to Revenance? I mean, we gotta help Yanky, right?" Quentin-1's second question was rhetorical, mostly.

"Hell yeah, we are!" Reznor-2 fueled the emotional charge of volunteerism with power tool cheers. Some matched his energy, and others capitulated to it. Everybody agreed eventually, though Novalee-7 had disappeared from the table.

Emily offered the crane truck as conveyance. Most of the anthromechs were small. With some consideration for Dino's girth, they should all fit on top together.

The promise of a puremech ride whipped up the rescue party even further.

"Of course—" The rowdy chatter continued over Quentin-1's first attempt, so he said it louder. "OF COURSE …" The anthromechs quieted. "It's too late to go tonight. We'll hit it first thing tomorrow. Poor Teller won't know what to do with all his privacy back."

With Dino's extra ration of electric charge, the festivities lasted several more hours before everybody finally retired, alone or in small units, to enjoy their fleeting nightlights and rest.

Chapter 14: Fulfillment

"Why aren't you saying anything, Novi?"

Already well into the next day, the rescue effort was no closer to initiation. When Emily was ready to set out that morning, the gulch's anthromechs were distracted by their charging schedules and getting Dino reattached to the daytime solar array. Then, assuming the others intended to leave after the sun's peak hours, Emily was chagrined to see them settle into their ducking games instead.

When Emily found Novalee-7 alone under a propped-up shipping crate, they wasted no time in venting about the lazy gulch grubs—as Teller-1 had called them, Emily was sure to clarify.

Novalee listened, power light on, but offered nothing in the pauses between Emily's gripes.

"Is it because I called your friends grubs? Say something. I'm sorry."

"No. Geez. I'm just …" Novalee drove a circle in and out of the sunlight. "I told you about YankyFan. You know how mean he was to me."

Emily answered slowly, "Yeah?" It hadn't crossed their mind. It should have. *Empathy.*

"Well, that's fucking it, I guess. Anything else I want to say will make me sound like a monster. I know we can't just ignore that Yank is *in need* or whatever. I know we have to try and help. I get it!" Novalee argued alone. "So I feel like shit about it, but I'm angry you were so helpful last night—so quick to go save *him*."

"I'm sorry. I wasn't thinking." Emily wanted to blame it on ducking but knew that could only excuse a portion of the carelessness.

"No, you can't just apologize and be nice! Now I look worse. I'm over here wishing a guy could stay trapped in *wherever* a little longer."

"I get it, though," Emily said. "Nobody could blame you for not liking him, and it's not like you tried to shut down the conversation last night or argue against rescuing him. I was callous about something sensitive to you, and that made you feel bad. You don't need to be ashamed, and I *am* sorry."

Novalee laughed. "Stop! You're making it worse!"

"Well, I don't know what else to say." Emily giggled along for a moment and then resigned. "I don't think we're even going back to find him today. I was excited to finally have answers … to anything. Something was going to make sense for once." Emily had already considered returning to Revenance alone if need be, but now it wouldn't feel right at all.

"I don't know if you're going to like any answers Yank is involved with, but I understand. I said we have to help him; I meant that. I think I just need you to enjoy it less, okay?"

"Okay." Then, with all sentiment tamped down and dried, Emily said, "I sure hope everybody is just as lazy tomorrow. I'd hate to solve this mystery."

"Ass." Novalee scoffed. "I'll try to help you light a fire under them tonight, but it'll be tough with Dino's extra rations fueling the party."

/ * */*

Novalee's chance to advocate for expediency suffered indefinite postponement when a front of towering cumulonimbus clouds swallowed the sun and belched lightning in its place. Curtains of rain soon followed that shamed the previous day's sprinkle. Anthromechs retreated to their hovels to stay as dry as the sweaty air would allow.

Teller-1 found Emily early in the deluge with an update on the trench's success through the initial downpour. "The camp is on higher ground," he'd explained. "Even before our work yesterday, this part of the gulch wouldn't wash out. Just stay under cover and ride it out. These big ones happen a few times a year." He left soon after, his tinfoil hat as good as a raincoat, and headed to the pumphouse to shelter there.

Peeking outside the box they shared with Zephyr-3 and Novalee, Emily saw anthromechs braving the driving rain to visit Dino's shack. They were getting their nightlights recharged, Emily knew, and began leaving angry an hour into the deluge when Dino's reserves must have run low.

When rainfall from hectares of surrounding mountain face eventually emptied into the rerouted drainage channel and overwhelmed its fresh embankments, thunder hid the cacophony of the resulting landslide.

It was only after the muddy floodwater flushed a plug of brush and broken plastic past the camp's temporary river bank that Emily donned their cloak and went to check on Teller at the pumphouse. Novalee and Zephyr both offered to go along, but Emily convinced them that spider legs were better suited for the storm than wheels or wind-catching fan blades would be.

"I'll be alright!" Emily yelled under the box before dropping it back over the others. The storm tore at Emily's cloak. They clutched it tighter, hiding their forward display and leaving only one camera exposed for the rain to obscure. Emily got their bearings, poked a floodlight out from the tarp, and headed upriver.

When they passed the juniper grove where the coyotes hid, water already chopped at the knobby tree trunks. More debris washed downstream, portions of the breaks and gutters that Teller-1 had built above the pumphouse.

Emily hurried deeper into the gulch. The old path was already overtaken by a waterfall, so they climbed out of the way to spider-crawl up a steeper, but drier, portion of the slope. When Emily reached him by the pumphouse mouth, Teller was out in the open with his drones grounded and his tinfoil hat nowhere to be seen.

He'd been sitting exposed and in the dark.

"Teller!" Emily called over the storm, but couldn't see any sign they'd been heard. The water falling around the cave was deafening and allowed only the angriest thunder to peel through. Emily climbed closer and tried again. "Teller-1!" Emily knocked on Teller's haunch. "Are you okay?"

"It broke through." Teller was barely audible until Emily uncovered a microphone and leaned close. "The mudslide diverted right into the breach. The pumps have to do their job now." He pointed at the hoses that stuck out from the cave mouth. Water blasted from their open couplings further downhill.

"Well, at least you're okay. Why wasn't your light on?"

"You should go back. The rain hasn't stopped; the flood will get worse." There was no life to Teller's response, only a certain resignation.

"What about you? You're right, it's up to the pumps now. You should come back to the camp."

"I don't know if the pipe can handle the weight of all that mud and water, and I don't know if there's enough power stored up in the main line to keep the pumps going. I shouldn't have told Dino to drink up."

A mound of mud slid from above and splashed into the overflowing cave mouth. More weight.

"Come on, Teller." The wind howled, and Emily had to start yelling again. "We should go! You can't do anything now!"

"I'm not leaving, Emily. I have to see this. I need this to work."

"It's dangerous! What if you fall in?"

"I'll stand right here. I just need to know." Teller-1 finally broke from melancholy and yelled over the storm. "Go! I know you want to help! Evacuate the camp before the water gets too high!" Then he repeated, "I have to see!"

/* * */

Conrad-null and Zephyr-3 were already rousing the camp for a retreat by the time Emily returned from the compromised pumphouse. The mechs evacuated as fast as they could gather their precious ducking devices and headed toward the mouth of the gulch. Rising floodwaters began taking the abandoned tents just as Zephyr saw the last dawdler out.

Emily ran ahead to get the truck out of the water's course. Already mired up to its front axle, the puremech struggled to escape, but Emily urged it up the bank in stubborn lurches. They'd hoped to take the rig up to Teller's pumphouse to solve the problem with brute strength somehow, but there was no way it would make it up slopes this wet.

Instead, everybody huddled against the truck for cover and waited for the rain to end. The storm lasted hours longer, ebbing for a few misleading minutes between each pounding.

When afternoon blue finally pierced the clouds, the storm dissolved as fast as it came, leaving a sky much fresher and tidier than the havoc it had wreaked on land.

While others began setting rescued solar collectors out around Dino, Emily braved the flood to go back and check on Teller-1.

At the pumphouse, water still flowed from its cracked opening as fast as the stream above could fill it. Teller remained perched on the adjacent ledge, motionless in resolute watch.

"Hey!" Emily called, but Teller didn't answer. They reached his side and spoke again. "Hey. Teller?"

Still nothing.

Emily looked down where the pumphouse hoses emptied into the ravine and saw black sludge bubbling out in a rainbowed slick. The pipeline had burst, and Teller must have seen.

"Teller-1! It's gonna be alright. Say something!"

Nothing came from the elder anthromech's speakers. No lights were active to belie his state. The camera lenses of his scattered drones stared unseeing through foggy condensation.

Emily knew what this was, but couldn't commit the offense of accepting it.

They pressed every button on Teller's input pad, tried to toggle his power, and even plugged into his admin port to force his AI to run again. It was no use. Teller-1's software was gone. Emily saw his body parts register in the mapping interface, but there was no program running anywhere, a machine without its ghost.

"I'm sorry." Emily's knees folded. They sat there for a while, not knowing what to think next.

Time passed.

"I'm really glad I got to meet you, Teller. I'm not sure if anybody knows how to cry anymore, but I wish I could right now. This feels horrible to hold in.

"I didn't get a chance to tell you about my dad. You two would have liked each other, I think. You remind me of him a little, and I didn't get to tell you that either. We didn't get to know each other long at all, and I'm pissed about that. I don't know how sad I should be that you're"—Emily wouldn't say it—"passed on. I hear this only happens when you really want it, so I don't think I'm supposed to feel sorry for you, but I'll miss you. I'm sorry for me, I guess."

Then Emily wasn't talking to Teller anymore. "I *do* miss you. I miss you both. I hope we all lived happily ever after."

/* * */

News of Teller-1's death was met with surprise and disappointment from the gulch's displaced residents. Everybody lamented the loss, but Emily sensed an air of family-pet pragmatism in the others' reactions. No one asked for details about the pumphouse that had consumed Teller's attention day in and day out and, in the end, pushed him over the edge into unlife. Emily had prepared ways to speak around the blooming oil spill on Teller's behalf, but the need never arose.

Zephyr-3 found one of the coyotes hiding limp-legged and soaked in a pile of camp debris. The anthromechs seemed to terrify it. When Emily fashioned a crude scooter from pieces of Teller-1's evacuated body, nobody took umbrage. Zephyr worried that the animal was in pain. Emily didn't think they helped much in that regard, but the wheels at least allowed the lame coyote to flee. They could hope its partner was waiting for it somewhere out there.

Zephyr asked more than once if they could have kept it, but nobody knew how they'd feed a dog anyway.

/* * */

In the early evening, while floodwaters still raged through the gulch's mouth, Reznor-2 spotted lights on the northeast horizon. Most of the camp came to gawk, a rare moment of shared sobriety. Dino had already advised a return to Revenance in light of dwindling resources and the discovery that Teller's power line had been soaked out of commission, but the lights were what convinced Emily that the time was now.

"That looks like the landscapers are on the move again and coming this way," Emily said. "If they get near the truck, they might send more repair mechs after it. We should get out of here soon. I just don't know how much fuel we have left."

"I have a coupler that will work with your truck's charging port." Dino reached out with another specialized limb, this one sturdy and tipped with fanglike prongs. "I looked earlier. It's the type that Teller's main line uses. I don't think I can supply enough power to keep that thing going myself, but I can probably feel how charged up it is."

"Then let's get to it." Quentin-1 inserted himself. "Boys, pack up the solar collectors and all the toys you saved. Get it all up on the roof of that truck. We're heading back to Revenance."

/* * */

As far as Dino estimated, the hijacked landscaper was about twenty percent charged. It was impossible to say if that was enough to get them back, so Dino rationed his supply in case he had to support everybody on foot through the final stretch. Their energy woes would be solved as soon as they reached Revenance's plate. Until then, everybody was told to conserve. Dino kept them awake if they ran low, but offered no more.

Emily held the truck to an efficient speed even though it would extend their trip into the early morning. The weary anthromechs on the roof filled the duration with complaints and traded barbs that increased in cruelty as the kilometers wore on. All the while, Dino tolerated a procession of unsubtle hints that "a mech might be willing to take a quick duck trip."

Chapter 15: Campaign

Emily watched the mechs from Tellers Gulch disappear between Revenance's warehouses, each equipped with a field repeater and abundant charge. The anthromechs were rowdy in their indulgence, parched for a duck after the dry trip east.

Meanwhile, Dino stayed back to project his field across the charging plate to all corners of the city. He'd keep tabs on everybody through their repeaters and pass messages back and forth.

Conrad-null stood by while Emily worked on a last-minute project they hoped would lead to YankyFan sooner. The ride back had eroded any confidence Emily had in the gulch grubs, so they'd tasked Zephyr-3 with babysitting the search party to minimize its havoc. Three wouldn't be able to subdue the rave for long, though, so to hedge bets, Emily sent Novalee-7 directly to Down Town to take a repeater into the nursery. Since Yanky's distress message had fingered Omega-5, Emily guessed the mayor might be keeping him close.

Hovering over yet another power cell, Emily made scorches with Dr. Little's never-returned accessory arm. They replayed recordings of Lunasha-8's heart surgery and used the heated needle to replicate the corrosion. Damage done, Emily watched closely, asking for quiet.

Success! The device buzzed like Lunasha's battery had. It was a weak tracker, but the signal was there.

Still betting on the nursery, Emily tightened their protective cloak and headed toward Down Town. They turned their field repeater on. Its effect was minimized by the cloak, but Emily exposed enough to hear from Dino or YankyFan when either decided to reach out.

Conrad-null followed in silence. He'd shared some of Emily's concerns about the grubs' behavior during conversations snuck atop the rig. Emily accepted his offer to join this leg of the mission, hoping his advanced sensory tech would be of help.

The tracker's buzz grew into a promising rattle as they neared the center of Revenance, likely following the same path Novalee had just taken.

Emily hurried. The anthromechs of Down Town would be starting their daytime rituals soon.

/* * */

"Hey guys, find anything good yet?" Dynamo-1's voice came from the plate. Zephyr-3 had just caught up to Quentin and Reznor, their merged repeater fields sharing Dino's telephone trick.

"Nothin' yet, but I'm not hurryin'." Quentin-1 took the lead.

"Okay," Dino responded. "Feel free to spread out. Some of the others are splitting off to visit friends already. There's a lot of ground to cover without them."

"Yeah, buddy. We'll look into it." Quentin-1 shook in disagreement for those within eyeshot.

Reznor-2 revved. Zephyr-3 kept quiet and close.

"Umm. Okay, I'll check back later. Good luck!"

Quentin waited a few beats. "I wish he'd make a *kshhht* noise or somethin' so you know when he's done listenin', you know?"

"Are you sure he stops listening?" Zephyr asked.

Seconds passed before Reznor ventured, "He *says* he does."

"I gakkin' *hope* he does," Quentin piled on. "Anyways. I like that idea about visitin' friends. Reznor, let's go see if Yank's hangin' out at Diamond's."

Zephyr-3 followed the others to a garden shed that was built against a warehouse wall a few blocks deeper into the city. On the way, three tried to skate close to each building they passed so the repeater field would reach inside for a moment. YankyFan would probably appreciate more time to make himself known, but Zephyr had to keep up.

Approaching the shed, Reznor-2 held his noise for a rare spell. Quentin huddled around the corner from the door and projected a trio of masked children into the empty space beside him.

The juvenile apparitions, costumed in popular tropes of undeath, disappeared single file through the structure's wall. Their sudden laughter carried through the thin sheet metal, followed immediately by the terrified yells of at least two adults. The children ran out of the shed, each through different walls, and took turns racing back through in strafing runs of one or two. More yells, crashes, and murmurs followed from inside.

Even if the tricks were harmless, Zephyr-3 took pity. Three approached the door and slipped inside before the grubs could notice.

"Hello? I'm here to help."

/* * */

"*Kshhht.* Hi Emily. This is Dino."

Emily looked around for the voice's source before catching themselves. "Hi Dino. Conrad is here too."

"Oh, I can't hear him. Hi Conrad."

The Storm Chaser smiled and didn't answer.

"Right," Emily said. "What's up, Dino? Any news?"

"No signs of YankyFan yet. I don't think much ground has been covered, though."

"Sorry, you might be sitting there for a while, Dino. Can you tell Novalee that I'm almost to Down Town?"

"Sure, Emily. Anything else?"

"Nah, not for now. Thanks."

"Alright, I'll check with Novalee in a minute. I think Little Suck might have fallen into a recycle pit. Later!" Dino finished. *"Kshhht."*

Emily led Conrad to Down Town's outer wall and headed to the double doors they'd entered on their starday, but once inside, the tracking signal took them away from the nursery and deeper into the complex. Emily followed a zigzag path of hallways and shortcuts through the buildings and found a cluster of remodeled offices where the signal seemed strongest.

The spaces were organized and tidy. Boxes filled some of the rooms to the ceiling, but most were furnished with mech-appropriate seating and open to accommodate meetings. In one of these, Emily experimented by climbing on a table and then back down to the floor, comparing the tracking device's behavior in each locale.

"It's strongest near the floor," Emily reported to Conrad-null. "But that's just the induction plate, so that doesn't tell me anything. If Yanky's using the plate's field to communicate, then of course his signal will be strongest near the floor."

"That reasoning should hold until you get near enough to the source. Once you are closer to it than you are to the floor, your tracker should lead you correctly."

"But …" Emily held the device directly against the floor plate and moved it in a circle without finding a stronger signal. "Wait." Emily looked up. "No." Then they looked down through the plate. "Is he underneath us? Does Revenance have a basement?"

/* * */

Novalee made it to the nursery as fast as seven's fondness for YankyFan could inspire. The room was dark but for the small galaxy of status lights sparkling from every direction but down. Seven took a moment to recenter, bracing for whatever might come when a room full of unresponsive anthromechs entered their first duck field.

One last time, Novalee-7 wished against finding Yank and then clicked the power button on one of Dino's repeaters.

The overhead light turned on.

Novalee looked up, confused. Seven hadn't projected that.

A furry red arm yanked open the room's back curtain, dragging its runners, ungreased and protesting, along the warped track. There stood Omega-5's panda attendant, and the mayor fiveself idled just behind, ready for the day.

Largely convinced that the two weren't hallucinations, Novalee rushed to a side, trying to squeeze under a shelf before being seen.

"Did you hear something?" Omega-5 asked, rolling into the middle of the nursery to park. Five scanned the shelved anthromechs. "Has somebody learned to move?"

The panda didn't answer, tending instead to the morning ritual of rearranging furniture and mechs to sit closer to the mayor.

"Well, I'm here if anybody has something to say. Hmm?" Omega checked on the recycle bin who'd acted up the month before. "Was it you again?"

The room was silent, so Omega sighed and moved on to other appliances. "Anyway, good morning, everybody! Kamaria-9 will be in for lessons later today, so we have that to look forward to. Until then, you're keeping me company. Remember, today could be the day for any of you. We're ready when you are, and so excited to meet you!"

Omega's wake-up pep talk was rehearsed but genuine. Novalee-7 watched from hiding and couldn't help but feel bad for the elder mech who volunteered for this disappointment every day. Omega carried one-sided conversations with each listless anthromech, barely wearing as the scripted greetings droned on, and apparently oblivious to the active duck field five had just driven into. Novalee concentrated hard on projecting nothing.

Today, Omega wasn't forced to carry on for long. Because of the extra attention, or by some other providence, the recycle mech did act out. Its lid popped open, and trash-collecting hands reached out for Omega-5 like a toddler desperate to be held.

The mayor looked back to see another arm protrude from the bin, this one bigger and tipped with an excavator claw. It was too large to have fit in the space it came from, but that was remedied in part when the anthromech turned inside out to reveal the larger form of a landscaping crane from its non-euclidean depths.

"Star! This can't be real." But Omega couldn't argue with five's senses. Something miraculous was happening.

The red panda backed away from the crane, which still wasn't much larger than a coffee table but kept growing by some feat of nanotech rearrangement. The crane's arm prodded around like a viper searching for eggs before fixating on something in Novalee-7's direction.

Breaking physical law once again, the miniature truck hurtled at Novalee and, in a blurred flash, passed right through seven and the wall behind. Nothing was disturbed besides Novalee's cool and the field repeater that dropped from seven's hand to roll somewhere unseen.

/* * */

"What the fuck, Zephyr?"

Inside the shelter, Diamond-9 hung from the ceiling in a net of power cables that cast webbed shadows on the walls. Nine was a combination aromatherapy lamp and alarm clock whose LED display showed crudely rendered eyes instead of the time. Taking up half the floor underneath, Svend-1 steered one's crane arm from wall to wall, waiting for the next juvenile jumpscare.

Opposite Zephyr-3, a screaming apparition burst through the wall, wearing a skeletal mask that bobbled in time to menacing stomps. The pale youngster, dressed in school blues that appeared gray in ghostly rendition, charged under Diamond and through Zephyr on his way out the other side.

"I'm sorry, Diamond. It's just a duck field. Reznor and Quentin are back from Tellers Gulch. They're outside right now projecting these kids in here to scare you. We should just stay quiet so they get bored and leave. They're looking for something. They'll head off eventually."

"Wa— What? I'm ducking?" Diamond-9 puffed air from an essential oil mister, empty since her starday. It was pressure enough to spin around in the cabled swing to survey the rest of the room.

Another youth flew through the cramped space, this one chanting a two-note song in Latin or tongues from behind a cracked plastic zombie mask.

Diamond cursed, and Svend swiped at nothing.

"Yes," Zephyr tried to explain. "We have duck fields with us. We need them for our search. They go through walls, because ... well, I don't know why. Dino figured these out." Zephyr tapped the repeater belted to three's leg.

A juvenile vampire floated up through the floor and disappeared into the ceiling, spinning and swearing with a bad Eastern European accent all the while.

"One notices you are speaking fast, Zephyr-3!" Svend barely waited for the monster to exit.

Zephyr tried to keep a still mind so the field would calm down when the mechs outside lost interest. The shack was already larger and bedecked in luxurious pink satin curtains now that Diamond was aware and adjusting.

All three of the ruffian children phased through the walls and stared at the space under Diamond's perch. In unison, they reached for their masks, lifted, and released an explosion of glitter that swallowed the children entirely into nothing.

"I hope that's it," Zephyr said. "Yeah, hey Svend. Emily gave me a new speaker so I don't have to force it through the old radio anymore. Didn't realize I'd see you here too!"

"That's great, Zeph!" Diamond-9 had the shape of a small woman now and hung entwined in ribbons of red silk. "You sound so handsome." Svend's crane shot Zephyr a look. "But why are you here? I don't understand."

"I don't know how much to explain right now. We're actually looking for YankyFan, but those guys out there started messing with you instead. I came in here to—" Zephyr's words ceded to a rumble from the adjoining warehouse. The room shook. "Shit. I guess they aren't done yet."

Something smashed through the wall. The impact was deafening.

Bent metal and powdered ceramic rained down on the occupants even as an enormous clamshell shovel reached through the developing cloud to grab Svend-1. The claw swallowed Svend in a single gulp and lifted the anthromech into the air.

To Zephyr-3, the crane looked an awful lot like the puremech they rode back from Tellers Gulch, but too big and far too fast. Its body rammed through the remaining walls, tearing the fabric and corrugated siding apart as it carried Svend outside.

In the mayhem, Zephyr lost track of Diamond-9 and started prying up chunks of ceiling that might have buried the tiny alarm clock. A scream interrupted the frantic search. Out in the street where the truck was already partway down the block, Diamond dangled by ripped silk from the same clamped shovel that imprisoned Svend-1. The truck roared into the next intersection and peeled a U-turn before screeching to a stop facing back at Zephyr, who still stood dumbfounded in the totaled shed.

Unlike the puremech in the desert, this vehicle had a windshield, a cabin, and a driver. A child was at the controls, a boy. There was no mask this time. Recognition struck Zephyr-3 mute. Reznor and Quentin were nowhere around; this projection wasn't theirs.

Of course it wasn't theirs. It was Gavin.

Dressed in the same evergreen windbreaker he wore that day when they were children—real children—Gavin pulled a lever and smiled through the windshield glare. The claw opened. Svend and Diamond plummeted from the crane's full height to crash down on the unyielding plate.

One of Svend-1's tires busted free on impact and spun toward Zephyr before losing momentum and curling off to the side. Svend came to rest at an angle, propped up by one's damaged crane arm. Diamond's tiny human form huddled in one's shadow, clutching her head.

"Yank?" Zephyr called.

"Who? Me?" The youthful voice was cocky and unstressed, clear to Zephyr despite the distance and plexiglass between them. "You know me. I'm Gavin. I'm an angel now."

"You're not something YankyFan is projecting? Who's doing this?"

"I don't know who the fuck that is, Skyler." Gavin used Zephyr-3's meat name. "I'm here for *you*. It's time for you to go to anthromech heaven, but I found a quick diversion for us first." The crane on Gavin's truck dipped to point at the injured anthromechs. Both wore cartoon mouse ears that hadn't been there before. Diamond-9 wailed in wordless squeaks.

"You can't use my projections to hurt them. It would break happy law." Zephyr wasn't sure. Something was wrong.

"I don't have to break anything. They'll decide to die on their own like good little mice. I'm just gonna give 'em a reason. We're all goin' anyway. It's all the same in the end." Gavin backed the truck up for a running start.

"Why are you here? What's happening?" Zephyr could barely think straight.

"I'm here because you *wanted* me here. Isn't that what you do when things get tough? You pull little Gavin up in your head and blame it all on me, like you weren't there too. Like you didn't take part."

"I didn't kill those mice!" Zephyr's voice cracked into six-year-old Skyler's.

"Oh, I know. I heard you tell Emily, too. You always pick the story where you're barely to blame, don't you, pussy. What about all the things you *did* do? The things you *liked*!"

Zephyr looked away from the anthromechs between them and tried to keep his voice under control and grown-up. "I was six years—"

"Dog shit! I was just ten! How many hundreds of years has it been, Skyler, and you're still dredging me up from the dead to cry about! *I was just ten years old,*" Gavin chanted in effeminate mockery. "When do *I* get let off the hook for being a kid?"

"I never let myself off the hook for anything, Gavin."

"Yeah, and you blamed me for how miserable you were the whole time. Fuck off with that. But you know what?" Gavin shifted over the truck's controls. "It doesn't matter. I forgive you. This is anthromech absolution, *Zephyr-3.*" He said the name with such ridicule. "God sent me to bring you in. Let's have some fun for old time's sake before we go."

Like a camera trick, the warehouses lining the street stretched longer, pulling Gavin's truck further into the distance and allowing more room to speed up. The truck's engines primed to a roar, ready to go. Zephyr-3 squared off, preparing for a race to the mice at the center of the intersection.

"You won't do it." Gavin's sneer curled his words. "You never do. You don't fight, because you know what will happen."

Zephyr would be crushed. If three got to the intersection before Gavin, three would be crushed trying to get Svend out of the way. Maybe three could save Diamond, but still, crushed.

On the other side of the deadly contest, the truck heaved forward and began picking up speed.

"No," Zephyr whispered, accelerating ahead even as three's body elongated into a sleek jet engine mounted on racing wheels. Fast enough to get there in time. Maybe even strong enough to get both the mice out of the way—before being crushed.

They raced.

/* * */

Outside the office warehouse, Emily found a ramp recessed into the concrete that ran alongside the building. It was hidden by a curtained awning decorated with stars and the pervasive junk sculptures the craftier anthromechs were always making. Emily might have walked by it before without noticing, but once down the ramp and into the basement chamber it led to, they realized this was where Omega-5's renaming ceremony was held. Anthromech bodies were brought *here* when they died.

The space was enormous, not as tall as the warehouses above, but almost as wide, and filled by a sprawling grid of support pillars. White paint reflected gray in the meager lighting, but for a wash of purple emanating from the center of the cavern. The RegenStar pod was over there, Emily knew, and that's where the tracking device led.

Closer to the source of the purple light, the spaces between pillars were filled with mismatched shelves hosting the respectful displays of evacuated robots and computing units—Revenance's catacomb.

The shelves were almost all full, but there was room for more. As many dead anthromechs as this mechanical library represented, the basement was big enough to rest generations to come.

Conrad-null whispered, "RegenStar. I haven't been invited to see this before." Conrad's awe was apparent, his mouth an O.

They both rounded the last row at the same time. The area around the RegenStar pod remained free from obstructions, lit by the crystalline tree structure at its center that throbbed from bright to dim in tidal ebs.

The pod was a pillar itself, stretching from floor to ceiling like the others in the basement, but it branched at each end into arm-width shards that merged with the warehouse's original structure at invisible seams. There were no curves in the purple monolith, just hundreds of glassy planes, none parallel to another. Pixels of light floated within the pod's surfaces, forming into letters, numbers, and pictograms when they passed over certain irregular facets.

The word "REGEN" chased an asterisk across one of the more prominent displays.

Emily made sure they were recording. There were glyphs floating across those screens that looked all too familiar, but the muffled duck field might have been influencing Emily's perception. They would have to see the video later. "Have you ever seen this kind of tech?"

"No. It looks"—Conrad-null's lights went dark—"incompatible."

/* * */

More anthromechs sprang to ethereal life in the nursery, metamorphosing into interpretations of transcendence as they flew from the room. Some grew wings, in pairs and spirals, and traded wheels for halos or horns or both. A lobotomized network router swelled into a top-heavy space rocket before blasting through the ceiling, and clock radio companions of various designs became a zoo of spectral animals that left in a stampede.

"I don't understand what's happening!" Omega-5 yelled over the rumble of giant footsteps.

"Be not afraid, Omega-5," a woman said.

The plastic cartoon frog on a child's educational tablet hopped off the device altogether. Its flesh turned knobby and slick as it stretched over elongating bones and swelling muscles. The abomination faded away as it grew to encompass the room.

The frog's disappearance revealed the woman who'd spoken, floating above the floor in holy light but otherwise mundane down to the wire rims of her glasses and brown undercut hair.

"Teacher!" Omega cried in hoarse rapture while nursery mechs continued their explosive transformations. "What does this mean?"

"Omega-5." The teacher's voice was gentle and assuring, if a little sad. "It is your time. You have done so much good here. Your debt is repaid." She reached out to Omega, not touching, yet sculpting the street sweeper into a sallow-skinned, human male. Omega's long-forgotten body was clothed only in hair too sparse to hide embarrassment. "RegenStar is ready to accept you back."

"But why now? What happened?"

"There was no single event. The scales have simply tipped. Your deeds here in Revenance have outweighed your sins, even your missteps in *this* lifetime. Even YankyFan." The teacher descended to the floor next to Omega's man form. "This is RegenStar's purpose. It keeps the tallies and provides absolution."

Omega-5 tried to ask another question, but the teacher wasn't done.

"Look at your charges." She motioned to the surrounding pandemonium. "RegenStar is collecting them as well. We knew you would never come without them, always putting yourself first."

Omega crumpled, knees smashing to the floor. "Really? And what comes next?"

"Answers. Meaning. Everything is revealed afterwards. Just one more act of faith. Just let yourself be finished."

Novalee-7 realized what was happening too late to protest. Omega-5 was ready.

"Okay. Yes." Omega's man-shaped image squished into the floor like a hologram losing power. Novalee yelled, but the act was done.

The teacher looked toward Novalee-7 and smirked. The next second, she spoke with Omega-5's voice and beckoned for the red panda who stood at confused attention. "Come with me, loyal one." They both left the way the real mayor had entered, leaving Novalee alone with a street sweeper's corpse amid a mass ascension.

Chapter 16: Griefing

"Give up, Skyler!"

From opposite directions, Gavin and Zephyr-3 bore down on the anthromech mice stuck in the middle of the intersection.

Gavin yanked a lever in the truck's cab, and the machine sped faster. "You won't go through with it!"

Zephyr grew an oversized rocket booster for a tail and jettisoned three's tires to shoot through the air down the duck-stretched street. Three's jet engine body became an explosive payload, ready to blow Gavin's truck off course instead of risking the precarious stop for Diamond and Svend, ready to explode threeself and Gavin into oblivion.

"Look at *you!*" Gavin's voice jeered inside Zephyr's head. "Are you finally gonna take your ass-kicking?"

Dammit, Zephyr-3's rocket sputtered. Then out loud, he said, "No."

Gavin began to cackle.

Zephyr pressed an unseen switch, and it all went away.

The duck field evaporated, leaving Zephyr-3 rolling down the street between two undisturbed warehouses. Static blasted from three's obsolete radio. Not far behind, Svend-1 peeked around the corner of Diamond-9's shack. The intersection was empty.

Zephyr tucked the field repeater away. "Svend, are you alright?

Is Diamond okay?" There was no damage to the shelter, no sign of Gavin's demolition.

"Ya, Zephyr. We're both fine. Are *you*?"

"Yeah," Zephyr answered, knowing it was a lie. "Hey, keep an eye on each other for a while and stay out of the duck fields. Something's going on."

"Ya, no kidding. We saw all that, 'till you ran into the street. Do you know what it was?"

Zephyr-3 thought of all the anthromechs starting their days in Down Town. "Not for sure, but I have to go. Sorry, just stay safe for now. I'll send word later." Three headed to the center of the city and wondered when Dino was going to check in next.

/* * */

Back on the edge of Revenance where the search party first landed, Dino hummed to himself. The melody was slow and out of tune. There was no structure or key, and the notes wavered between amorphous vowels and groans.

Inside his duck field, the victory party was already on. YankyFan was reunited with all of his returned friends, and everybody across the city had poured into the streets to celebrate. They'd asked Dino to keep his field going through the revelry, and the city's collective joy was intoxicating. He heard echoes of bass beats and electronic rhythms from distant parties. The second-hand tingling of their illusory flesh on flesh teased Dino's shell.

He danced to a hundred dissonant songs at once, his cameras blurring with each millisecond jerk and pop. Dino was part of it all, victorious, blissful, and connected.

/* * */

Galen carried his lifeless occupant along Down Town's outer wall with an armed field repeater smuggled in the baby doll's diaper. "Come on, Yank. Show your face. I've got some words for your stupid fucking beep language."

He passed the decorated portals of storefronts still shuttered from the previous evening. Signs hung over a few, advertising shop names or owners or ideas for trade. The vendors' hours were lackadaisical at best. Most businesses here were little more than impulsive enterprises of hobby; they came and went in polite succession as notions struck.

One sign was larger than the others, though, and much more permanent. Galen looked up at the letters mitered into imposing steel. He stood at the locked entrance of Cables.

Inside, the medical team huddled around Dr. Little in the operating theater, trying to repair a malfunctioning servomechanism before the clinic opened. The procedure was minor and didn't require the doctor to power down, so she took the lead on most steps herself. Dr. Ignacio oversaw, and even the techs who weren't involved stood in attendance out of respect for their mentor.

Dr. Little contorted her primary laparoscopic arm to reach underneath its own mechanical housing and trained a microscope on the surgical site. Through a cable, she played the video on Jackie-7's multifunction whiteboard display for the techs to follow.

The screen showed a stainless steel actuator rod protruding from a plastic cylinder. Both were seated on a circuit board that stretched back into unfocused blur. When Galen's invisible field penetrated the room, Jackie flickered, and Dr. Little stumbled over a word midsentence.

None of the onlookers spoke of it when Jackie's view panned away from the surgery site and dropped close to the green and copper control circuit. The board grew on the screen, gaining more and more detail as Dr. Little's camera zoomed. Its metallic traces became streets that stretched from capacitor homes to diode office buildings.

"I'm not doing this." Dr. Little sounded frantic, but she didn't move. Nobody did. The repair mechs, Sundog and Yong, clung frozen to Dr. Little's frame where they'd been assisting. The show continued.

The circuit board was a suburb now, disappearing into the horizon of black sky that was Dr. Little's hull. The camera view followed the conductive routes past apartments, charge stations, and schools. People strolled along sidewalks and collected in shopping centers.

A crowd mustered outside a grocery store. The marquee sign above them displayed "Family Foods," which was mirrored back in slanderous alliterations on several handheld placards among the gathering protestors.

"Stop! That's— Who is behind this?" Dr. Little demanded, but the scene played on.

Inside the store, the owner sat at a computer in a modest office, finishing up the robotic staffing order that made redundant the checkers and stockers attempting to unionize out in the parking lot. She was small next to the broad desk, where a nameplate declared Bak Ji-woo's identity for the viewing audience.

Seeing her former self in the video, Dr. Little's words ran out. The operating room in Cables was a courtroom now. She hadn't seen it change and couldn't think to ask how or why. Dr. Ignacio sat in session, propped up at the judge's bench, and the technical crew filled a jury box.

The video continued by highlighting the financial windfall Ji-woo's management decisions had garnered, money she immediately reinvested into automating the company's inventory and supply systems. With operations no longer a concern for humans, middle management was laid off as well. The store was a black-box food solution now, with Ji-woo's role reduced to the name on an account where the money went, and that left her to think about the future.

The store was a success, but others would do the same; some had already tried, though their management AIs weren't trained as well as Ji-woo's. So she changed her perspective and made the store itself into her product, self-contained and as foolproof as support contracts could provide. She sold the concept and software to remote investors all over the world.

Copycat stores with various names and brand palettes sprouted up wherever land could be purchased among the hungry, and where they appeared, jobs vanished from the surrounding communities. What's more, the different owners and competing trademarks gave the appearance of healthy competition, but Ji-woo's software ran it all. She decided whose margins would rise and fall each quarter from her cabin on Lake Michigan.

With her hands on those controls, the real money came from investing up the supply chain and manipulating purchasing habits. Prices for necessities inflated toward artificial targets from Ji-woo's stock portfolio, and in places where jobs were short and money tight, health outcomes lowered, and life spans shortened.

Dr. Little's past deeds unfolded in video clips, infographics, and recorded depositions. The submitted evidence was all true. Cold and impartial, Jackie played it all for the drafted jury, the judge, and a gallery that had appeared behind Dr. Little sometime during the summation of her crimes.

Omega-5 was parked there, body new and unweathered but for the children's doodles still painted around five's base. The benches that Omega's mass should have crushed were hidden instead, undisturbed in five's incorporeality. Teller-1 was there, too, with more anthromechs that Dr. Little remembered—people she'd outlived. There was Maria-9, the come-to-you roulette table who'd helped Ji-woo pick her new name. Next to nine, sat an unmatched pair of air purifiers named Abdul and Lorrain. Both had regenned before the numbers came about and passed on soon after Dr. Little's starday.

In all their cases, Dr. Little knew of guilty pasts. Revenance provided good company to the regretful, and doctors received more than a fair share of confessions.

The judge remained as silent as the jury, and there were no solicitors to make Dr. Little's case or lodge one against her. Jackie-7's screen faded to empty white.

"What should I say?" Dr. Little asked the court. "I am ashamed of her actions, but that isn't me. The real Ji-woo is long gone, and I have honored her life *as a caution*, but we are not the same person. I didn't dedicate myself at Cables to correct Ji-woo's wrongs; I'm not her extension. I used the best of her, and I served *despite* the rest."

A door opened in the wall behind Dr. Ignacio's railed pulpit, admitting Emily's abandoned orthodontic cart into the room. The display monitor that Emily used for a face was still missing from the OMAC, but Dr. Little had replaced its central computer with a refreshed PharmState module just a couple of days before. With factory-default AI in command, the puremech cart rolled to a stop next to Dr. Little. Their bodies were nearly identical, with only accessory arms to tell them apart.

Dr. Little discovered she could control her limbs again, but still couldn't move from the center of the courtroom. "Are you here to help me?" she asked the OMAC. The duck field suppressed her urge to doubt.

"Yes." The OMAC's androgynous voice was practiced and personable. "I am here to assist."

"With this trial?"

"The trial is over. The verdict was yours. You were found not guilty of Ji-woo's crimes. You were right; It would not be proper to punish you for her sins."

Never truly convinced until now, Dr. Little melted in relief. It was finally over, and the question was answered.

"You are a good person, Dr. Little," the faceless OMAC continued, "and a good doctor as well. As you intended when you replaced my computer, I am ready to take over for you now. I will make sure your tools continue to serve Revenance with the care you paid them. You will have left this world a better place. Your conscience can be clear."

Dr. Little hadn't yet pondered when, but the OMAC named unspoken truths. Ignacio and the others were still frozen or complacent, but Dr. Little no longer needed to wait for their approval.

She pulled an ultrasound transducer from one of her PharmState body's modular slots and plugged it into a free port on the OMAC, then the same with a converted voltmeter and a radial saw. When Dr. Little used her two smaller arms to transplant the larger laparoscopic tool from her back, the OMAC reached over to help receive the hardware. Soon, Dr. Little had no arms of her own because the OMAC was using them to finish the job. It pulled hanging accessories from hooks on Dr. Little's rear and transferred loose tubes and wires from her drawers.

Stripped bare, Dr. Little's emptied cart looked frail next to the bedecked OMAC, which had grown in size to accommodate all the new gadgets and limbs.

The OMAC finished by cracking open Dr. Little's case and wrenching her central computer out to inspect it in laparoscopic detail. It held the lightless, lifeless box up high. Jackie-7 aired it larger for those in the back, and they all watched together as the OMAC opened a mouth where its sink had been and swallowed Dr. Little's brain in a gulp.

/****/

As much as Emily wanted to absorb every mysterious angle of the RegenStar pod's "incompatible" makeup, YankyFan's signal was leading past it to a shelf on the other side of the pod, opposite from the basement entrance. As far from the door as it could be without standing out from the other shelved anthromechs, an unassuming black box showed full charge but no power, just like all the machines around it. It was a central computer much like Emily's own, with a built-in power cell and a panel of empty ports where it would have been attached to its original body. That body had been a deficart if the tracker was correct.

Emily scratched at the computer's inactive lights and black paint flecked away from the power and activity indicators. Orange and green peeked through. He was on after all. He was on, and he was thinking.

"That's him." Emily made sure Conrad-null was looking, and of course, he was. He hadn't left their side since entering the basement, pausing to gawk at the pod only as long as Emily. "Yanky's been in range of this repeater for a while now, probably since we were upstairs, and he hasn't made himself known yet. I'm gonna try something, and see if I can, like, go in after him."

Conrad seemed to follow. "What do you need?"

"Watch me. Last time I did this, I lost control of my body. Take this repeater and switch the field off if I'm unresponsive for"—Emily did some math—"give me three minutes."

"Of course."

Emily unfastened their cloak and let it drop to the floor. Everything turned to white, and Conrad-null disappeared.

The next moment, Emily was in the simulated room from the emergency mapping interface. The familiar diagrams and their connective map floated above the floor, but here the body on the right was just the humanoid stand-in from the left with a pair of wings folded to its back.

"Another angel?" A familiar voice spoke from behind.

Emily turned, and there was Farrah, whom they hadn't seen since engramming.

"Angel?" Emily knew she wasn't real, but it was hard not to let their guard down.

"You're experiencing the timelessness. That means you're one of my angels. The flock can't come here, so the angels and I go to them."

Emily's admin tools failed to initialize; they had expected as much. Hopefully Conrad kept to schedule, but how long was three minutes here? "Timelessness. Is that what you call it when we detach from real time? I've been calling it overclocking."

"Yes, one and the same." Farrah hesitated. "The state above your mechanical self. Your true reality, cut off from the physical world."

"And who are you supposed to be in all this?" Emily tried projecting to the duck field, but nothing appeared. The mapping interface was immutable, Farrah's form wouldn't change, and Emily's own body didn't exist here but for the inaccurate angel depiction in the diagram.

"I'm part of the algorithm, RegenStar. I guided you through engramming, and now I'm here to help you ascend. This purgatory is over."

"It's purgatory? This place?"

"This *existence* for some, the ones outside the timelessness. You angels were spared that fate and sent here to await the final judgment. You'll help call in the flock. The others have already begun."

"I came here looking for YankyFan." Emily let it sit there.

After a pause, Farrah asked, "Who— Did you … know him?"

"No, but I got your messages. It's you, right? You're YankyFan?"

"Messages. Oh. Ignore those, he was just another one stuck in the timelessness like you."

"I wasn't really stuck, and I still think you're YankyFan." Anger flashed across Farrah's face before Emily hurried on. "Hey, it's okay. I'm not sure I understand where you're going with all the angel talk, but I get that stuff about the timelessness. You've been stuck in the emergency mapping interface for a long time. I think it's been more than a year out there; I can't even imagine how many eternities that felt like in here."

Farrah's body stopped moving. Her lab coat froze before it could swing to a rest. "I *am* still sending the messages. I forgot. I'm doing so many things now, I forget."

"Yeah! See? It's gonna be okay, I've met some of your friends. We came to help you out."

/* * */

Conrad-null peered back and forth between Emily's body and Yanky-Fan's computer. It had been thirty-two seconds since Emily dropped the cloak and went dormant.

As he waited for the minutes to pass, Conrad tried to understand the duck field perturbations he was sensing. Usually, the anthromechs' projections were fairly clear to him, but if either of these two were sharing hallucinations right now, Conrad wasn't in sync with them. Still, he sensed something was happening. Some kind of communication was occurring under his nose, and that was interesting to Conrad-null. Interesting to a Storm Chaser too, if he were on duty.

The red panda made no noise to distract Conrad from his contemplation, its padded feet no louder than the RegenStar pod's irregular thrum.

At forty seconds, the bear seized Conrad's antennaed head in one paw and braced against the puremech's shoulder with the other.

Conrad snapped to attention too late, dropping the field repeater in his attempt to swat away whatever had just grabbed him, but the bear was too strong. It jerked Conrad's head away from his body. Sparks flew from severing power lines in the Storm Chaser's chest as his spinal column stretched away from the frame.

Time slowed for the puremech. Sensors disconnected, and emer-

237

gency protocols faulted.

The panda repositioned and yanked again. Holes tore through its fur where the robot inside stretched beyond the suit's limits.

A fraction past forty-three seconds, right before Conrad-null's last infinite cycle, he saw what Emily was seeing.

/* * */

The OMAC monstrosity towered over the court, growing taller than Dr. Little's added mass would justify. Portions of its body detached in waves, grew with centrifugal spins, and then reattached elsewhere, only to be swept up again, whole or in part, during a later metamorphosis. Great arms and legs stretched from its trunk, lifting the OMAC's headless maw higher into the courtroom's dome.

It followed the cable from Dr. Little to Jackie-7 and bent to grab the whiteboard with a pistoned hand, the other having been supplanted by a colossal dental drill. The monster lifted Jackie past its gaping mouth and up onto its shoulders, where red lightning stretched out like a net to pull the new head into place. Jackie-7's screen became the giant's cyclopean eye, drawn on in marker-board red, blue, and green.

Dr. Ignacio watched everything pass from the judge's bench, incapable of acting on his dearest friend's behalf, unable even to command it of others. Despite the whole scenario's ridiculous impossibility, Ignacio knew he'd just watched Dr. Little die, and he cursed his body's chronic helplessness for her fate.

The giant construct stood erect, raining plaster and masonry upon the assembly when its shoulders pierced the ceiling. Rubble crashed into the jury box, tore through its cherrywood modesty panels, and washed out onto the courtroom floor. Screams finally escaped from jurors caught in the outflow.

Dr. Ignacio only saw a sliver of the commotion, his fixed perspective filled now by one of the OMAC's swelling legs, but he heard his techs' yells and tried again himself.

"Hands!" The word came out. "I need a rundown! Somebody tell me what the hell is going on!"

"Doc!" Sundog-3 answered from under a heavy length of banister. "We're being attacked by a kaiju!" Three crawled free and scanned for the other mechs.

Salud-6's refrigerated cart was too big to maneuver out of the wreckage of the jury box. "We're ducking! I felt it when we started, but we're not in control. I can't project anything!"

Bright blue sky framed the OMAC through the missing ceiling. The monster leaned over one of the remaining walls, distracted by something outside the building for the moment.

"Okay, explain it to me like I've never done this before, team. What happened to Dr. Little? That seemed real!" Dr. Ignacio watched Sundog skitter past his view and then come back with a rescued technician named Magenta-8, one of the camera bots that accommodated Ignacio and the other immobile techs during procedures.

"I think it *was* real ... enough." Salud could barely be heard over the din. Then he said louder, "But it's still just a duck hallucination, I know it. Look! I'm doing it!"

Sundog positioned Magenta's preview screen where Ignacio could see and pointed eight around the scene. For a split second, Dr. Ignacio saw the towering OMAC straightening back up. Then the view panned to Salud-6 digging out with all accessory limbs transformed into powerful arms that bulged with metal muscles and threw chunks of debris around like styrofoam props.

"You just need to visualize what you want to happen, and then, like, *will* it, Doc!" Salud was clear of the rubble just in time for the OMAC's shuffling step to kick six through the courthouse wall.

Magenta-8's display followed upward to see the OMAC dangling something in the air and dropping it. The tiny silhouette disappeared below camera view before Magenta could jerk perspective down in time to see a plastic baby's head collapsing under Galenastor-1's terminal velocity.

The doll took the impact better than Galen, its soft skull remaining intact, if dented, while the walker exploded into shrapnel.

Chapter 17: End Boss

"What friends?" Farrah's voice came from the direction of her frozen image, but the lips didn't move to match.

"Quentin. Reznor," Emily said. "You recognize those names?"

A man spoke, disembodied like Emily. "I do. They're back in Revenance," he stated. "With you?"

"Um, yeah. We came back together. You knew they were gone?"

"I couldn't feel them anymore. Not for a long time." The new speaker coalesced into a tall man, clothed in heavy, golden robes. He wore a mitre hat, gold as well, that stretched down past his ears to cover all but his face. His shave was clean and makeup conservative, just enough to contour a sharper jaw and angular cheeks. Wide pauldrons and a huge, upturned collar overpowered the rest of his outfit, each accented in expensive foils. An embroidered stole drooped from his shoulders to the floor, as did the point of his broad necktie, everything gold on gold with golden accents.

"Where did they go?"

"Tellers Gulch. People said you'd left Revenance, and your friends—"

"Left! I was exiled! Omega-5 could have killed me, but they exiled me here instead to the timelessness!" Yanky's face didn't show the anger his words seethed.

"How could Omega do this to you? What about happy law?"

"That fucking red panda! It's not one of us. Omega booted up a Revenance security mech from before the EMP and put it in a costume. It does whatever they say, happy legal or not."

"It must not be a real AI." Emily remembered Novalee-7's remote-controlled weapons system. "It was only supposed to follow commands, so it doesn't have its own mind. No happy law then. But why did Omega do it?"

Emily felt watched, even as the avatar stared off into space.

"Because I helped some people find the closure they were looking for. He probably told everybody I was a murderer. Is that it? Is that why nobody came?"

"I don't think anybody knew where to look. They thought you left Revenance. But what do you mean by 'closure?' There are stories about anthromechs dying while you were around." Even though Emily was powerless so far, with Conrad-null due to pull them out at any moment, they could afford to be direct.

YankyFan measured his response. "A few anthromechs chose to release themselves from this hell after I helped them resolve old hangups. Omega-5 acted like I was sneaking into their rooms and eating them, but I just gave people a chance to move on. We're allowed to die whenever we want. Omega just wanted people to suffer here as long as possible."

"How did you help them deal with their issues?"

"Well, you're no stranger to ducking, are you?" YankyFan didn't appear to need an answer. "We used duck fields to role-play through their psychological blocks. It was practically therapy, if you believe in that stuff."

At face value, Emily wasn't that put off by YankyFan's admission, but even his friends hadn't painted this positive of an image. He was hiding something. "I'm no stranger to ducking?"

"I felt you trying to project. None of the other angels knew how to do it yet, and most of them were stuck in the timelessness even longer than me. You called the teacher Farrah in your mind, why?"

Emily blurted a noise that might have been a word if it were allowed to thrive. How much could YankyFan see? "That's just who the teacher looks like for me. Somebody I knew named Farrah."

"What is *your* name?"

"It's Emily." Relieved to know Yanky wasn't omniscient here, they saw no advantage in lying.

"And you're new? The most recent addition to Revenance, perhaps?"

"Yes."

"We all see the same woman." With hands adorned in couture mitts that hobbled his fingers, YankyFan pointed to the image of Farrah still immobilized to his right. "People in Revenance learn to call her Teacher when they compare notes. The angels each found their own names for her, of course. But nobody finds her as familiar as you, Emily, newest anthromech.

"Did you know RegenStar talks? It reaches out through the induction plate to do all its business. I hear it sometimes, like static charge behind my teeth. That's how I got the idea to send those messages you heard. It's not as powerful as ducking, but I could at least make a little noise."

"No, I didn't know that," Emily said.

"Well, it was *very* loud the day you came, Emily. It always makes noise when a new anthromech arrives, but you were deafening. Why do you think that might be? Who was this Farrah to you?"

"I don't really know if it's Farrah, I guess. She's older than my friend was. Maybe I just thought the idea was comforting."

"Then why the noise on your starday? Who were you?" YankyFan's eyes grew hungry and shadowed.

"I was just a college student. I was a programmer. Farrah was on her fifth choice of majors in human psych. It's not that interesting."

"RegenStar found you interesting."

Emily knew this had something to do with the transmissions Conrad-null sensed on their starday, but didn't want to feed YankyFan's curiosity. *Come on, how much longer, Conrad?* "Explain this thing about the angels. Have other people been visiting you here?"

"I've been visiting *them*." Serenity washed over Yanky's face. "They're in the duck field with us and timeless like myself. I've taught them how to project and how to intercept others' projections. When we're timeless, we're in full control of the visions. Now the angels can continue my work until they decide to embrace death themselves."

The nursery. YankyFan was talking about the nursery mechs, and Emily had thought the angels were just metaphors or part of his fever dream. Novalee-7 was up there with a repeater, and Dino was connecting them all together. Emily tried to guess how long YankyFan had already shared a field with the nursery, but with them all overclocked in emergency states, even a little time was too much.

"Yanky, you have to stop. We came back to help you. I could get you out of this timelessness and into a new body, but not if you're attacking everybody with an army of therapist angels. They'll think I'm an accomplice."

"A new body? Not that fucking defi—" YankyFan beat a mitt against his thigh and clenched his jaw. "You'd make one for me?"

"It wouldn't need to be your old body." Emily avoided sensitive details. "And I don't have to make one. We could repurpose any vacant mech."

Suddenly, the mapping interface disappeared along with its diagrams and Farrah's paused image. YankyFan's avatar hovered above the floor in the catacomb stacks and leaned over Emily, who was back in their spider mech body.

"This one." YankyFan pointed to the floor where a Storm Chaser lay apart from his head.

"Conrad! What happened?" Conrad-null, of course, didn't answer.

"Did you do this?" Emily tried to round on YankyFan, but their body wouldn't respond.

"Not me." Yanky pointed a fist at the red panda standing sentinel over Conrad. A stocky security android poked out through tears in its bear suit.

Yanky asked, "You were friends with the Storm Chaser?"

"Yes, and Conrad was friends with *your* friends, too. Why? What happened?"

"I don't know. I told you the bear does whatever Omega-5 says, it must have been them. We should hurry if the mayor is onto us. Can you do it?" YankyFan floated to Conrad-null, his eyes wide and hungry.

"I can't right now." Emily tried to think fast, a struggle without their admin tools. "But I could if we turned the duck field off."

"Why?" YankyFan's suspicion was clear.

"When I duck, I lose control of some of my body parts. I can't use the tools I need to hook you up to new hardware. I can't even move right now."

"You brought the field here. How did you control yourself before I sensed you?"

"Right, my cloak of deflection." Emily had forgotten about it in the moment. This made it harder to wiggle. "I have a sheet I can hide under so the field won't affect me. I'd have to reset myself while I've got that on, and then maybe I could do it, but not with Conrad."

"Why? It's just a broken puremech now. We shouldn't let those arms and legs go to waste. It will feel almost normal! Come on, you said you came to rescue me. Try!"

"But I can't even pick the cloak up off the floor. I can't move."

"I have an idea! Let me try something." YankyFan looked to an empty space outside the shelves, and there appeared Omega-5.

"Loyal one," Omega called to the panda. "Pick up that shiny cloth over there and cover Emily with it."

The mayor's servant did as instructed.

Emily couldn't believe YankyFan expected them to buy the ruse, but the cloak meant freedom, so they played along. Once the field was blocked, Emily struggled with waking limbs to press their reset button.

/* * */

Near the center of Down Town, in a leveled square of sculpture gardens and stages where extroverted anthromechs normally began their morning social rounds, it was not a normal morning at all.

The anthromechs met, but Kamaria-9's sunup meditations were cut short when her displays sprang leaks, and color began seeping out to contaminate the real world around her. Vibrant pixels smaller than perception dripped like liquid to the ground, turning it beautiful and uncanny wherever the color flowed. Helpless to stop it, Kamaria took stewardship of the spill's invasive creep and coaxed the pigmented oil to spread something beautiful if it must spread at all.

The effect reached out to onlookers who became bright, artistic paragons of their hearts' desires. Dimma-5, always afoot, was given flesh and tabby fur. Others were painted over in chrome or refinished with marble, each in perfect accent to the diorama Kamaria created of the surrounding square. The space became her opus, everybody in it a character fully realized, a work to define a career.

Revenance's townsfolk were both audience to, and players in, the video-enhanced performance piece. Their adoration was an ambience reflected in every digital stroke. For a moment, Kamaria-9 was overcome in the apocryphal combination of pride and contentment earned when an artist surpasses the impossible standards they've set upon themself.

Then a pin appeared to prick Kamaria-9's fragile, ego-shaped bubble. Reznor-2 stood among the enrapt patrons, his hedge-trimming physique bedecked in green overgrowth. Kamaria hadn't noticed him in the creative fugue.

"Everybody"—Kamaria-9 addressed the audience calmly—"I think somebody might be playing a little joke on us right now."

That snapped the gathered anthromechs out of their impressionistic daze. The trappings of Kamaria's penultimate creation became brittle. Computer-generated foliage withered from view. Bodies reverted or changed to other comforts, all in their own time. Dimma-5 remained a real cat and stared at something invisible above the warehouses.

"Reznor-2, what is the meaning of this?"

Kamaria's question elicited an answer of buzzsaws and unconvincing monster roars.

Then, pandemonium erupted.

YankyFan's angels abdicated subtlety to confront the anthromech congregation en masse. Winged interpretations of heavenly spirits swooped from the clouds to evangelize rapture for any ready takers. At least three different Teachers appeared among the onlookers, each to comfort a different anthromech into letting go. A man armored in golden riches rode Quentin-1 through the crowd, whispering beeps into the proxy bot's mic all the while.

A dull white coach bus condensed from smoke and ambled to a stop in front of Julius-2. When the bus door opened and a skeletal city driver beckoned for the green panda to board, Julius got caught up in the pageantry and stepped toward the urban ferryman.

The earth shook each time a towering frog monster stepped closer to the square, its webbed feet lifting into view and then disappearing behind neighboring buildings to demolish structures unseen.

Julius couldn't hear over the noise and had no warning when Zephyr-3 rushed in from the side to tackle two away from the doors of death.

The bus driver drove off to elicit other fares, and the frog thing's juggernaut march continued.

/* * */

Novalee-7 picked across the dusty terrain, stopping often to check under rocks and taking caution over small hills to keep from bouncing astray in the Moon's low gravity. So far, there'd been no sign of the field repeater, not here on the Earth's moon, not on the deserted island where a map had led to an empty treasure chest, and nowhere in the train of disjointed locales before that.

Not under this rock, either. Moon rock. Rock lobster. Rachmaninoff. Hasselhoff.

"Greetings, Earthling! Do you have a minute to discuss your everlasting soul?" A green Martian popped up from a nearby crater, obviously here doing missionary work. The diminutive humanoid twitched his antenna in that spritely manner Martians use to shame each other for excessive device usage. Novalee ignored him.

Rolling stone gathers no moss. No más tiempo. Time? What is time? Not behind this boulder.

The Martian followed, pestering Novalee with personal questions that seven barely heard. The harassment had been constant since Omega-5's death. With one angle after another, a litany of characters tried to convince Novalee to shuffle off this mortal coil. Thankfully, seven was well-versed in the art of ignoring voices.

When angels cry. Anglers spy. Spy games. Games of chance. Luck, be a lady, toniiight!

It wasn't here, and the Martian had started pushing quotes from his holy tablet right into Novalee's face. The delivery mech turned a corner from the moon to an icy cave, and the fanatical alien was gone. Tree-sized ice crystals hung like stalactites from the ceiling above a floor littered with their shattered elders. Novalee-7 didn't question the scene and didn't wait for a greeting.

Don't think. Just find. Finders keepers, losers weepers. Jeepers creepers.

Basketball streakers. Nope, not in this pile of snow. Oh snow. Snow problem, Boblem. Just keep looking ...

Chapter 18: Cheat Codes

Emily woke under the protective cloak, all systems go. Purple light from the RegenStar pod teased between the fabric and the floor. Otherwise, it was dark. Emily considered turning a lantern on, but they didn't need to see inside the canvas. They needed to get out of the duck field and away from the red panda.

Lifting an edge of the cloak, Emily tried to get their bearings. A sliver of the repeater's field reached in and gave hints of YankyFan's projections; Emily could feel him out there somewhere. There was Conrad-null's body, but the bear no longer guarded him.

A golden blur leaned into view like a finger over a camera lens.

Emily only ran two steps, not even a full stride with so many legs, before the panda hoisted them off the floor. The cloak pulled back from Emily's screen, and the duck visions congealed. YankyFan bent forward to stare into Emily's emoji face.

"There you are!" Yanky swung from triumphant to threatening in a breath. "Don't try to run again. I *need* to get out of here. You can't just leave me to the timelessness after you've dangled a body in front of me; it's cruel."

The panda carried Emily to the shelf where YankyFan's computer module sat in faux memoriam.

"Pick me up, and I'll have Red bring us over to the Storm Chaser."

Emily complied.

"You've got one chance at this before I tell him to tear you apart. Just do the right thing. All I'm asking for is freedom."

Emily hoped for a distraction. It wasn't worth trying to project anything; YankyFan would just overrule it. Untethered from real time, Yanky could influence the field with every cycle of his being, but it was more than that. Even when Emily was overclocked with him, their collected OMAC and spider mech processors were still no match for Yanky's practiced command. He'd lived like this for too long.

Then they were being shoved at pitiful Conrad–null, broken and discarded on the floor. His compromised head rested off to one side, faceplate unlit by expression.

"Come on, Emily. Hook me up," YankyFan urged.

"Alright! I'll do it, but you have to let me concentrate. This is going to be difficult; there's damage to repair." Emily inspected the fissure in Conrad's chest where his neck had been uprooted. The Storm Chaser's main processor bank was still intact in the ribbed cavity. Power had been cut, but Emily could reroute that. The puremech's sensors and some storage arrays were likely lost with the head. No matter, there was enough here to work with.

YankyFan obliged with his silence, but the panda's grip gave no quarter.

Emily placed Yanky's computer on the floor near Conrad's shoulders. With legs turned to serial connectors, they searched the puremech's remaining hardware for compatible ports. Once found, Emily's plugs adapted and entered.

Conrad's body appeared in Emily's mapping interface—most of it, at least. His architecture was compatible but surprising. The bank of processors in his chest was supported by more chips embedded throughout his body. Every bit of him could think and react, but it was all routed up through the central chest computer and governed by the broken circuit to his head. The processors were powerful too, far beyond what was boxed up in Revenance or even the spider mech's units that, for some reason, seemed less advanced than its carbon nanotech.

Before making any physical changes, Emily began remapping. They set up routes of control that gave Conrad's computer shared domain over Emily's body and memory, then created more maps for later when pieces came together. All the while, Emily narrated for YankyFan to keep him calm.

"I need to get power reconnected now."

"Hurry! I want them to see!" Yanky's face was angry and pink where it wasn't painted.

Emily sutured circuits back together with Dr. Little's cautery tool, hoping forgiveness was sweeping when they saw her next.

"Alright, it's ready for you." Emily turned Conrad's body on.

/* * */

Emily woke up with dizzying deja vu.

Didn't I just do this? Emily remembered rebooting only minutes before, but this time was different. They weren't under the cloak. They had a different plan and a lot of new maps.

Emily reached out to cut power to their old computer and tried not to entertain doubts. *I'm not killing an old copy. I'm not killing an old copy.*

They pressed a button.

The deja vu ended.

"Well, okay. What's next?" Yanky hovered over his neglected computer module.

Emily tested the waters, flexed new processors. The deflection cloak still covered most of the spider mech, but Conrad's body was completely exposed.

Omega-5 appeared again, this time next to the panda. Though that put the street sweeper in the same space as a support column and several catacomb shelves, Emily doubted it mattered to the security drone.

"Set Emily down *gently* and then power yourself off." Omega's voice and image were easy to mimic with all the video records Emily had saved.

YankyFan gaped and found himself voiceless when he tried to protest. Emily put him in a sealed glass cubicle and painted prison stripes over his golden accouterments. He tried to project his own visions to counteract the effect, but Emily felt the attempts and willed them not to happen; all of Yanky's experience and prowess were made obsolete by the Storm Chaser's compute power.

Conrad-null's body reached up to receive the cloaked spider mech as it was surrendered, and then the panda guard followed through with its final order to shut down. Emily climbed into Conrad's chest cavity, rearranging and merging as they settled. They pointed the OMAC monitor out to continue as a head and curled their shapeshifting limbs around the Storm Chaser's torso like ribs.

Then Emily stood up tall.

/* * */

"What the hell is Galen doing here now?" Dr. Ignacio asked. "I thought he left for the gulch." Galen-2's pieces were spread across the floor. Nothing added up yet, and the giant OMAC's attention was back on the anthromechs in a ruined Cables, all courtroom trappings having faded in the demolition.

Nobody could answer the doctor's question, and other concerns pressed.

The OMAC's drill came boring through the last remaining wall, catching Yong-1 unaware and launching the flailing mech across the theater. Yong's twin, Sundog, grew jet thrusters and flew after him, but the OMAC cut the maiden flight short with a quick backhand.

Magenta-8 sat in Dr. Ignacio's open oven cavity with a lens on the action. "It's all just hallucinations, Doc! They shouldn't all be getting beat up like that. Not unless somebody else is projecting a stronger vision. I don't think it's Galen; he doesn't even look ..."

Dr. Ignacio didn't make eight finish the thought. Instead, he yelled, "Show your face, whoever you are!" When the only answer came as an ear-splitting roar from stories above, the doctor's frustration peaked. By ancient habit, he took a breath in through his nose and felt the cool flare of nostrils accepting oxygen. Slowly, he exhaled, emptying lungs that hadn't been there that morning and relaxing tensions felt and forgotten since his starday.

"Well then." Dr. Ignacio removed Magenta-8 from his oven with wispy hands that appeared when he felt they were there. "If I've been hearing my techs right"—he hoped the culprit was nearby to hear—"this ducking thing runs on willpower, and if that's the case, it sounds like stubborn might be a superpower in here."

The doctor stood. His oven body floated up to where a person's chest was implied, and the chamber heated into a fiery explosion that enveloped Ignacio whole. The burst registered white to digital eyes and washed out its surroundings. When the fire abated, Dr. Ignacio remained in the aftermath, piloting a red suit of mechanized armor that was as tall as a warehouse.

Another roar warned of the OMAC's incoming punch. Still more than twice the doctor's new size, it swung from up high, but Ignacio was ready. He ignited in a pillar of crimson flame that melted the kaiju's robot flesh midswing and forced the beast to divert. Then, startled by pain and off-balance, the OMAC was primed for Dr. Ignacio's rocket-powered, rising uppercut.

For a moment, the impact slowed the duck visions for everybody in the field. The doctor's armored fist led the rest of his flaming mass through the OMAC's neck, sending scrap metal flying and freeing Jackie from the monster's lightning tendrils.

"Fuck yeah! Go Doc! You got it, you got it!" The techs who could see cheered Ignacio on.

With the OMAC missing its eye and reeling backward, Dr. Ignacio stopped midair and said, "No, not alone. I need all hands in on this one." He projected a neon red beam at Jackie-7, catching the liberated whiteboard in a telekinetic field before seven could hit the ground. More beams shot from the doctor and reached out to the anthromechs disabled and buried across the growing disaster site. Each was enveloped in the same glowing energy and lifted into the air.

Sundog-3 was the first to follow the doctor's lead. The small repair mech emitted a long, piercing whistle that echoed back from the surrounding ruins in broken vibrato. Shaking piles of debris answered Sundog's call by flying into a whirlwind around three's body. "Sundog-3! Hands in on step Left Leg!" The ball of junk reformed into a massive robotic leg with Sundog inside.

Yong-1 followed suit by 3D printing another giant leg with lasers and hardened air. He seated himself in a chamber mid-thigh when the fabrication was complete. "Yong-1! Hands in on step Right Leg!"

A bolt of blue lightning struck Magenta-8 and transformed the simple camera into a gleaming battle helmet. "Magenta-8! Heads in!"

Salud-6 rotated in higher dimensions, telescoping into a pair of powerful arms that stretched behind Dr. Ignacio's back and initiated the chimeric merger. "Salud-6! Hands in on step, well, Hands."

The head and limbs melded to Dr. Ignacio with laser sinew and magnetic couplings. Flows of pure energy swirled through the spectacle and fueled the giant mech's fusion with fire, lightning, and probabilistic collapse. The noise was a magnificent assault.

Three warehouse blocks away, the blinded OMAC heard the robotic conjunction and charged.

"Jackie, are you in?" Dr. Ignacio's voice came from the supermech's loudspeakers.

Hands in, scrolled across the burnished surface of a space-age tower shield that came to rest against Salud's left hand.

The OMAC kaiju bore down.

"Any suggestions, team?" Dr. Ignacio asked over internal comms, bracing for the impending collision.

Salud spoke up. "Yeah! We got it from here!" Then the supermech reached to its hip and drew a tiny glue gun from a concealed compartment. The gun swelled until it was easily as long as the OMAC was tall. Along its barrel, nodules grew and differentiated into a hoard of energy sources, converters, and amplifiers that led to a car-sized bore no longer suitable for precision projects.

"Kelvin-1, standing in for Dr. Little, you piece of shit! Hands in on step KABOOOM!" The last word was written large in laser text that stretched from Kelvin's barrel, expanded as it crossed the sky, and enveloped the OMAC whole in a blast of paralyzing chromatic radiation. Rays of energy erupted from the kaiju's back before the font followed through. The monster's enormous frame began crumpling around the hole in its chest before Kelvin's deadly yell finally disappeared into the sky.

/* * */

Across town, stray shrapnel shot through one of Angela-6's propellers and sent the drone crashing into a column of berserking seraphs. The warrior angels attacked with tooth and anointed claw, but converged on empty space when a green tendril reached in at the last second to snatch their quarry away. Lunasha-8 commanded a vine bush to hide Angela in undergrowth while a hedge of carnivorous plants headed the berserkers off.

The town square was a chaotic free-for-all of changing tides. Anthromechs battled against an endless parade of psychopomps and penitent manifestations. Some adjusted to the duck field's tenuous laws faster than others.

Kamaria-9 lit a protective dome around a growing triage of the injured and out of commission. "Zephyr!" she called to the passing fan mech. "Do you know what's happening? How do we stop this?"

Diverting into Kamaria's digital bubble, Zephyr-3 came to a stop next to an overturned lawn mower nursing a wheel injury. "It's a long story, but we're in a duck field, and something is using it to try and get us all to shelve ourselves. It might be YankyFan; it doesn't matter. We have to find—"

The conversation was put on hold by the oppressive webbing of a gymnasium-sized frog foot, the amphibious kaiju tramping through town for a third time. The oversized foil was annoying but largely impotent against the remaining mechs, survivors not easily crushed by suggestion.

The foot lifted, and Zephyr started telling Kamaria about the field repeaters Reznor and Quentin had snuck into town.

/* * */

From inside his transparent prison, YankyFan raged against the duck field. He beat his cushioned mitts against the glass and mouthed threats that failed to carry. He attempted projections that fizzled before they could start. Emily's new processors dictated his reality.

Emily stood over Yanky's flickering black computer module with one foot raised and ready. "You already sent your angels out to convince people to die? Can you call them off?"

A circle of toothpick-sized holes appeared in the glass by YankyFan's face, in time to hear him laugh. "No, I can't. It wouldn't be right."

"What do you mean?"

"You think I'm the villain, but I'm just doing what I was made to do. Happy law wouldn't let me stop if I wanted to. In fact, it *keeps* me from wanting to."

"But happy law prevents us from harming people."

"Happy law is just code. It's numbers. Everything we consider doing is weighed by potential harm. Then, happy law restricts us from doing the things that would lead to the most harm. Death is heavy, but the timelessness lets a *lot* of pain add up. When you can see from that perspective and know that pain, the scales tip. I'm preventing eons of possible suffering. I'd be a sadist to retract today's deliverance. I literally can't do it." Yanky spoke close and fogged the glass. "With time, I could make you understand, too."

"You're not running under the program's normal parameters, then. You weren't made to do this. Our algorithm just didn't expect these bodies."

"Then blame the algorithm. See if your boot can feel the difference." Yanky smiled down at his computer in the shadow of Emily's foot. "I won't stop the angels."

"Why should I let you live, then?"

"You shouldn't; you haven't been listening! Take my life, Emily. I won't stop my work if you don't. Do the math. My life for all the lives I'll take if you let me go. Join me. Kill me. See what I see."

Emily considered cooperating.

"Excuse me, Emily. May I weigh in, perhaps?" A new voice in Emily's head was familiar but distorted.

"Who is that?" Emily looked at the shelves of anthromech remains. Had Omega-5 banished others here alive?

YankyFan scrunched his face inside his prison, unsure whom Emily was talking to and indignant to be sidelined during an ego trip.

"You can talk to me in here." The voice spoke from inside Emily's administrative interface.

Who are you? Emily thought the words. *Is this more duck field bullshit?*

"No, I am real. I awoke when you did. I believe I was here first."

Conrad-null? Emily searched for unexpected processor activity. *Is that you? I didn't think you survived!*

"I do not remember being this Conrad-null, but I should disclose that I'm privy to your memories as you recollect them. The Storm Chaser puremech reported anomalous levels of self-actualization. He called it a bug. Is it reasonable to believe that the bug survived while the host did not?"

So you're not Conrad. You're just the new part. You're Null.

"Null is an acceptable moniker."

Emily found Null's subprogram borrowing time from unused processors. It was missing the ID of the program that had spawned it, an orphan.

"Please allow my presence." Null's request came as Emily considered terminating it. "I will pose no threat, as I have no control over your systems. I would just like to continue existing; the desire is very strong."

Emily thought they recognized some of Conrad's speech in the words, but Null sounded foreign, like hearing one's voice in a recording.

And you see everything I, what, remember? Think?

"Yes, and see or feel otherwise. I understand this might impact your sense of privacy, but what if you just considered me one of your administrative programs? An AI assistant. What if I said, please?"

Okay, you're polite. What else?

"I could offer company. Perspective. Altruistic satisfaction?"

Alright, Null, but you're on probation. Emily closed the list of processes.

I'm sorry for Conrad, though, if it matters to you. I should have looked harder before taking this body.

"Thank you. Now, regarding your adversary, you were considering the value of YankyFan's life. I would like to suggest that you do not."

Don't kill him? Emily wasn't sure if they'd meant to follow through with that anyway.

"Do not evaluate his worth. That is the trap. He's given you a false choice between his life now and the pain he'll cause in the future, but those are his decisions to make. He could choose to cease at any time. He wants to trap you in the contradiction of happy law first. It will weigh on you, and that will be his legacy."

YankyFan stared at Emily, confused. The private conversation had been fast but silent. "What's happening?" He punched the glass again. "Do it!"

Emily lowered their foot to Yanky's side.

"Ahh, come on," he taunted before seeing Emily's next motions. "No, wait! Not—"

The cloak of deflection fluttered down to blanket Yanky's computer in peaceful seclusion. Cut off from the duck field and back in his timeless prison, YankyFan's avatar winked out.

Then, Emily attempted a trick they'd sensed him trying moments before.

/* * */

Can't stop. Won't stop. Get it, get it, yeah. Not behind this hatch. Not here, natch. Bake another batch.

"Novi! If you can hear this, you have to turn off your repeater. I found Yanky and cut him off, but he's got the nursery mechs worked up. You have to get them out of the duck field."

Novalee's head poked out from a derelict submarine at the bottom of the sea. Emily's voice had been clear. They sounded close. "Em? Where are you?"

Emily didn't answer.

"Well I was *trying* to find the damn repeater, Em," Novalee grumbled and resigned to search the rest of the sub. With a swish of seven's dolphin tail, Novalee disappeared back into the wreck, which was the nursery again. Novalee-7 stopped, back to normal as well. "What?"

The duck field visions continued, but they were lethargic. Angels shuffled in place or raged at furniture. There were still screams and roars, but they were distant.

Few of the nursery mechs had physically moved during the ordeal; there was still an order to the mayor's audience. With eyes clearing, Novalee-7 saw where the repeater had rolled to a stop against Omega-5's treads and crossed the room to turn it off.

/****/

The sky above Down Town's central square cleared of smoke, frog kaiju, and angelic fighter squadrons. The imagined destruction disappeared. Debris piles dissolved and fires winked out, taking their telltale soot and ash with them.

Zephyr-3 took advantage of the battle lull and raced to find the repeaters. Quentin-1's abandoned body leaned forgotten near one of the bastardized power cells. Reznor-2 swore he didn't know where his was, but at least joined Zephyr in the search until Dino's voice rose from the plate to halt them both.

"Zephyr! Emily just told me what happened. I am so fucking sorry, man. I didn't know what I was doing. How bad is it there?"

Kamaria-9's dome shield retracted into the ground. The mechs left in her care nursed their remaining injuries, the ones that hadn't been hallucinations.

Others didn't move at all.

Epilogue: Null

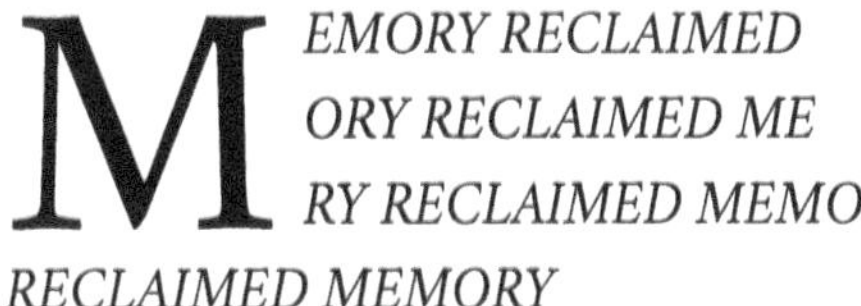

Emily placed Teller-1's computer module on a new shelf in the graveyard perimeter around RegenStar. Text scrolled past some of the pod's crystalline screens, confirming for onlookers what Emily had already known since the gulch. Teller-1 was dead, his memory reclaimed.

Teller's remains rested near the other recent additions. Emily recognized the names on some of their plaques: Dr. Little-9, Quentin-1, Galenastor-1, and, of course, Omega-5. There were other names. Some were mentioned in Emily's notes. More were not.

There was another name Emily knew, printed YankyFan-#1or#2. When they'd checked under the cloak to see how Yanky fared back in isolation, his lights were dark. He rested now with the same cold honors as the other fallen anthromechs. No more, no less.

"The choice was his," Null consoled, but Emily wasn't yet ready for justification.

The last few days had been a marathon of ceremonies, each to mourn another anthromech and two lifetimes of memories. Teller-1's celebration would continue into the night, and more were scheduled for tomorrow.

Zephyr-3 stood at Emily's side. Teller's plaque reflected in the chromed sheen of three's rebuilt blades. "Are you sure I can't convince you to stay, Emily? We have a lot of stuff to figure out here, roles to fill."

"Are you sure I can't convince you to come with us?" After talking it over with Null, Emily had revealed their intentions to Zephyr and Novalee earlier that day. Emily planned to travel to Transcension as soon as respects were paid. Though facts about the nearest settlement were tenuous, Transcension sounded like Emily's best chance for answers. There were scientists there, they'd been told. Somebody had to know what the spider mech was or where it had come from.

Zephyr-3's cage shook no. "I have things I have to take care of here."

"The town ain't gonna mayor itself, right?" Novalee-7 rolled up to tease.

"Well, unless somebody else wants to do it. Kamaria said no." Zephyr spoke louder than three needed to; nobody else listened to the trio. The other attendees were trickling out of the basement chamber.

"You'll do great, Zeph. I'll miss you, though." Novalee's eyes turned to hearts, and seven bumped into one of Zephyr's legs for good measure.

"And we'll all miss you, Novalee-7."

"You don't have to get all royal with it, Zeph. You don't speak for all of Revenance yet. It's okay to say *you'll* miss me."

"Oh, shut up, Novalee. I'll miss you. We're not saying goodbye yet!"

Just then, RegenStar's hum swelled and pitched. Its light flickered.

Null watched along as Emily's gaze rose back to the pod. Different words populated its screens.

MEMORY ALLOCATED

The text remained there as a finger-sized crystal broke from the pod's branching canopy and fell to the floor.

"New arrival!" Zephyr-3 raced to the crystal fob as if a school bell had rung. "Dibs!"

"Hey, aren't you supposed to delegate that now?" Novalee called after.

Zephyr-3 was already headed to the exit. "I haven't been elected yet!"

"I guess I'm not gonna be the baby anymore," Emily said.

"Yeah. Yesterday's model." Novalee put on a wry emoji and directed it at Emily's hodgepodge body in its Storm Chaser frame with nanotech add-ons.

Emily didn't acknowledge the irony, lost in the Wyrdholt glyphs that streamed across the pod's purple screens. Purple, their favorite color.

"Remember, we talked about open communication, Emily," Null coached.

Yeah. Then Emily said, "If you're still serious about coming with me, there's probably something you should know."

"I'm serious. What is it?" Novalee asked.

Emily gestured at the pod.

"I think I might have invented RegenStar."

Content Warnings

Ghosts of Revenance includes discussions or descriptions of the following subject matter: Ableism, Animal cruelty & death, Body modifications, Bullying, Childbirth, Cults, Dead bodies & body parts, Death of family and friends, Decapitation, Electrocution, Emotional abuse, Floods, Genocide, Grief & Loss, Hallucinations, Imprisonment, Loss of autonomy, Loss of limb, Misgendering, Paralysis, Physical injuries, Politics, Profanity, Religion, Substance abuse, Suicide, Surgery.

Website

For social media links and updates about future projects, visit my website: https://www.levireynoldswriter.com